Creepy Campfire Quarterly
#1

Edited by
Jennifer Word

EMP Publishing
www.emppublishing.com

Creepy Campfire Quarterly
#1
Compilation Copyright © 2016 EMP Publishing

Cover design by Maxmart ©2016 Jennifer Word by Licensing Agreement c/o 99designs.com

ISBN: 0692597719 (paperback)
ISBN-13: 978-0-6925977-1-2 (paperback)

CONTENTS

Introduction
1

Vixen – Sylvia Greenwich
6

Wealth and Hellness – Gregory L. Norris
18

Insider Trading – John H. Stevens
33

Ghost of Big Bend – Nicholas Paschall
42

Last Supper – M.B. Vujačić
47

Hungry – Robert Stahl
61

Love Feast – Emilio DeGrazia
71

A Story for the Boys – John Teel
84

Pieces of Me – Craig Steven
91

A Slippery Customer – Marlena Frank
102

One Good Deed – David J. Gibbs
109

The Susurrus of Cerulean Snow – Randy D. Rubin
121

Eden Saw Play – Stephen McQuiggan
125

Entangled – Katherine Sanger
131

They Live in the Trees – Daniel Marrone
137

A Letter to Michael – Edward R. Rosick
147

Bad Bone – John Howe
154

Sheol – Paul Stansfield
161

At Day's End – Leonard Apa
172

About the Authors

183

INTRODUCTION

Greetings Creepy Campers! Welcome to the inaugural issue of the new *Creepy Campfire Quarterly*, or simply the CCQ. In this introduction, I simply want to tell you a couple of simple stories. Or maybe these are stories *about* stories. The main theme to take away from all of this is simply partaking in the art of storytelling, because, really, doesn't all art, in every medium, and every facet of human entertainment simply boil down to a story being told? In photos and paintings, sculptures and music, plays and films, television episodes, and even the news. In rumours whispered down hallways, or spread like the flu across the Internet, to scrapbook albums, 'catching up' over coffee, to wedding toasts and classroom presentations, and sadly, even obituaries and funeral eulogies – everything is a story. And I've got a few to share with you. So let me tell you a story.

The original *Creepy Campfire Stories (for Grownups)* anthology was simply that: a single volume of collected horror short stories from various authors. The anthology quickly became known simply as the CCS. The open call for the anthology was launched on the EMP Publishing website on May 13, 2015 and was the first open call launched by the publisher (moi), who had only registered the company a month earlier, on February 15, 2015. Being an entirely new company, my team wasn't certain what to expect, but we anticipated a slow and meager trickle of stories from authors. We weren't even certain we'd receive enough submissions over the slated four-month period to actually fill a full anthology. We were looking for roughly 65,000 words of quality and spine-tingling horror. What we got overwhelmed us. By the way, 'we' includes my two amazing associate editors, Theresa Huffman and Kimberly King, without whose tireless efforts, I would never have been able to get through our slush pile, but I digress.

To recap: *Creepy Campfire Stories (for Grownups)* began as a stand-alone anthology, launched on May 13, 2015. The response from horror writers was phenomenal. In less than four months, we received over 220 submissions from all over the globe, from the UK, including London, Ireland, Scotland & Wales; Italy; Belgrade, Serbia; Germany; Poland; Australia; New Zealand; Western Cape, South Africa; The United States;

and Canada! The quality of the stories streaming in was so exceptional that we were able to fill a full, 65,000-word anthology with absolutely amazing and high quality horror stories in less than two months! In fact, we had to close our submissions early, moving our end date back from September 13 to July 13! This led to some brainstorming and the first blooming idea of making *Creepy Campfire* a 'franchise', not to mention some hefty revelations about the current horror authorship that abounds.

Closing our anthology's submissions so much earlier than originally planned left many authors shut out. It soon became clear to us here at EMP (Electromagnetic Pulse) Publishing, that there were just far too many quality horror writers out there to fit into one single anthology. We began brainstorming and landed upon making the *Creepy Campfire Stories (for Grownups)* **brand** an annual publication, every Fall/October, (hence the first 'franchise' rumblings), but as submissions to our original anthology continued streaming in, and the quality of the stories continued to astound us, we quickly realized that even an annual publication still wouldn't fully accommodate the high number of amazingly talented authors of horror/extreme horror that exists today. We wanted to be able to publish, PAY and showcase as many new, up-and-coming horror writers as possible, as well as provide a new publishing outlet to already established horror writers who were starved for new places to submit their ongoing hard work and showcase their talent.

That is when the idea for turning *Creepy Campfire Stories (for Grownups)* into a quarterly publication was born. Why not turn the *Creepy Campfire* anthology brand into an ongoing publication? It wasn't long before the *Creepy Campfire Quarterly* (much like the CCS) simply became known as the CCQ. The original CCS anthology was released on September 3, 2015. However, submissions for the new CCQ had already opened. In fact, we'd received over thirty subs for the CCQ **before** the original CCS was even published.

And now, here we are, releasing the first issue of the CCQ! Much as with the subs to the CCS, we received so many amazing stories for the CCQ that we unfortunately had to close submissions for two quarters, as we've already been able to fill the first THREE issues of the CCQ. In less than four months we've been able to slate 3/4ths of the first year of the CCQ's life. It looks like this 'franchise' is here to stay for a while. So now, onto the tale of what inspired *Creepy Campfire Stories (for Grownups)* to begin with.

Another story.

I was born and raised in Anchorage, Alaska. My hometown is rich in Native Alaskan culture and education. In elementary school, every year, we'd study a different tribe, from the Tlingit, to the Athabascan, to the far North Inuit. I have fond memories of carving mini Totem poles in art class, and once, a walrus from soapstone. Over the years, there were multiple field trips to various Alaska Native cultural museums and galleries, as well as many in-school (and all-school) assemblies to enjoy various Native tribes who would travel all over the state to schools and colleges, performing their dances, singing their culture's songs, playing their beautiful instruments (I recall a caribou hide snare drum, once), and sharing their oral stories (native myths and legends), which were always preserved specifically through live storytelling.

In fact, Storytellers are a "thing" in Alaska. Storytelling is a bona fide art form in the North, in the Arctic Circle and all along the Yukon, to name only a few places. Extreme emphasis was (and is) placed, when educating children, both native and non-native alike, on the importance of the art of passing a people's history and culture down throughout the generations specifically through oral storytelling. After all, in the middle of the harsh winters, in small villages in the Alaskan wild, previous to the 19th Century, oral storytelling was the *only* way to pass down these tales of culture and history.

Storytelling is a revered thing among many cultures, tribes and clans, all around the world, in fact, and I was first introduced to this 'phenomenon' as a very young child, up in Alaska. There were (and still are) dozens, if not hundreds of professional Storytellers who make their living in Alaska visiting schools and continuing to share ancient tribal stories and legends. I recall a school assignment in fourth grade where we had to emulate the specific narrative style of Native personification. Example: 'How the Caribou got its Horns', expertly told by an ancient looking Tlingit man during an in-class visit. What followed was the assignment for each child in class to write their own version of this specific storytelling method. I think mine was something to the effect of, 'How the Squirrel got its Bushy Tail', but I honestly don't remember. We wrote our stories down, but the ultimate assignment was to read them aloud to the rest of the class, to honor the tradition of oral storytelling.

And so, while learning from a very young age to love reading books (I devoured them), I also learned to simultaneously and equally love the art of hearing stories be told. And there was no shortage of camping trips by my family during the very short (3 month) summer season, each year, when we'd receive a glorious respite from the bitter, harsh and snowy winters. I learned to love those (hundreds of) camping trips over the years, specifically for the inevitable stories told 'round the campfire every night.

As expected, the majority of those campfire stories were, by nature, of a darker bent: scary, suspenseful, spine-tingling, as they say.

And so, the final building block was placed for my love of books, stories, oral tales, and most specifically – scary stories. For some reason, I enjoyed the darkest tales the most, for they got my heart racing, my breath held, and my imagination fully engaged beyond any other genre. I love many genres of story, but horror is my top pick (shrug). So when I launched my own publishing company, some 25 or 30 years removed from those first early childhood experiences, laying the foundation, in fact, for me becoming not only a writer, but (perhaps, inevitably), a publisher – it was no surprise that EMP Publishing's first open call would be for an anthology specifically designed to honor my own innate love of horror stories, while incorporating my specific fondness of the oral tradition of passing stories around, via campfire.

In fact, all the traditional native stories were generally passed down around campfires at night, to keep warm, to entertain, and after the daylight had been spent upon building, hunting and gathering. Campfire stories have existed since before the printed word, and even before modern language, when early, nomadic tribes of Neanderthal couldn't take their cave drawings with them, or found an easier time relating their stories through sounds, body movements and hand gestures.

Storytelling was born from oral tradition, not print. It is the most ancient form of art, relating information, facts, myths, legends, history and culture that our human race has. And so, I wanted to honor that ancient and enduring practice (despite the dispersing of said publication in print form) in the only other way I know how – by bowing my head and giving my utmost and honorable praise to oral storytelling. A very longwinded way to explain why the original CCS anthology, and now the CCQ, is specifically named *Creepy Campfire*. It incorporates both my love for the spoken tale, as well as the spooky. And so far, the idea seems to be appreciated and eagerly anticipated by authors and readers alike. If you are reading this, then that makes you one of us: a 'Creepy Camper'.

So welcome, my Creepy Campers, to the first of hopefully many issues, for many years to come, of *Creepy Campfire Quarterly*, or simply the CCQ. While it is a quarterly publication, the CCQ is anything other than your average 'digest' or 'magazine'. The CCQ will be releasing a new issue every three months, four times a year, and each stand-alone issue will be a full-sized *anthology*. We'll never release a single issue that is less than 50,000 words in length (this issue you are currently reading runs at 78,500 + words, in fact).

Introduction

The CCQ is a quarterly anthology, something a bit different from any of the current horror mags and other publications out there. We are also unique in that our entire issue, *each* issue, is devoted to storytelling. You'll never find any columns, articles, interviews, reviews or editorials in the CCQ. Just good and scary horror tales. We will never busy our pages with ads of any kind, either. We will eventually provide a link in the back of future issues (beginning with April 20, 2016's issue #2, in fact) where subscriptions to the CCQ can be purchased, but that's it.

The CCQ simply publishes great horror stories by talented authors. That's it; the CCQ is a rather simple concept, yet, surprisingly, a fairly novel one. We've dropped the *(for Grownups)* moniker, but these are **not** YA yarns, be warned. Each issue will span from the sometimes dark, yet comic; to the downright EXTREME horror tale, but no story in here is for the weary, nor the minor of age. Enter, if you dare, and partake of the newest modern horror tradition.

Welcome to the Campfire.

Jennifer Word
January 4, 2016

VIXEN
Sylvia Greenwich

"According to Indian legends, Fox Lake got its name from a spirit said to haunt the woods around Enderby," Ellis said, naming the town nearest to the lake. "The story goes that if a brave unfaithful to his squaw saw a fox on the shore of the lake while he was out in his canoe fishing, the man was doomed to drown. If he saw the fox while he was on the land, hunting or working or whatever, his body would be found ripped apart in the woods, mysterious animal markings on his flesh. They say that even today, the cheating man better beware of the fox spirit, or else something terrible will happen to him."

Ellis thought it was a pretty cool story. She liked spooky stories, the scarier the better. And what better story for a trip to a cabin in the deep, dark hinterlands of the northern Maine woods?

Eyes on the road, both hands on the wheel, Mark shook his head, familiar look of scorn curling up one side of his thin mouth. "Where'd you get that crap, El? And which Indians, anyway? Probably some nonsense made up by the locals to suck in rubes from down East, like us."

Ellis's joy died, and she sat back against her seat, pulling her long legs up to prop her feet against the dash, only remembering, just in time, how much Mark hated when she did that. He always complained about having to clean dirty footprints off the leather.

"C'mon, Mark, it's a good story. Don't you get the chills, just thinking about it?"

Mark shrugged and shook his head again. "No, I don't."

And that, right there, was why they were on this trip, she thought. Mark never believed in anything interesting. He always demanded evidence, practically requiring mathematical proof for even the simplest things. God could appear before him, glowing white robes, big beard and all, and Mark would ask to see His birth certificate and two forms of photo ID.

Mark's practical nature had once appealed to Ellis, who'd never dated anyone as serious or stable as Mark before. Usually, her boyfriends were the passionate, moody, artist types, drifting in and out of her life like the various people who had shared her loft in the Village over the years. At

6

twenty-eight, she'd been tired of living hand-to-mouth, tired of always being left behind while her friends and lovers went off to see the world.

When she'd met Mark, he'd seemed heaven-sent. Marrying him had promised Ellis a solution to all the uncertainty and chaos of her earlier life. If he was a little stuffy, she'd figured some of her impulsiveness would rub off on him, eventually.

But here they were: a year after their marriage, driving up to what Mark predicted was going to be "some craptastic hellhole" one of her "stoned-out hippy friends" had offered them the use of, trying to see if they couldn't get themselves back in the same book, never mind on the same page of their lives.

Thankfully, the cabin turned out to be pretty nice. Mark grumbled about having to start the generator, but the place had everything they could ask for: running water, electricity, a big fireplace, and a porch that faced a stunning view of the isolated Fox Lake. Side-by-side in the matching Adirondack chairs on the porch, they could look out at their little inlet along the shore and see no other habitation.

"Isn't this romantic?" Ellis cooed, leaning over the arms of their chairs to rest her head on his shoulder.

"Isn't that uncomfortable?" he countered.

Ellis sighed and went inside to get them each a beer.

After dinner and more beer, Mark seemed to loosen up. He built a fire in the fireplace, and they fed each other S'mores, laughing at the inevitable smears of chocolate in the corners of their mouths. Laughing led to licking led to passionate sex on the woven rug in front of the fireplace. Ellis was nude, straddling Mark, just about to ease him inside of her, when a harsh, loud noise – quite near the cabin – startled them both into freezing, listening hard for a repeat of the sound.

It came again: an inhuman, strangled shriek, and again, closer still.

"Whatever it is, it's moving fast," Mark observed in a hush. "Maybe a big water bird flying over?"

"It sounds like it's in a lot of pain, whatever it is," Ellis said, getting up to go to the window in the kitchen, which looked out onto the driveway and the forest behind the cabin. She couldn't see anything beyond what the weak glow of their fire illuminated through the window.

"Come back here," Mark said, and she obeyed.

***

She was just about to reach her climax, Mark straining silently beneath her, never one for expressing his pleasure, when the sound returned, even louder than before, coming from just outside the cabin door.

Ellis turned her eyes toward the door, losing the rhythm of their lovemaking as she held her breath, afraid that whatever was making that horrible scream would somehow get into the cabin.

"Hey," Mark protested, grabbing her hips to urge her to move, and she resumed her somewhat distracted motion, even as part of her waited to hear the sound again.

Mark was thrusting hard up into her, reaching his silent climax, when the shrieking came again – this time from the porch on the lakeside of the cabin. Fearing what she'd see, Ellis turned her head toward the big picture window there, squinting against the firelight to try to make out what was outside.

Was there a shadowy figure hulking in the window? She gasped, forgetting all thoughts of pleasure, and pulled away – Mark slipping unceremoniously from her.

He grimaced and said, "You're dripping on my leg!" as she stood up and walked toward the window, stopping mere inches from the glass, cursing its reflective surface that allowed her only a vision of the ghost of herself, naked and damp.

She felt the wetness between her thighs and turned away, too unsettled to cross the last few inches of space and press her face to the window so that she could see out.

Mark, meanwhile, had gotten up to clean himself, and the bathroom door was pointedly closed. Like so many other things Ellis was easy about, Mark didn't like sharing a bathroom and was very particular about what should be private and what should be public between them.

By the time she'd had her turn and cleaned up, he was up in the loft, snoring away. She sat for a long time in the slowly dying light of the fire, eyes skittering every few seconds to the picture window looking out over the lake.

Finally, when there'd been no sound for at least an hour, she climbed wearily to the loft and settled in next to Mark. She was almost asleep – riding the waves of lucid dreams down into deeper rest – when the scream came again, seemingly directly overhead, as though whatever were making it were on the roof.

She started upright, staring at the ceiling, shaking Mark with a hand and whispering, "Wake up! Please, wake up!" Ellis knew Mark would tell her she was being silly, but she couldn't help but feel that this thing, whatever it was, was stalking them, deliberately waiting until she'd almost relaxed, before screaming, as if to make her scared all over again.

After the last outburst from above, though, nothing else happened, and eventually, Ellis fell asleep. She dreamt of blood-red foxes with long, sharp faces and big, vicious teeth, and she awoke feeling haunted and out of sorts.

***

Mark was gone. She smelled coffee that had sat too long on the warming plate, and when she came down the loft ladder, it was to find the dregs of coffee turning to tar in the carafe, but no other sign of her husband.

Expecting to find him out on the porch, she walked out there barefoot, hugging her arms against her chest at the surprising coolness of the morning air.

No Mark.

Ellis walked back through the cabin to the door on the driveway side, opened it and looked out. The car was where they'd parked it, no sign that it had been moved. No sign of Mark, either.

She searched for a note Mark might have left to tell her where he'd gone, but found none. Worried now, Ellis retrieved her cell phone from her duffel. Jerry, the friend who'd offered the cabin, had told her that service out there was spotty at best, so she wasn't surprised to see no bars.

Sighing, she put the phone back, and then Ellis slipped into her Birks, intending to walk down to the lake. Maybe Mark had taken a walk around the shore?

From the edge of the water, she could see only a short way along the inlet in each direction. As far as she could tell, she was the only one on the beach.

Unless he'd gone into the woods…

But that wasn't like Mark. Not a nature lover, it had only been the promise of free lodging that had gotten him on this anniversary trip to begin with. A walk in the woods wasn't his style.

Ellis was staring – unseeing – out over Fox Lake, imagining the worst: that Mark had decided on a swim and caught a cramp or had been chased into the woods by the screaming thing they'd heard last night.

What if it had been a rabid dog?

What if there was a bear or a coyote in the area?

Worse, what if it was some lunatic escaped convict?

Just as Ellis's speculations were reaching hysterical heights, Mark floated into view in the cabin's little canoe. He was talking on his satellite phone, which he'd insisted on bringing, saying it was the only way he'd agree to go to the middle of nowhere in "North Buttfuck, Maine."

Snatches of his words carried over the water – "miss you" and, "Hey, sweet" and, "I'm sorry" – before he caught sight of Ellis on the shore. Dropping his voice to a low hum and hanging up, he waved to Ellis with the hand holding the phone and put on a big, false smile.

He paddled inexpertly toward the shore, fumbled the landing, and almost tipped over before Ellis steadied the prow with her foot and helped him drag the canoe onto the beach.

"Business?" she asked, handing him the lie almost graciously.

"Yeah, just Larry at work," he explained. "Something about a surprise inspection at the building site. He was freaking out."

"No problem," she lied, figuring it was her turn. "So long as he remembers that it's your anniversary." The reminder wasn't really for Larry.

"I told him not to call me again," Mark agreed, wrapping an arm around Ellis and turning her up the beach toward the porch. She wanted to duck out from under his arm and move away, wanted to wrench the truth out into the light and have a screaming fight to clear the air.

She wanted Mark not to be fucking the firm's newest secretary, Melody, behind her back.

***

Who could have known, when the Boho girl from the Village had married the steady, reliable engineer that it would be *he* who'd cheat on *her* and not the other way around?

Just as she started to swivel out of Mark's embrace, Ellis caught sight of movement just down the beach. "Oh," she said, turning out of the bracket of his arm and pointing. "Look!"

There, not a hundred yards away, was a red fox vixen and four kits. She came down to the water cautiously, looking along the shoreline, before lowering her head to drink while the kits wrestled in the gravel of the beach, nipping playfully at one another and yipping in short, sharp bursts.

Just then, looking over her shoulder suddenly, as though startled, the vixen caught sight of the couple. She gave a sudden, piercing bark, as of an animal in pain, and herded her kits back into the umbrage of the forest in a blur of red fur, there and then gone.

"So that's what we heard last night," Mark said. "Mystery solved. And you were all worried," he teased her, putting his arm around her again to pull her back toward the cabin. "Let's have some breakfast," he suggested, nuzzling her ear. "And then we can take the canoe out or go for a walk. Would you like that?"

Since those were both things Ellis would ordinarily enjoy and Mark typically hate, she figured he was sucking up, trying to make it up to her that he'd brought his whore on their vacation, in a manner of speaking. But she didn't let on like anything was wrong, except for maybe a little stiffness in her shoulders beneath his proprietary arm.

***

The day was pretty good, when she let it be. Almost, Ellis could forget that her husband was screwing around behind her back. Almost, she could overlook the way the eminently sensible, always focused Mark, sometimes got this far-away look on his face or lost the thread of their conversation. Almost, she could pretend it didn't hurt that it wasn't she who made him dreamy-eyed and befuddled.

***

They were inside after dinner, playing a vicious game of Gin Rummy – Mark played everything as though he were in Olympic trials – when the vixen's bark sounded loud and clear.

"She must be just down the way," Ellis said, abandoning the game to check the picture window, cupping her hands around her eyes and pressing against the glass so that she could see. It was dark in the trees, of course, the only light coming from inside the cabin, but where the path widened at the beach, the gravel was limned in silver from a half-moon that reflected off of the water.

Silhouetted at the edge of the lake, was the fox – sitting in regal profile – reminding Ellis of the jackal statues she'd seen in the Egyptian exhibit at the museum. As if the fox sensed her audience, it turned its head toward her, and by some trick of the light, its eyes glowed yellow, as if lit from within by infernal flames.

"Now, that's creepy," Mark commented, making Ellis gasp and jump away from the window. She hadn't heard him come up behind her.

She slapped him hard on his bicep and said, "Don't sneak up on me like that!"

He chuckled like she'd said something funny. Mark often made fun of her for the things that frightened her – the gap between the platform and the train in the subway; homeless men who muttered to themselves at bus stops; taxi cab drivers who didn't speak English.

Stung by his usual cruelty and still pissed that he'd called his girlfriend on their anniversary, Ellis recalled the Fox Lake legend Jerry had told her when he'd given her the keys to this place. Ellis gave Mark a sidelong look and said, "It must have been looking at *you*."

There was a long space of tense silence. It was the closest she'd ever come to confronting him about his infidelities, and he seemed surprised by it.

Then he laughed – an unpleasant, nasty little sound – and said, "Or you."

But she wasn't unfaithful, Ellis thought later, as she got ready for bed. Sure, she'd had to make out with Jerry to get him to give up the keys to the cabin, but 'no penetration, no litigation', as her friend, Jeannie, was fond of saying.

It wasn't adultery if there was no actual sex, right?

As if answering her question, the fox shrieked again, sounding so much like a woman's scream – being cut off by strangling hands – that Ellis shuddered and closed her eyes, wishing the sound away.

It wasn't for her. It couldn't be. Besides, it was only a stupid legend, just like Mark had said. Right?

The vixen screamed again as Ellis was climbing into bed beside Mark and a second time before her head even hit the pillow. The shrieks continued in irregular bursts, two or three at a time and then nothing for several, long minutes, during which Ellis would hold her breath, muscles taut, eyes straining into the darkness as if she could see through the wall and outside to where the fox was calling.

Why was it hanging around their cabin? Why did it scream like that?

Ellis thought of waking Mark up to ask him, or at least so that she didn't have to be alone with the awful sound, but she dismissed the idea almost as soon as she had it. He'd make fun of her, call her foolish, suggest that she'd seen one too many horror movies.

He'd make her feel – as always – that she was irrational, a complete idiot.

***

Ellis remembered a time when life hadn't been scary, when nothing really bothered her. Sure, she had some silly fears, but they weren't entirely unfounded. After all, if the cabbie couldn't speak English, how could she be sure he'd take her where she wanted to go? And people had gotten their feet caught in the gap between car and platform; she'd read about it in the *Post*, hadn't she?

No, on the whole, Ellis had been pretty happy with the world, before she'd married Mark. It was only since their marriage that she'd started to feel like everything she thought or said was immature and dumb.

She hated that he made her feel that way about herself, that he could *make* her feel that way.

From outside, the vixen screamed again, and the sound seemed to echo and carry, as if it were coming from all directions at once. Shivering, Ellis got up and climbed down the loft ladder, intending to make herself a cup of cocoa. While the water was heating, she thought she'd build up the fire, but when she walked over to the basket, she discovered they had no more wood.

"Damn it," she groused. She'd asked Mark to bring in more, but he'd said he didn't feel like it and that he'd get it in the morning.

Ellis weighed her options. The wood was stacked in neat rows on one end of the lakeside porch. It was only a few steps from the sliding door to the pile and back. She could tiptoe out, grab an armful, and be back inside in fifteen seconds.

Plus, she hadn't heard the fox in several minutes. Besides, she reminded herself, the fox wasn't really dangerous, not like a wolf or a bear would be.

Having talked herself into it, Ellis walked barefoot to the sliding door, unlocked it, and cracked it open an inch or two so that she could hear more clearly.

Nothing.

It was so quiet she could make out the faintest sound of water lapping gently against the stone beach down by the lake.

She peered through the darkness at the shore, where she'd seen the fox earlier.

Nothing broke the line of sight between her and the faintly shimmering water of the lake.

Reminding herself that she was a brave girl – not the scared, silly thing Mark made her out to be – Ellis slid the door open far enough to slip outside and walked with deliberate strides to the woodpile. She loaded up one arm with enough wood to last a couple of hours and turned back toward the door.

The fox was standing on the porch stairs, one front paw poised, to step onto the deck itself.

Ellis jumped in place and swallowed a scream, juggling the suddenly unbalanced pile of firewood to try to keep from dropping it. Who knew if that might startle the fox into attacking her or something?

"Hey, pretty," she tried, voice hoarse from fear. "What do you want, huh, girl?"

As if in answer, the vixen turned its eyes from Ellis and toward the sliding door, which was standing open, just as Ellis had left it.

"Oh, you don't want to go in there," Ellis cooed, easing the wood out of her arms until she was holding only a single piece, perhaps three feet long – split unevenly and narrowing to a splintered point on one end – like a large, unwieldy stake used for destroying the hearts of vampires.

The vixen regarded her for a few moments as if reading Ellis's mind, and though her heart was frozen with fear and the hand holding the makeshift weapon was shaking, she stood her ground and tried again to coax it away from the door.

"No, honey, that's not a place for you," she reasoned, as if the fox could understand her. Ellis took a tiny step forward, bare foot scuffing on the wooden porch deck. The vixen's right ear twitched at the noise, and she lowered her head an inch or so – a low, warning growl coming from between her almost smiling lips.

Then, without another glance at Ellis, the animal padded across the deck, over the threshold of the open door, and into the cabin itself.

Heart hammering in her throat, cold fear-sweat breaking out over her body, Ellis whispered to herself, "What should I do? What should I do?" Tears pricked the corners of her eyes as she stood there indecisively, holding the piece of pointed wood until she felt splinters piercing the skin of her palm.

Still, she clutched the weapon, as if she could wring an answer out of it, and then she realized that, if nothing else, she had to warn her husband that there was a wild animal in the cabin.

"Mark!" she called, her voice hardly loud enough to be heard over the pounding of blood in her ears. She gathered her courage and tried again, this time louder. "Mark!"

No sound from within the cabin. Creeping silently to the door, Ellis held her breath and peered around the end of the woodpile and into the cabin through the door.

The vixen stood in the living room, halfway between the door and the ladder to the loft, looking directly over her shoulder at Ellis. Ellis let go of a shuddering breath and felt her insides turn to ice at the fox's steady regard.

The creature's eyes glowed an eerie yellow, too bright for the scant light of the dying fire's dim red embers.

Ellis clenched her bladder, suddenly afraid that she'd wet herself, and tried to convince herself that the fox was just a curious animal that had wandered into their cabin. Just because it seemed like the fox could read her thoughts didn't mean that it could.

Mark would tell her that she was being foolish, and Ellis tried to comfort herself with thinking he was right in this case.

"Go on, get!" she called, waving the stake in her right hand, weakly, in the fox's direction.

With supreme disregard, the vixen turned her head back toward the ladder of the loft.

"Mark, wake up!" Ellis shouted, seeing the fox take a step toward the ladder.

She didn't think an ordinary fox could manage the steeply canted stairs, but she couldn't be sure.

Ellis took a deep breath and stepped through the sliding door, nudging it open further, not wanting the fox to feel like it was trapped.

But the fox wasn't even looking at her.

"Get away from there," she tried, voice quavering with fear. "Shoo!" she cried, brandishing the impromptu stake.

The fox set its front paws on the first rung of the ladder.

Sidling toward the couch, Ellis picked up a decorative pillow and threw it at the fox. It missed, landing with a dusty *woomph* a foot to its left. The fox didn't seem to notice or care. With a flash of color, it surged up the steps, unnatural speed making its figure blur like red smoke in the indistinct light of the shadowy room.

Ellis cried out and raced to the foot of the ladder, staring up at where the animal had disappeared. From this angle, she couldn't see the creature, but she knew what its target must be. There was no way this was an ordinary fox; it moved like no animal Ellis had ever seen and with a purpose that suggested it could think and plan.

Swallowing a cry and holding back tears, Ellis took another shaking breath and reached for the ladder railings. Realizing that she couldn't climb with the stake in her hand, she tucked it into the waistband of the boy-shorts she usually wore to bed. It rubbed uncomfortably against the soft skin at the small of her back, and she could feel a splinter working its way into the flesh of her hip, but she ignored the discomfort, intent on stopping the fox from hurting Mark.

Even if it was a spirit animal out to wreak vengeance on her cheating husband, Ellis had to try stopping it. Maybe this weekend had proven that she and Mark were through, but she certainly didn't want to see it end in bloodshed.

No, she wanted to divorce Mark the old-fashioned way and get the nice, tidy sum they'd agreed to in their pre-nup.

Reaching the top of the ladder, Ellis peeked over, half afraid that the fox would be waiting for her there with its sharp teeth bared in a snarl.

But the fox had its back to the ladder; it was standing at the foot of the bed, staring up at Mark's sleeping figure. Ellis forced herself to clear the top of the ladder, steadying herself against the railing that spanned the breadth of the loft on the cabin side. From its place, the vixen turned its head – yellow eyes alight with an eerie intelligence – and then leapt onto the bed, making for Mark's throat.

"Get away from him!" Ellis shouted, rushing forward, stake raised in both hands, like the slasher in some late night gore fest.

At her shout, Mark awoke, sitting up on his elbows, staring blearily at Ellis, who was rushing the bed, weapon ready.

"What are you doing?" Mark cried, a sudden fear in his voice and on his face. A little part of her (that wasn't concentrating on the fox's next move) was gratified to see the usually stoic Mark lose control of his emotions.

"Look out!" she screamed, as the fox lunged for Mark's throat, its jaws closing around the fragile flesh, blood jetting from the punctures as he screamed and struggled.

Ellis brought the stake down toward the fox's exposed back, aiming for the place between its narrow shoulder blades. She stabbed at it, blow deflected by one of Mark's arms, waving wildly in an attempt to defend himself.

She raised the stake a second time, as the fox deepened its grip on Mark's throat, savaging him now, blood splattering the cream down comforter, the white pine headboard, and Ellis herself.

"No! God, no!" Mark shrieked, and Ellis brought the stake down a second time, plunging it into the fox's side, feeling the animal hesitate, feeling its muscles and bones give as she put her weight behind the weapon and pushed it deeper.

"No! Stop!" Mark cried, efforts to resist the fox's attack weakening as he lost too much blood. His voice came in a harsh gurgle, barely audible over Ellis's heavy panting as she yanked the stake from between the faltering fox's ribs and struck again, harder still, stabbing the soft meat of its partially exposed belly.

The fox's movements ceased, light dying in its eyes, as it slumped over Mark's bloodied chest, teeth still clamped to his throat, where the blood pulsed slow and slower, still. Through the slick red waste of his torn throat, Ellis could see a darker red line, his artery pumping weakly as his heart gave out.

"No," Ellis whispered, touching his cooling cheek with her blood-slick fingers. "No," she said again, pulling at the body of the fox. It made a thick, wet sound as it struck the floor beside the bed, but she didn't care about that now. All she cared about was the way the spark of life in Mark's eyes was fading, pupils fixed; gaze distant as he slipped away from life and from her.

Suddenly cold, shivering with shock, Ellis draped herself over her dead husband's body and let the dark that ate at the edges of her vision overtake her in an obliterating wave.

***

At the wake, Jim Kosmo and Nick Richards stood contemplating the closed casket.

"I guess she tore him up pretty good," Jim observed.

"Yeah, I didn't think she had it in her. I always made her for the airy-fairy sort, you know? Peace, love, free sex –all that hippy shit."

"Maybe it was drugs," Jim speculated.

"That's gotta be it," Nick agreed. "Though, you can't really blame the girl for going ballistic, if it's true that she found out about Melody."

Jim laughed and nodded. "Yeah, Melody was one hot little number." Mark had brought her to a couple of get-togethers at Nick's place.

Nick gave Jim a look.

"What?" Jim asked, unable to interpret his friend's expression.

"You didn't hear about Melody?"

Jim, who didn't work at the same firm as Nick, shook his head. "What about her?"

"Weirdest thing, man. The same morning the cops found Ellis wandering through Enderby, with Mark's blood all over her, Central Park police spotted Melody's body in some bushes just off the jogging path. They said it looked like she'd been attacked by wild dogs or something. They figure maybe someone's pit bull got out of hand and the owner tried to cover up the killing."

"Geez, that sucks," Jim answered. After a short, respectful pause, he added, "I'd have liked a piece of her."

"Your wife would kill you," Nick observed.

Jim laughed.

WEALTH AND HELLNESS
Gregory L. Norris

5 x 7. Silver. In the unforgiving white glare beyond her dimming vision, Ruth saw that the little picture frame was tarnished. The elegant, delicate scrolls were caked in a darkness they wouldn't likely be rid of again in her lifetime. And after she stole her final breath, what then? The picture torn out, tossed into the garbage pail at the side of her bed, presently containing a few candy wrappers and plastic from whatever pharmaceutical sponge or instrument of torture had been opened by a nurse or nurse's aide. Someone would claim the frame; it was sterling silver. But the picture…

Ruth Elizabeth Lester forced her gaze higher and greeted the eyes of the young man captured in that lost moment. He looked happy. Maybe he was, though she didn't think so. His smile owed to the photographer. College graduation? No, high school. He hadn't made it long past this snapshot frozen in time.

There were instances lately, too many of them, when Ruth couldn't remember who he was, only that he'd died in a car accident. Now, the truth sat heavy on her shoulders and fed whatever dark creatures lived in her gut and the regret that tumbled through her bloodstream.

"Jacob," Ruth whispered.

For a terrible second, she felt all the emotion drain as it got ironed off her face. Then the caustic sting of tears invaded her eyes and, for the thousandth or millionth time, she wept for her dead son.

***

"And how are we today, Ms. Ruth?" the chirpy, chipper young woman asked.

Ruth assumed the nurse in the plum paisley scrubs was Mimi, who worked the weekday shift at Hutton Hill, though it was difficult to tell one body or voice from another when everyone paid to care for your health and wellness in the last of your days among the living acted like your best friend and was so happy to see you. She'd never had so many cheerleaders. A whole cast of partygoers present to celebrate the end of eighty-three years, a jumble of months, and who knew, anymore, how many days.

How was she? Her entire body felt like one giant bruise. It was as though every cut, every scrape her skin had ever sustained, dating all the way back to childhood, had surfaced up from scars long healed and stitched together.

"Fine," she settled for, instead.

Mimi—she wasn't sure who her new best friend was—wandered over to the wheelchair wedged into the small space between the hospital bed and the outer wall of the bathroom. "Are you sure, Ruth?"

Ruth remembered the tears, her latest over Jacob. Proof lay in the wadded tissues clutched in her good hand. What was the point of lying? Still, she hadn't been the type to bemoan life's many sinkholes. Maybe-Mimi leaned down and checked the sling. Tenderly, of course—the adjustments were merely mimes, motions run through and something to do out of compassion, because, that was what was expected of party guests waiting for you to blow out your candles at the last big hurrah.

The breaks in her arm: three, according to the unreliable information ping-ponging through her thoughts, were healing on their own, no cast or surgery required. Still, the miserable slowness, and so much agony.

***

She'd slipped out of the wheelchair, her second home after the hospital bed, which trapped her body at night but couldn't keep Ruth's mind from wandering back to people and places from the past. She'd fallen asleep in the chair, breaking a promise she made to herself never to do so, because, in the chair, she was able to move about. It wasn't the same as walking; still, the closest thing to it at the end of her life.

What Ruth didn't tell them was why: because she was running, carried along by the wind. Running around the shiny exterior of Lester's Variety during the store's best and happiest years. Running toward the alley, which opened up on the patch of backyard behind the building. Inside the fence, somewhere between the pickets and the back door leading up to their homey apartment above the convenience store, she heard Jack and Jacob having one of their father-son talks. Her heart galloped in anticipation of joining them. Ruth's legs sped faster. And then, the world erupted in red-hot agony, and the dream cracked apart. So did arm bones, Ruth later discovered.

She woke on the clean white linoleum floor of Room 209 at Hutton Hill, the nursing home for well-to-do old ladies. The pain was so intense that it drove out the fog, and Ruth remembered everything. The convenience store; long gone now. Her husband, Jack; gone longer. And

Jacob, whose body had been so mangled in the wreck that they'd held the funeral closed-casket. That pain knew no rival, not even breaking her arm in three places.

The Italian woman on the other side of the privacy curtain, Ruth's unwanted and loud roommate, screamed for help. It was the one time Ruth was grateful for the woman's big mouth.

***

Three weeks later, the pain roused Ruth awake. She unstuck her eyes and gazed to the foot of her bed, where Death stood dressed in maroon hospital scrubs. The air thrummed with its usual undercurrent of electricity, the pulse of machinery, and televisions playing in other rooms. The white glow from the hallway outside the room did little to illuminate the man's face, though she could tell by his silhouette that he was, indeed, a man.

Death held a penlight in one hand. He flicked it on and off, creating an effect Ruth equated with distant thunderclouds pulsing with furious energy. The storm stood frozen, watching her. A chill gossiped over her flesh, creating an unpleasant sensation in counterpoint to the burning from deep within her bones. He stared. Ruth's skin dimpled in goose bumps.

She conjured her voice. "Hello?"

The man answered with an exhale, snorted through nostrils, nothing more. And then Death walked out of the room. Invisible ice encased Ruth's body. She waited, breathing no longer simple or even an involuntary thing. She forgot to blink until her eyes started to burn, and sleep remained elusive until one of the nurses checking in saw that she was awake, and brought Ruth her next dose of pain medication.

***

Lester's Variety had been more than a place to buy cigarettes, beer, and cold cuts. One whole aisle was devoted to seasonal items—coolers and suntan lotion in the summer, and beautiful gift notions during the holidays. That's where the silver picture frame originated, Ruth remembered, during the too-short spell of clarity following her disturbed night.

The store was gone. So, too, were husband and son. She was stuck in a present whose reality was pain and infirmity of both body and mind. Limbo, land of lost souls.

One of the Mimi's washed and dressed her and, with another Mimi's assistance, eased Ruth into her wheelchair for another day no different than the one before. The pain in her broken arm helped her to ignore the unforgivable invasion of hands touching her that Ruth always choked down and suffered through in silence. She welcomed the warmth of the long, gray sweater, draped over the shoulder of her injured arm.

"Looks like we're gonna have snow today," one of the Mimi's announced in a cheery voice before exiting the room.

Like that news mattered or was reason for saccharin smiles. The last time Ruth had sampled the outside world, she was being whisked away by ambulance to the hospital, her arm in pieces. And the cold on that journey, untold days in the past, had gotten deeper into her marrow through the breaks. Sometimes, she overheard the nurses complaining about the stifling heat inside Hutton Hill, after they removed their birthday party hats and thought the guest of honor wasn't listening. Truth was, she always felt cold, even under the extra blanket in the prison that was her bed.

Right before Death moseyed back into Room 209, Ruth sat staring at the tiny, oblong patch of real estate her life's end occupied. In the apartment over the store, there'd been big rooms filled with plenty of furniture, books, and drapes she'd ordered from catalogues sent to Lester's Variety by vendors. There were rugs—a big oval one, dark green, though, for a moment, her mind colored it cobalt blue. A gallery of family photographs—snapshots of happier times—filled the hallway between the bedrooms and bathroom.

The photograph of Jacob, on top of the nightstand near Ruth's bed, was the last survivor to have escaped the hallway; the last relic of Ruth's life apart from the frail living corpse that still, somehow, held onto so many ghosts—the memory of the china they ate off of daily, with its butter-yellow stripe around the edges; the fancy plates for company and special occasions, Blue Willow; the night of the phone call, and how that deep *ringing* right before she lifted the receiver off the cradle had gotten into her and stayed, was still echoing in the dusty corners of her psyche, proclaiming the news of Jacob's death.

One photograph in a tarnished silver frame, set beside an impersonal altar of tissue box, plastic water pitcher, cup and straw, and a plastic vase with one silk flower, a gift from unknown hands. All sat beneath the stark white glow of the light from which the call button's tentacle snaked, along a length of drab beige wall.

Briefly, Ruth pined for the apartment. She'd kept the place immaculate, and had loved their small, guarded backyard. Jacob had wanted a dog, but there was Lester's Variety to run, a store that provided them an above-average life. She'd wanted to entertain—dinner parties, using the good Blue Willow china…

But always, there was the store.

A shadow cut across the top of the nightstand and engulfed Jacob's photograph. Ruth seized in place and returned to the present. A blur of crimson color materialized at the corner of her eye. She attempted to turn the wheelchair, using her feet. The pain in her broken arm reasserted its pull.

The earth moved beneath her. No, Ruth realized, it was only the wheels under the chair. Death's hands turned her around to face him directly.

"Hello, Ruth."

"Well, hello," she said in her usual voice, which always accentuated the positive, even as her insides clenched from the negative energy she felt radiating outward from the man in the crimson scrubs, who towered over her, seemingly at a height of a hundred feet.

Their eyes connected, and the cold inside Ruth's bones worsened.

"*'Go say hi to Ruth Lester'*, they all said. *'Ruth's the sweetest, kindest soul'*," the man said, his voice deep, friendly.

Ruth instantly sensed it was a ruse. Decades had passed since some smiling customer had approached the register at Lester's Variety, intending to steal whatever was inside the cash drawer. The store had been robbed a total of seven times during its existence, and all of the criminals had spoken in that same, slippery voice, before revealing their true intentions.

"I told them," he continued, "you don't gotta tell me. I knew the Lesters a long time ago. Nice people. Especially that Ruth."

The man hunched down so that his face was close to Ruth's. Too close. She caught the thick stink of his cologne on her next sip of air and drank in the image of his face—long, mean, despite the smile, especially in his eyes. His mean, dark eyes drilled into her.

"You don't remember me, Ruth? Sam Tillman? I was a pal of your son, Jacob. You know, before…"

He mouthed a sound meant to mimic screeching tires, followed by the *kaboom* of an explosion.

Ruth listened, too stunned to react. Her lips moved of their own will. "A friend of Jacob's? How nice."

The man's smile flattened. "Yeah, nice. How's the arm? Heard you landed pretty hard on it."

His hands moved to adjust her sling, only this time, fresh stings rippled outward in concentric waves, engulfing her entire body, and Ruth knew the pain was inevitable, because she saw it telegraphed, first, in his smile.

"How's that feel, Ruthie?" the man taunted more than asked.

She bit back a howl. The fear she remembered, from the man's first visitation at night, manifested in day—a snowy one, by all reports. The scream built in her stomach and clawed its way up her throat. Ruth ground what remained of her teeth and readied to release the shriek.

The man straightened. "You let Sam from the old neighborhood know if there's anything you need, dear Ruth."

He shuffled toward the door, and she got a better look—this former friend of the dead boy in the photograph wasn't the size of a skyscraper anymore. Tall enough. If he were the dead boy's friend—*Jacob*, proclaimed the voice in her thoughts—he'd be in his late forties now. A tattoo snaked along one of his arms. The smirk on his mean face unleashed pins and needles over her skin. And deeper. Deeper than marrow. Soul?

"See you soon, Ruth," Death said. Then he winked at her before exiting the room.

***

Ruth sat paralyzed, fearing to blink, to breathe. The male nurse's name—*Sam Tillman*, that's what he said. Frozen in the wheelchair, she focused on his name, attempted to etch it into her grey matter through concentration. That was his name. Sam. Tillman. Tillman's Salvage and Scrap Yard.

The place jumped out of the background of muddy memories and she could almost see it clearly, a two-dimensional automobile graveyard on the bad side of town. Bad kids. Jacob was having problems with the Tillman brothers. Jacob wanted a car for graduation. Car accident. Dear God, the man in the crimson scrubs…he'd *mocked* Jacob's death. Who could be so cruel?

Ruth caught herself drifting past the rusting, sepia wrecks of Tillman's Salvage and Scrap Yard and turned the shoulder of her injured arm, just enough, so that a bolt of exquisite red pain shattered the fog and left her head clear of distraction. Ruth imagined the jolt as a ballpoint pen, then as a threaded needle, and wrote his name out, in cursive.

Sam Tillman, he knew my son.

Ruth choked down a dry swallow and maneuvered her feet along the floor, closer to the nightstand. She reached for the cup. The water was warm, but she drank it down through the straw until she drained the cup.

Knew my son, she embroidered in her thoughts. *And he knew me.*

***

It could have been days later or only hours—in the jumble of concentrating on Sam Tillman's name, to the exclusion of most else, Ruth lost track of time—when she overheard the birthday party revelers as they worked on the other side of the privacy curtain.

"So nice. And funny!" one of the Mimis said, in a voice not meant for anyone else's ears. "He knew exactly what to do. Somehow, it was a loose battery cable."

"You're lucky," another Mimi said. "I feel so much safer knowing we've got Sam working here."

She heard them moving around, wrapping and taping. Presents for the party? The privacy curtain was closed fully around Ruth's little oblong patch of real estate. She imagined herself sitting inside a gift box, bolts of ribbon spilling down from a giant bow. Wheels moved across the white linoleum—the cart upon which the birthday cake sat, perhaps?

Movement stirred just beyond the curtain. Something snagged and dragged the curtain aside, enough for Ruth to see the stretcher as it slipped past, containing the shrouded corpse of the loudmouthed Italian woman from the bed next door. Sam Till…no, *Barbara*…had been in fine voice, not long before. Clearly, the birthday celebration was for Big Mouth, not Ruth. Barbara had blown out her candles. The Mimis could focus on other shindigs, other funerals, now.

The curtain fell back into place, and a silence far worse than the loudest of her roommate's jabbering settled over Room 209.

He said he was coming back, warned the voice in Ruth's thoughts. *That boy who knew Jacob. The scrap yard kid. Tillsbury…no, Tillman. Sam Tillman!*

***

Food had long ago renounced its taste and pleasure. For a while, Ruth loved frozen yogurt, particularly the chocolate brownie variety served for dessert in Hutton Hill's dining hall, but even that had waned.

One of the nurse's wheeled Ruth out of the room and down the corridor, toward the elevator.

"Barbara," Ruth said.

"I know. So sad, but it was her time."

Ruth pondered the partygoer's statement. "Do you know when I'll be getting another roommate?"

"Soon, hopefully," the nurse said. This Mimi's voice boasted a soupçon of Spanish accent. "Until then, be sure to enjoy the quiet. Rest, Ruth—get that arm back to where it was for the next tennis match."

Ruth laughed, even as the sense of dread thickened around her. "Is it still snowing?"

"No, dear, that was days ago. It's just cold and miserable."

"And Tillsbury?"

"You mean Sam? Sam Tillman?"

"Yes, him. That rotten punk from the junkyard. I don't want him playing with Jacob. He's too rough—and a bad influence. Every time Jacob comes home from that place, he's covered in scratches and bleeding!"

Mimi hesitated. Ruth wondered if she'd trapped her thoughts inside the tiny section of clarity where she attempted to sort out memories, names, and faces, or if she'd spoken them aloud.

"Ruth, you have the wrong guy," Spanish Mimi said. "Our Sam, the new nurse—he's a gentleman. So nice, so sweet and kind. We're all lucky to have him here. You'll see."

The elevator reached the ground floor, dinged, and its doors trundled open. Standing outside was Death, dressed in crimson hospital scrubs.

"Sam," Spanish Mimi said. "Ruth and I were just talking about you."

Ruth gazed up. The man's mean eyes captured hers, and their cruelty intensified, in league with his slippery smile. "Were you? All lies, I hope."

Spanish Mimi snickered and wheeled Ruth past the lobby, a turn right, and then another, into the lunchtime bustle of the first floor dining hall. She sensed his cold stare tracking her to the table beside the big window that looked out on the courtyard, presently draped in a coat of pristine white. A thick soup of meat-and-gravy smells and coffee sitting too long on burners, mixed with perfumes and sweat, hung over the place.

Spanish Mimi guided her wheelchair into one of two vacant spots. Colleen—the woman's last name eluded Ruth's memory—sipped either tea or some of that burned coffee, pinkie finger politely extended.

"Hello, Ruth," the Grand Dame of their dining table announced.

"Hello, dear."

Ruth nodded to the other lady at the table, all that now survived of Colleen's court. The two women were engaged in eating their dinners. Ruth's soon appeared—some kind of meat, pork or turkey, she assumed, cut into tiny bites; starchy mashed potatoes under a glaze of brown gravy; and bright orange cubes she guessed were carrots. One round bread roll and a single pat of butter. Tea with skim milk. She moved the food around on the plate with her fork more than she actually ate anything.

"Do you need help, Ruth?" one of the Kitchen Mimis asked.

Ruth lifted a glop of potatoes and gravy, showing them she didn't need spoon-feeding. She wanted the tea more than the rest. Anything to feel warm again.

"Terrible about Barbara," said Colleen.

Ruth roused from the fog and attempted to focus. "Barbara?"

Colleen rolled her eyes toward the vacant seat. "Your roommate. *Ex*-roommate."

News travels, thought Ruth. *Especially bad news.* "Have you seen that new man? Tall and mean. He was a friend of Jacob's."

Colleen tittered in that theatrical manner that drew attention from other tables, something the Grand Dame ate up as heartily as select castoffs from the rest of her court's unwanted lunches, like bread rolls and butter. "You mean that nice man, Sam? If I was thirty years younger…"

The statement went unfinished. More laughter. Saying nothing, Ruth lifted the plastic cup containing her tea and sipped.

***

The joy of food was gone. For lunch, which was also Ruth's breakfast, following the daily morning humiliation of being washed and dressed, she forced herself to eat. Dinner was usually a small carton of skim milk, maybe something sweet, though even dessert had lost its appeal.

She sat in her wheelchair, her eyelids fighting the pull of gravity. It could have been a dream, but she was almost certain it was a memory. Jacob, sobbing. The Tillman boys, whose family owned the junkyard of rusting cars and car parts, had chased him home from the bus stop. Ripped his clothes. The skin beneath one of the tears, bled.

"What happened?" the younger version of Ruth Lester asked. Before the boy could answer, she demanded, "Who did this to you, Jacob?"

"Sam."

"That Tillsbury boy?"

Ruth reached for the phone, that rotten crier of doom, whose ring haunted both dreams and the background of her waking hours. The Ruth who dialed was an elderly shell with a broken arm in a sling.

"Yes, I want to talk to you about your boys. Especially Sam, and what he did to my son, Mister Tillman!"

Jacob tugged at Ruth's gray sweater. She turned to face him. He was older now, barely eighteen, and clearly scared, according to the look on his face. "Be careful, Mom—Sam's back."

Ruth's eyes snapped open. The confines of the apartment evaporated. Room 209 at Hutton Hill Nursing Home rose up from the fog and solidified in its place.

"Ruthie, wake up," Death cooed in a sweet voice. "I brought you something."

Sam Tillman's face leaned down, right into Ruth's. Her heart attempted to jump out of her chest and into her throat.

"You-!"

"Shhh, Ruthie, just a couple of friends from the old neighborhood, hanging out here, catching up. How you doing today, sweets?"

He cupped her chin. She twisted away. Tillman pulled her face back toward him, hard enough to hurt. She thought about the call button, still within reach. She'd ring for help and, surely, help would arrive…unless he told them not to come. Then what? Try to convince whatever Mimi was on duty that she was being terrorized by the new favorite son of Hutton Hill? Hadn't she already tried that? Nobody believed her claims about Sam Tillman.

"Please," she attempted. "Whatever happened was a long time ago."

He dismissed Ruth's statement with a snort. "I got a long memory, lady."

Ruth persisted. "Whatever I did to make you angry…your mom, would she want you acting this way to me? I'm a mother, too."

Tillman released her chin, caressed her cheek, and, at first, the gesture seemed kind. Soon, his touch was overly familiar – unwanted.

"You sure are, Ruth. Go on, drink up."

Tillman reached for the small carton of skim milk on the nightstand and aimed the straw at her trembling lips.

"Drink up, mommy."

She caught his malevolent smile again. Every instinct told her no— *don't drink it, Ruth!*

"Do it," Tillman growled.

Ruth took a tentative sip. The second made her gag. She choked down the swallow as the sharp odor of urine struck her nostrils a fractured second before the taste ignited over Ruth's tongue. She pushed the carton away, sputtering.

"What? You don't like my little happy hour cocktail of piss and milk?"

He laughed and straightened. Turning, he entered the bathroom. Ruth heard the glug of evidence being dumped into the toilet, followed by the flush that washed his guilt away. She reached for the water cup—empty— and then the pitcher. Tillman intercepted her wrist and yanked the pitcher out of her hand.

"No, you rotting old snatch, you get to choke on the taste of my piss. Just like that fucking dick-smooch son of yours. You uppity, rich fucks, thinking you were so much better than us. Do you know what my mother did to me after you called to complain about me and my brother and your kid? We were only roughhousing with him. Know what she did to me?

That was a day at the circus, compared to what the old man did after you banned our family from your shitty store, and he had to go to the next town over for his beer and smokes. You want to see, huh?"

Ruth attempted to look away, but Tillman lifted his scrub shirt, and there were the scars—nearly perfect, round burn marks, drilled into flank and stomach. Scars from the ghosts of cigarettes past, she realized.

"Oh, no, Ruth-baby, I'm not done with you. Not even close, bitch."

Tillman smoothed out his scrub shirt, flashed his slippery smile, and shuffled toward the door.

"You have a great day, too, dear Ruth," he said, loud enough that she imagined other patients and nurses overhearing the exchange.

Bile rose up Ruth's throat on a sour burp and painted the back of her tongue. The contents of her stomach threatened to follow. Somehow, she willed the vomit into staying down.

Oh God, dear God...

Ruth began to pray. To God. To whatever saint, martyr, or deity would listen. To Jack. To Jacob. To the late Italian Big Mouth, who'd woken her up so many times with her endless babbling and snoring. She forgot the woman's name, but figured the least she owed Ruth was a good word with the Powers Above.

And then it struck her—a concept that would have seemed crazy, if not for her predicament.

What if Sam Tillman had murdered the Big Mouth to get her alone, to further isolate her from prying eyes and loose lips?

***

Ruth sank into the darkness. She didn't want to sleep. Sleep gave Tillman yet another advantage over her. Age, exhaustion, and the pain medicine all conspired against her, and, despite her promise not to, Ruth floated off, wondering about his accusation—*banned from the store*.

We reserve the right to refuse service—the words jumped out of the depths and played in the foreground of her dream. There'd been a sign posted on the glass door with the jingling bell that announced customers had entered Lester's Variety. After the funeral—Jack's—Jacob had gotten into another scrape with that Tillsbury punk. *No, Tillman*, her inner voice barked.

"Since you can't keep your son from acting like an animal and beating up on my boy, I have no choice but to ban you—all of you—from my store!"

The humorless, hulking brute that smelled like ashtrays and motor oil had gone off on her, using the kind of language that cemented Ruth's resolve. "The apple and the tree," she'd calmly stated, while reaching for the phone. "Yes, Operator, give me the police…"

She'd been terrified then, more so than she ever thought possible, but no Tillman was going to bully this widow around, even if he was twice her size. And no Tillman brat was going to get away with beating up on her son.

"Fuck you, bitch," spat the long-dead memory of the Senior Tillman.

"You fucking bitch," the son whispered, shocking Ruth out of the dream.

She woke to the on-off click of the penlight, now aimed right at her eyes. Pain pulsed between the flashes.

"That's right, it's me again, you dried up cunt. Skeleton crew on tonight at the Hutton—the minimum staff required. Just you and me, together, Ruthie."

A hand slid over her cheek as the penlight went out and stayed dark. Ruth gasped.

"Only the two of us…"

The hand slid lower, down Ruth's throat, over her nightgown and the shriveled lump of her left breast. She let out a yelp, which she imagined vanishing into the ether, smothered by all the other sounds of nightlife in Hutton Hill.

A hand clamped over her mouth, silencing any additional temptation to scream for help. The hand groping her breast pinched, savaged. Tears invaded Ruth's eyes.

"Go ahead, tell them," Tillman chuckled, his voice barely above a whisper. "Nobody will believe a senile old gitch like you. *Dementia*, Ruthie. You talk crazy shit all the time."

She attempted to bite. Ruth Lester had faced off against dragons before—seven thieves and Old Man Tillsbury, the chain-smoking, alcoholic mechanic among them, even if standing up for her son, against Death's father, had sewn the seeds that had germinated into this dark moment.

"Tomorrow, Ruthie," Tillman said, and released her. "You just wait for what I've got planned for you, bitch. Wait 'til you see what's coming next…"

He spit at her and stalked out of the room.

***

The clarity of her thoughts wouldn't last, she knew. Ruth imagined herself holding onto the details, each fact a bird with flapping wings attempting to escape her grasp.

"Mimi," she said to the woman who washed her body.

"Mimi?" the Spanish girl laughed. "Ruth, Mimi hasn't worked here in a jillion years. You know very well, I'm Altagracia."

"You won't let him near me, promise me you won't."

"Him? Who do you mean?"

"That boy. The one who was so mean to my son. His family owns the scrap yard. Will you please call the police?"

"There's nobody like that here at Hutton Hill—you know everybody cares about you. You're just confused again, Ruth."

"That man—*Tillman*!"

"Sam?" Spanish Mimi giggled. "He's a big teddy bear. Every time one of us has car problems, there he is, saving the day. Man's a mechanical genius!"

"But…"

Spanish Mimi finished drying off Ruth and fixed her with a fresh adult diaper. Then, with another nurse's assistance, they dressed her, seated her upright in her wheelchair, and made sure she was as comfortable as possible.

"You won't let him hurt me," Ruth pleaded. "You'll check in on me, won't you?"

"I swear," said Spanish Mimi. "Cross my heart."

And then they left her alone.

***

At lunch, as was always the case, Colleen held court and Ruth pushed the food around on her plate. She eyed Colleen's butter knife. Because they cut her meat, Ruth's own table setting consisted only of a napkin and fork.

The fork, with its four tines, seemed a better weapon for defense, anyway. During an interlude from Colleen's theatrics, Ruth wiped the fork on her napkin and slid it under cover inside her sling. The metal lay cool against her epidermis and helped her to keep a grasp on those many thought-birds scrambling to fly away.

***

She sensed his approach, even before he entered the room. Ruth's heart beat a tattoo in concert with his footfalls across the linoleum, or, perhaps, in response to sensing his dark intentions coming closer, closer.

"Hello, Ruthie," he said. "You're looking particularly lovely, today."

He closed the door. The doors had no locks, but the Tillman punk didn't need them. He created a temporary lock by wedging what looked like a screwdriver or scalpel into the thin space between door and frame.

Death grabbed hold of his crotch. "Wouldn't want anybody interrupting our fun."

"Spanish Mimi promised to call the police on you," Ruth warned. "You stay away from me!"

"Altagracia? Her shift's over, and all the other nurses on this floor are busy. It's just you and me now, Ruth."

"*No*," Ruth said. "You're a rotten boy, Sam Tillman. I'm calling your mother. *Help!*"

Death hurried over and clamped a hand over Ruth's mouth. She struggled, ignoring the pain in her shattered arm. The pain became her ally. She used it to locate the weapon, scrambled old-but-capable fingers into the sling, gripped metal that wasn't cold any longer, but warmed by her body's heat, and withdrew.

She took aim and lunged. Ruth swore she heard the pop, as well as felt it, as the fork's tines punctured the soft meat beneath Death's chin. Tillman howled and drew back. Drops of red rained down. Her aim for his throat had missed; still, the jab proved effective. Tillman knocked the fork away and surged back toward her, and all else that followed was steeped in agony.

He pushed, driving Ruth's wheelchair backward, into the nightstand. Objects toppled off the altar. Then, he pulled her forward, and Ruth spilled out of the chair, onto the floor. Onto her broken arm.

The wave of pain crashed over her, so intense that Ruth's voice shorted out and she lost the ability to scream. Fantastic colors leapt before her eyes, as beautiful as brutal. Continents collided. So, too, did galaxies. She witnessed the supernova of numerous stars and the spiraling plunge downward of the universe into black holes filled with exquisite agony. *So, this is the end of life*, Ruth thought.

Jacob appeared beside her in the abyss. Her beloved son, taken too young from a world that needed his goodness: smiling at Ruth, seeming to beckon her forward. Only there was no accompanying tunnel filled with light and loved ones, and his smile, even at that horrifying instant, read as sad.

Darkness swept over Ruth.

"I have something to tell you, you rich cunt," Tillman said.

He straddled his body over her crumpled form. She smelled his breath, his cologne, his blood. Leaning his face down into hers, Death laughed.

"Always wanted you to know it was me. Yeah, that car accident, your faggot son—it was *me*. I was the one. Messed with his brake lines because of you messing with me."

A knock sounded. A woman's voice called out for whoever was in there to open the door.

"I did it, bitch," Tillman continued, unfazed. "*I killed your son.*"

5 x 7. Silver. Tarnished.

Ruth faced Jacob. She gripped the jagged shard of glass from the shattered picture frame containing her dead son's sad smile, and, focusing the last of her strength into the upward cut, she drove its point into Tillman's throat.

INSIDER TRADING
John H. Stevens

A white sheet fell from the sky. Ernie Hundley watched the snow accumulate from the window of his garden apartment. *There must be at least six inches already*, he thought.

He let out a worried sigh and looked at his watch. He prayed she would make it home safely. He wanted to apologize after this morning's row. Not that he thought it was his fault but he would apologize anyway. He always did.

***

"I think you should see my psychiatrist," Ernie said.

Nancy slammed her mug on the counter, ignoring the splash of coffee. She knew he would clean it up later. "Maybe you forgot that I'm the sane one."

Ernie retreated. "I haven't forgotten. It's just that I'm worried about you. You haven't been your usual self since…" Ernie's voice trailed off.

"Our baby died," Nancy finished. "It seems to me that you're the one who went fruit loops because of it. Seen any of your imaginary friends lately?" Nancy crossed into the hallway but not before flashing her twisted smile that consistently buckled Ernie's knees.

"You know I haven't. I'd still be in therapy if I had." Ernie shuffled after her. "The shrink said I saw him because I felt guilty about the baby's death."

Nancy reached into the closet and retrieved her coat. "Why would you feel guilty about that? *You* didn't kill him."

Ernie held the coat while she slipped her arms into the sleeves. "It's because I love you so much."

Ernie slumped against the wall. "I never told you the full story. The delivery was very premature. He was no bigger than my hand when they put him in the incubator. He looked so helpless.

"The moment I saw the doctor's face, I knew something was wrong," Ernie continued. "There were complications with the delivery. He said

33

you'd be fine, but we'd know more in the morning. As the hours passed, my legs cramped from pacing. I prayed so hard for both of you. The next morning, the doctor finally came to see me. When he asked me to sit down, I thought I'd lost you. When he told me your prognosis wasn't good, I was heartbroken, but at least you were still alive.

"I began to blame the baby. I got down on my knees—right there in the waiting room—and prayed. I told God I couldn't live without you. If he had to take someone from me, he should take the baby. An hour later, the doctor said you'd pull through."

Nancy zipped up her coat. "You're really crazy, if you think you had the choice of who lived and who died."

"I know that now, but that's why I started seeing, as you put it, my imaginary friend. Because of therapy, I know the man was a concoction of my guilty conscience."

"Therapy was good for you. To think, I had to threaten you with divorce before you'd go." Nancy paused at the door and tilted her head while staring at him. "You still think that man was real, don't you?"

Ernie nodded.

Nancy opened the front door. "You're Looney Tunes." The door slammed.

He saw Nancy slide into the front seat of her Ford Mustang. He didn't see her close her eyes and burrow her face into her hands. He also didn't hear her sob, "This charade has to end."

***

Ernie looked away from the window. "Where is she?" Patches tilted her head as if she didn't understand the question. Ernie smiled at the shaggy clump of unknown ancestry and sat on the couch. Patches immediately jumped up with him and nosed his hand. She received long strokes down her back for her efforts.

Bringing Patches home from the pound was a godsend for the dog, and Ernie. His being cured of seeing apparitions might have saved their marriage, but there was still a great divide between them. The presence of Patches was like a bridge over that chasm.

Patches was two months old when she was found rustling for food in a garbage can and was brought to an animal shelter. Patches had gray, wiry hair with indiscriminate patches of black, hence the name. With her overgrown, mangled fur and imploring eyes, she could have been a poster child for pet adoptions. Ernie patted her head. "You were the sorriest looking thing I ever laid eyes on. No wonder Nancy immediately fell in love with you."

In the two years since, Ernie couldn't picture life without their pseudo child. Nancy had become, "Mommy", and she called him, "Daddy".

"Your Mommy should have been home half an hour ago. I hope she's not in a ditch somewhere." Ernie gave Patches a final pet and returned to his vigil by the window. He knew thirty minutes was nothing in a storm like this. It could be another hour before she got home. If only she would call and let him know she was okay. He stared out the window, willing her car to appear.

A playful yap woke him from his trance. Patches looked from Ernie to the backdoor and back to Ernie, hoping he would pick up on the not-so-subtle hint.

"What is it, girl? Are you trying to tell me something?" Ernie teased. Patches ran to the door and glared at the knob while violently wagging her tail. "I'm coming." Ernie went into the hall closet, slid on a pair of slippers, and grabbed a coat.

Patches wedged through the door as it was opening and sprang up the four stairs to the outside door. Ernie was thankful for the enclosed back porch. He didn't have to bundle up on these cold nights. He knew he could trust Patches not to run away and he would pick up her deposits in the morning. A gust of wind greeted Ernie when he let her out and the snow pricked his face like hundreds of tiny needles. He slammed the door shut and quickly retreated into the apartment.

He left the kitchen, throwing his coat on the couch, to take up his post at the front window. He pushed away the window treatments. What a scam that was. The only difference between window treatments and blinds was the cost. He shook his head in amusement and peered out the window. There was still no sign of Nancy and the snow seemed to be coming down harder, if that was possible. *Why hasn't she called? Was she in an accident?* Patches' barking distracted Ernie from his visions of disaster. She was a good girl and hardly ever disturbed the neighbors by barking.

Ernie trudged to the kitchen window and looked into the backyard. The yard was eye level and Ernie only saw his reflection. He turned off the kitchen lights and returned to the window. He was able to make out a dark figure stooped over. Ernie's gaze followed the figure's outstretched hand and was able to recognize Patches backing away, still barking sharply.

Ernie flung open the backdoor and scaled the stairs in two bounds. He opened the outside door and whistled but Patches didn't come. Without thinking, he plunged outside and took four steps into the snow before the figure was visible through the onslaught of white flakes. Without his coat, the wind tore through his shirt and the snow seeped into his slippers, but he was only conscious of the black hood and the face hiding behind it. He gazed past the eerie shape and saw Patches looking back at him. The dog wanted to come to her master but didn't dare cross the figure's path. Patches let out a loud whimper, though Ernie barely heard it above the howl of the storm.

He took a deep breath and yelled, "Hey you!"

The figure straightened to his full height and turned towards Ernie. Ernie felt a chill down to his bones but assumed it was the weather, prayed it was the weather. He couldn't make out the face but felt the man's stare. Finally, being released, Patches ran past the figure and behind Ernie. She peered around his legs and let out one last bark before running to the door. Ernie broke the stare and moved toward the door himself, slowly at first, but quickly gaining speed.

He opened the door and Patches leapt down the stairs and waited by the kitchen door. A low whimper floated up the stairs. Ernie followed the dog but stopped short when he didn't hear the outside door click shut. The wind must have kept it from swinging closed. *How stupid could I be? I should have slammed the door and locked it.* Ernie gazed up the stairs and nearly wet his pants. The stranger had caught the door before it closed.

Ernie mustered up his courage. "I'm sorry, but you'll have to leave. This is for residents only."

"But I am a resident." The figure reached up and slowly lowered his hood. His long, stringy hair silhouetted his drawn-out, sallow face, but what startled Ernie were his eyes. They were jet black and appeared entirely devoid of white. "I moved in last weekend. I took over old Mrs. Murphy's place."

Ernie tried to make conversation but thought only of escaping the glare of the black eyes. "Did Mrs. Murphy move out?"

"No, she died."

Ernie wasn't sure, but he thought the stranger smirked. "She was such a nice lady. It's a shame."

The man laughed. "I don't think so. I got her apartment."

Ernie felt another shiver. "Well, I would appreciate it if you left my dog alone. I let her out by herself at night, but I'm out there first thing in the morning to pick up after her. The other residents don't mind. In fact, they all get along great with Patches."

"So, Patches is her name. I only wanted to get along with her, too. I was going to give her a treat until she started barking." He held out his gaunt hand and showed Ernie a dog biscuit.

"Do you always walk around with dog biscuits?"

"I happened to have it with me. I thought Patches would enjoy it."

"Only a dognapper would carry a dog biscuit with them, or a thief, to distract a dog while he robs the place. You keep away from my dog and my apartment." Ernie's voice wavered.

The stranger stepped down the first stair. "You don't want me to play with your dog?" He took another step. "You don't want me in your building?" He descended another stair. "People like you don't want me in their world. There's only enough room for you." His last stride brought him even with Ernie. "People like you make me sick."

Ernie wasn't a small man but he needed to lift his head to look at the stranger. Ernie was about to speak but was cut off. "In fact, I'd like to kill all the people like you," the stranger spit.

Ernie didn't wipe the spittle off his face. He was more than scared and found courage from somewhere past his humiliation. "I don't know what your problem is, but you better get out of my face."

The stranger snatched Ernie by the collar and hoisted him off his feet. "I'll get in your face if I want to. I'll feed your dog if I want to and there's nothing you can do about it."

Ernie grabbed the stranger's arms and held on. "Get him, Patches." Patches charged the stranger, biting at his ankles.

The stranger tried to kick off Patches but the dog kept coming. He tossed Ernie down and retreated up the stairs. He opened the door and stared down at Ernie. "You better watch yourself or I'll come for you next." He let out a laugh and stepped outside.

***

Patches scurried to Ernie and licked his face. Ernie hugged the dog. "Good girl," Ernie said between slurps. He slowly rose and took a long look at the door. Once he was sure the stranger was gone, he ran up the stairs and locked the door.

Ernie followed Patches into the apartment. Nancy was leaning against the kitchen counter with her arms folded. Relief washed over Ernie's face. "Nancy, thank God you're home. I was so worried about you."

A tear rolled down Nancy's right cheek. "I'm worried about you. It's starting again, isn't it?"

Ernie approached Nancy but pulled up short when Nancy's extended hands met his chest. "What are you talking about?"

"Ernie, I saw you." Tears were flowing freely now. "You were screaming, 'Get him, Patches', but no one was there. Then you ran up and down the stairs like you saw a ghost."

"Didn't you see him, honey? There was a guy in a trench coat. He was bothering Patches, so I went out to rescue her. Then, he followed us down the stairs and threatened me. He said he moved into Mrs. Murphy's apartment. I think we should call the police."

Nancy shook her head. "I think we need to call the doctor again. I saw you come down the stairs by yourself. You started yelling and flailing. Then, you ran up the stairs and locked the door. There was nobody there!"

"He was there. He looked crazy. You had to have seen him." Ernie's voice trailed off.

Nancy stabbed at the tears with the back of her hand. "It's been a long day. I think I'll go straight to bed. I'd appreciate it if you slept out here, tonight."

"He was there," Ernie pleaded.

Nancy brushed his cheek with the back of her hand. "I do love you. It's my fault you think you saw him. Maybe it would be better if I left."

"Don't leave me. I'll see the doctor again."

"I have to think. Good night, Ernie." Nancy quietly closed their bedroom door. She crumpled onto the bed. "It is my fault," she said to herself. "I don't know if I can go through this again."

***

Ernie stood in disbelief. She must have seen him. This wasn't like before. This time, he was physically accosted. A smile crossed his face and he patted Patches on her head. "That's it." Ernie crossed the kitchen and went down the hall. He walked into the bathroom and inspected his neck but nothing was there. Surely there would have been a mark from where his collar rubbed against it. He looked back to Patches. "You saw him, didn't you?" Patches wagged her tail and raised her forepaws to Ernie's waist. Ernie scratched his dog behind her ears. "Girl, it looks like it's just you and me, tonight."

***

Patches' tongue roused Ernie out of a pleasant dream. He pushed her face away and rubbed the sleep out of his eyes. He slowly rose from the couch, but stopped, suddenly. His hand moved to the small of his back. "Damn couch." He tenderly walked to the back door and opened it. Patches flew out the door and up the stairs. Ernie gently climbed the stairs and let Patches out. The sky was gray but at least the snow had stopped. He closed the door and returned downstairs.

He filled the coffeepot with water and started the morning brew. *There must be a foot of snow on the ground.* Then, it hit him. He had forgotten about the stranger. He must have left footprints in the snow. Ernie moved to the window but immediately forgot about the footprints.

He saw Patches hunkered down in front of the figure in the trench coat. The stranger lifted his hand toward the window and gave Ernie the finger. Ernie ran to the knife rack and grabbed the longest one there. He ran out of the kitchen and bounded up the stairs. He reached the door and jerked it open.

He never saw the punch coming. He stumbled backward off the landing and caromed down the stairs. He came to rest in a heap by the open kitchen door. He felt a sharp pain in his gut. He reached down and felt the knife protruding from his stomach. He stared at the red goo dripping from his hands as his eyes slowly closed. He felt the familiar kisses from Patches covering his face. Then he felt no more.

***

The paramedics removed the body through the kitchen. Nancy looked over the policeman's shoulder at the body of her deceased husband. "I've already told you. He said a man attacked him last night but I saw the whole thing. He was by himself. He had a problem a couple of years ago, where he saw imaginary people."

The policeman looked up from his notes. "We talked to one of your neighbors. She heard something crashing down the stairs. When she got to the landing, the door was closed and no one was there. Then, she saw your husband sprawled on the ground, near your door. I'm afraid it was too late."

When Nancy didn't respond, he continued. "We didn't find any footprints in the snow, besides the dog's tracks. We'll question the other residents. Maybe it was an inside job."

"I wouldn't upset them. I'm sure Ernie thought he was fighting his imaginary nemesis and lost his balance. Ernie didn't deserve this. I wish there was something I could've done." Nancy dabbed at her eyes with a tissue. "He refused to see the doctor."

Nancy hung her head, refusing to look at the policeman. They might be able to see the truth in her eyes.

The policeman closed his notebook. "We've got all we need, for now. We'll get in touch with you if we have any more questions. Are you going to be all right?" He received a nod in reply.

Nancy saw them to the door and plopped onto the couch. She turned on the TV, but gazed through it. After a few hours, Patches let her know that she needed to go out. She drifted to the door and up the stairs. A strong wind greeted her as Patches ran out to do her duty. *I hate winter. Now that Ernie's gone, maybe I'll move south, where it's warm.*

Nancy turned, but stopped, when she heard Patches barking. She swung open the door and saw a figure in a black trench coat with his hand extended toward Patches.

Nancy took a deep breath and yelled, "Get away from my dog!"

The figure reached up and pulled down his hood. He glanced over to Nancy and smiled. He threw a dog biscuit to Patches and strode toward her.

Nancy didn't move but she shook uncontrollably. "What are you doing here? I thought our business was done."

The figure stopped five feet before her. "I came for Mrs. Murphy, and since I was in the neighborhood, I thought I'd drop by and see how you're doing."

"Poor Mrs. Murphy died? She was such a sweet lady."

"Obviously, she wasn't, but that's beside the point. I'm surprised you recognized me. I guess I don't need this disguise anymore." The figure's face withered and turned pallid, but the pitch-black orbs remained. "Our deal is off. You were going to repent and change your life. Instead, you almost committed your husband to an insane asylum, because you didn't want to tell him the truth. I told you I'd be stopping by and checking up on you, but when your husband saw me, you told him he was crazy. I should have known that I couldn't trust someone who would trade her child's life to save her own."

Nancy stepped back from the figure. "A deal is a deal. Leave me alone."

"Your husband almost committed suicide from the grief. He always blamed himself for your son's death. He thought he saved your life by wishing your son dead, as if he had that kind of power. Too bad you couldn't tell him you bartered his child's life away. He might have really gone crazy, he might have killed you, or maybe you'd have gotten lucky, and he would have merely walked out on you. I was looking forward to seeing how that would play out. If he killed you, I would have gotten two souls for the price of one. It doesn't really matter, now. He's dead. I'm really sorry about that, but accidents happen."

"That's it!" A contemptuous smile washed over Nancy's face. "I'm afraid you won't be collecting my soul, after all. You took my husband's life by mistake. You owe me one. My husband's life for mine. That's the deal."

The figure contemplated. "I don't have much choice. I must admit, you do know how to haggle. It's a deal. Let's shake." A long, bony hand extended toward Nancy. She retreated into the doorway but the hand ranged closer.

"Stay away from me." The hand gently brushed Nancy's cheek. She took another step back and tumbled down the stairs. Her neck snapped when she hit the last stair, but it didn't matter. Her heart had stopped with his touch.

The figure descended the stairs and bent over her to collect what was his. "You always knew how to haggle, but you forgot one thing: I always get the price I want."

GHOST OF BIG BEND
Nicholas Paschall

Sitting around a campfire in Big Bend National Park, four teens slowly fed a growing fire tinder as they traded stories back and forth, elaborating on the various evils of the world that just happened to lurk close by. Emily, a Chinese girl with her hair up in buns, laughed at Jacob's attempt at making a man with a hook seem scary, while Sarah cuddled up to her boyfriend's arm as they listened. William, dressed in a modest, sleeveless green shirt, sat with his back to the darkness, one arm around Sarah. The four were in their nightwear as they were "roughing" it and planned to sleep in the tents they'd hiked up the trail with.

Jacob sat back down, throwing his hands up in frustration. "Man, I give up, I just can't scare you, Emily. You grew up with all that scary-ass Asian horror shit, the plain old classics here in America just don't cut it."

"Oh, your stories are all right, it's just that they lack a certain…" Emily said, tapping her chin in thought.

"Fear?" Jacob asked.

"Suspense?" Sarah tried.

William stayed silent and remained content, drawing circles on the small of Sarah's back where her nightshirt had ridden up.

"Passion!" Emily declared, flashing thumbs up to Jacob, who merely scoffed.

"Passion? You mean what I feel when I look in a girls' eyes? That isn't scary." Jacob said, waving her suggestion away.

"Uh-huh, passion isn't just about romance, you big lug, passion in anything can be a driving force behind good or evil. All of the best Chinese horror stories have passion in them!" She said, nodding as she scratched at a mosquito bite.

"Well, if you know so much, why don't you tell us a story with passion," Jacob said, earning a round of laughter from Sarah and William.

"All right," Emily said, a glint coming to her eye as she thought of a scary story. "I'll tell you a local legend with the passion that I know you've never heard before. I'll tell you the story of the Ghost of Big Bend."

"The Ghost of Big Bend?" Sarah repeated, earning a swat from William for interrupting.

"Thank you," Emily said, bowing slightly to William. "It all began many moons ago…"

***

Right here in Big Bend, before it was a park, it was just a canyon that America controlled, right next to Mexico. The border patrols regularly rode by on their horses, scouting out the terrain and reporting in whenever they found a caravan headed from the South. But one woman evaded them all, for many years. She lived off the land and trapped wild game, gathering water from cacti, and lighting campfires at the top of Emory Peak every night it was safe for her fellow Mexicans to pass into this country.

Her name was Isabella, and she had come to this country in search of freedom. But the U.S. government denied her citizenship, claiming she had no skills that would qualify her as a citizen. Devastated, she rode back in the wagon to the border with the other illegal immigrants, waiting to be dropped off in Mexican territory. It was then that she noticed the coyotes of the canyon running alongside the wagon, some ten to twelve of them. This gave her an idea.

Crawling out of the wagon, she shimmied around the side until she could see the driver. With the grace of a cougar, she leapt from her position on the wagon and onto the bollock seat, punching the driver across the temple, knocking him out cold. She took the reins and pulled the horses to a grinding halt. Before the coyotes could move in on her brethren in the back of the wagon, she pushed the knocked out white man onto the ground. He was dead within seconds, his throat torn out by one of the wild beasts. While they fed on his flesh, she ushered her compatriots out of the wagon and onto a trail headed north, to El Paso. She gathered the water that was given to the driver, as well as the food and gave it to them.

"Go on without me, I'll stay behind and take care of any white men that try and hunt you down!" Isabella said, ushering her friends onwards. She pulled the wagon to the side and set it on fire, before slaughtering the horses and letting the coyotes eat them as well. Looking at the ruined hide of the white man, she pulled his buck knife and examined it carefully.

"With this, I can fashion myself a poncho that will let me blend into my surroundings," she said, looking at the red rock of the canyon. She flipped the dead white man over and slathered his naked hide with blood before she began to skin him. It took hours, but she fashioned herself a full-length cloak and hood from the skin of the dead white man, sewn up with horsehair taken from the manes of the dead horses. The coyotes, now full from all the meat she'd blessed them with, howled their approval.

So, into the wilderness she went, buck knife in hand and suit of skin protecting her from the heat. She spent many years beneath the relentless sun, tracking down lost groups of Mexicans and guiding them back to the trail, all the while evading the Texas Rangers that had set out to investigate the grisly murder of the stage coach driver. They took it as an offense, that someone working for the government would be so ruthlessly dealt with. They vowed to bring the "animal" that had done this to justice, namely by shooting it.

Isabella was always one step ahead of them, though. By always feeding the coyotes whatever game she caught, she slowly domesticated a pack of them and had them patrol all around the canyon for her. Whenever they would see another white man, they would howl. Whenever she heard a howl, she would duck down against the dust and wait for the tracker to pass her by, his eyes not trained to see the tanned hide of a fellow White Man in the treacherous terrain.

The years crept by and Isabella grew lean from her hunts, and vicious from her attacks. She fought off mountain lions with nothing but her pack and her buck knife, which she regularly poisoned using the fangs of rattlesnakes and the stingers of yellow-banded scorpions. By this time the Rangers knew someone was out in the region, and merely labeled her as the Ghost; one minute she was there, fury incarnate with her quick blade flashing, but as the dust settled she was gone. Several Rangers lost their lives to her buck knife, while several others gained scars.

One such scarred man was Franklin Sneed, a hunter who'd joined the Rangers with every intention of tracking down Isabella the Ghost. He waited until winter came and the frost settled in, freezing over the canyon, dusting the mountaintops with snow. Then, he led in four men on horseback and began to track her, looking for human footprints in the patches of frost. When he found a set, he followed them.

The first set belonged to a small family of Mexican immigrants, a wife and husband with their little girl. Franklin ordered his men to shoot them and left them in the cold, to rot with the vultures, confident that Isabella was close by to see this happen. He hoped to infuriate her, have her make a mistake.

Unfortunately, she was close by, hiding in the tree line beneath her frost covered skin coat, hood pulled up over her ears. She went down to the bodies of her fallen countrymen and bathed her blade in their blood, swearing to the moon that Sneed and his men would pay. That night, as

Franklin Sneed and his four deputies set up camp, the winds carried the howls of the coyotes.

"What was that?" One of his deputies asked, sparking his flint and steel together in hopes of lighting a torch.

He never got past the first spark.

The following morning Sneed and his men found a bloody mess of packed ice and flesh leading away from their camp, down to a small river where the deputy lay dead. He'd had his throat slit and his innards eaten by hounds, with vultures now feasting off of his remains. Off of his back, the skin had been cut and laid against a rock, where a message was scrawled in blood.

"Turn back now and you will be spared," Franklin read out from atop his horse, before laughing. He turned to his deputies, who'd followed him on foot down to the river and ordered them to dig a grave for their comrade.

While they were busy with that, Isabella snuck into their camp and stole all of their gunpowder, filling their shot bags with sand, instead. None the wiser, the men came up and donned their gear for the ride that they faced in the coming day.

Around noon, they noticed a smoke plume rising from a crag in the distance, some mid-way up Emory Peak. Franklin ordered his men to investigate, and they all quickly scaled the steep cliff, only to find a small campfire with nobody tending to it. Standing there atop the cliff, Franklin and his three remaining deputies were stunned; who would climb all the way up the cliff to make a fire, and then not stay and use it?

They never got to find out, as Isabella had packed the stolen gunpowder down below in a crack in the cliff. Using the dead deputy's flint and steel, she lit the fuse that led to the small bomb, which blew the cliff apart at the base, creating a landslide down into the canyon, with Franklin Sneed at the top, fighting to stay alive.

Miraculously, he was only injured from the collapse. With a broken leg, he crawled out from under the rocks to find Isabella slitting the throats of his dead deputies, coyotes running wild through the mess, feasting on the fallen Rangers as she left them. Reaching for his pistol, he pulled the trigger, only to have sand pour out the barrel. Staring in horror as the Ghost loomed ever closer; she stood over him with a bloody knife, two large coyotes standing at her side, growling.

"This skin was getting a little ratty for me anyway. I think it's time I get a new one," she said, silencing Franklin's screams as she brought the knife down on his head.

***

"…And that's the story of the Ghost of Big Bend. The reason I tell you this sordid tale is that we're camping out right where the landslide occurred. Beneath this sediment and soil lay the bones of four Texas Rangers and their horses, one minus his skin."

The whole group stared at Emily, who merely smiled in response. Jacob looked over at William, who was as wide-eyed as Sarah. "Do you believe any of that story?"

"You don't have to believe it," Emily said, pointing up to a cliff set against the full moon. Looking to where she was pointing, the trio could just make out a pack of coyotes gathered near a small, smokeless campfire. "As long as we don't cross paths with her or make her think we're here to hurt her, we're safe."

Jacob stared long and hard at the hounds some five hundred yards up, before turning back to Emily. "Like I said before, you Asians have a whole different scale by which you measure your scary shit."

LAST SUPPER
M.B. Vujačić

This was it. This was the night.

Anna knew it the moment the clock struck nine and Rodger still hadn't come home. If it were any other man, Anna would've assumed he'd gone out for a few beers or gotten stuck in traffic. But not boring old Rodger. He would've done the responsible thing and at least texted her to let her know he was staying late.

Anna snorted, then lit another cigarette. She was sitting on the living room couch with an ashtray in her hand, her feet resting on the coffee table. One of her favorite actors was being interviewed on the TV, but Anna was damned if she heard a word of what he said. She couldn't stop thinking how, any moment now, cops would show up and tell her she'd become a widow and that they needed her to come identify the body. But, instead of relief, she felt a deep chill in her gut and sourness in her mouth, like she'd eaten something rotten.

The doorbell rang.

Anna sucked in her lips, snuffed out the cigarette, and stood up. Her hands shook, her legs feeling so stiff, she had to make a conscious effort to walk straight. She took a deep breath and looked through the peephole. The face on the other side was so pale she hardly recognized it.

Oh, Christ, Anna thought, and opened the door.

The man standing before her was in his early fifties. He wore an ill-fitting business suit that did nothing to hide his round belly; his face dominated by an endless forehead and the kind of mustache you'd expect to see on a whorehouse patron. His eyes were glazed and empty, like those of a porcelain doll.

"What the hell happened to you?" she asked.

"Anna, I...I don't know. Anna, I'm so cold," Rodger said, his voice trembling. His clothes were soaked.

"Well...Don't just stand there, you're letting the snow in." She went back to the living room.

Rodger stood in the doorway as if afraid to enter. His mouth twitched down, seemingly against his will. It wasn't until he stepped inside that Anna noticed the mud stains on his clothes, not to mention the way his shirt was torn at the front. His skin looked utterly bloodless, glistening with what appeared to be a thin layer of frost.

"Where have you been?" Anna said. "Hey, take your damn shoes off!"

Rodger ignored her. He walked to the dining table, leaving a trail of mud and snow, and took a seat. His eyes, still wide and glassy, stared at nothing. "I'm starving, Anna," he muttered. "I need something warm."

Anna wanted to shout, to tell him he wasn't going to eat until he cleaned this mess. But her mouth felt dry and her palms sweated so much, she had to shove them in the pockets of her robe to get them out of mind.

"Anna, please. I am so cold." His voice shivered like he was trying to keep his teeth from chattering.

"You, ah...there are some fish sticks in the freezer. I'll put them in the microwave."

Rodger opened his mouth as if to complain, then closed it again, his lips slack.

Slowly, almost on tiptoe, she went past him and opened the fridge. Rodger didn't move, didn't even seem aware of her, yet Anna couldn't help keeping her hand near the knife rack, wondering if he'd found out somehow. It wasn't until the fish sticks got that brown, crispy look that she realized she was practically hugging the wall.

"Oh, Anna, I am so afraid," Rodger said, sounding like he was crying.

Anna dumped the fish sticks and a chunk of bread on a plate, and placed it in front of him. By the time she realized she'd forgotten to ask if he wanted some cheese or ketchup or whatever, she'd already fled to the doorway. Her hands shook.

Rodger wasn't crying. His eyes seemed as dry and as glazed as they'd been a few minutes ago. He just sat there, looking at his dinner, his hands lying on either side of the plate. There was mud under his fingernails.

"I..." he said, so softly, she almost mistook it for a sigh. "I'm freezing. I need rest." He stood up.

"Aren't you..." Anna began, stopped, and cleared her throat. "Aren't you gonna eat that?"

Rodger said nothing as he walked past her. He stared straight ahead, his arms hanging by his sides like dead weights. The frost had melted on his face, making his skin look almost translucent.

"Rodger, you can't go into the bedroom like that. At least take off your muddy–"

The doorbell rang again.

Anna glanced at the door, then at Rodger, then back at the door. "Rodger? You expecting someone?"

But Rodger had already disappeared into the bedroom.

She put her eye against the peephole. Two cops stood on the porch. The peephole lens made their heads bulge toward each other.

"Oh, no," she said, backing away from the door. "Oh, Christ, no." Her arm bumped against the wall hard enough to sting, but she hardly noticed. *Prison.* She'd end up in prison for god knew how many years. They'd *rape* her there. Even if there were no male guards, it was full of those butch lesbians who injected all sorts of hormones to turn themselves into men and they–

Calm down, you idiot, her mother's voice said in her head. *If Rodger knew what you were up to, he wouldn't have come here. He's a loser, not a moron. Now, open the goddamn door and see what they want.*

"Okay," Anna said. "Okay, okay, you're right." She took a deep breath and looked over her shoulder. The bedroom was open, but there was only darkness inside. She closed her eyes and exhaled slowly.

More ringing followed by loud knocking. Anna opened the door.

"Good evening, ma'am," the older cop said. His nametag identified him as *J. BROWN.* "Is this the residence of one Rodger Marc Wilson?"

"Y-Yes?"

"Are you his wife?"

She nodded. "I am."

"May we come in, please?"

"What's this about?"

"Please, Mrs. Wilson," the younger, *M. GONZALES*, said. "We should not discuss this here."

"Umm...okay. Come in."

They beat the snow from their shoulders and their hats, and followed her into the living room.

"You should sit," J. Brown said, his expression grave.

"What's going on?"

He indicated the couch. "Please."

Anna sat at the dinner table, her fingers intertwined between her knees.

"Your husband was attacked while passing through a park not far from here. He was shot multiple times. I'm afraid he died on the spot."

"We believe it was a mugging gone bad," M. Gonzales said.

Anna looked at Brown, then at Gonzales, then back at Brown. "What are you talking about? Rodger came home half an hour ago."

They exchanged glances. Brown drew a little plastic card from his breast pocket and looked at it. "Is this Dorken Road, number two-oh-six?"

"Yes."

He placed the card on the table. Rodger's driving license. The photo on it made him look like a sex offender posing for a mug shot. "Is this your husband?"

"Yes. Where did you find this?"

"It was in his wallet," Gonzales said. "He–"

"Jesus Christ, he lost his damn *wallet*?" Anna stood up, went to the bedroom and flipped the light switch. "Rodger, the hell is the matter with you tonight, the police found your–"

The words died in her throat. There was nobody in the bedroom. Muddy boot prints led from the living room to the bed. The sheets, arranged that morning after Rodger left for work, were in disarray, their white surface splattered with bits of earth and frozen grass.

He hadn't even bothered to undress before lying down.

***

Rodger was dead.

Anna didn't believe it no matter how many times the two cops swore they'd seen his corpse with their own eyes. She went on not believing, all the way to the station, where they introduced her to two detectives who spoke in tones so convincingly solemn, she almost took them seriously when they said they were sorry for her loss. She kept thinking they must've made a mistake, even as the medical examiner unzipped the body bag lying on one of the metal tables, revealing the same mustached face she'd loathed for the better part of the last five years.

Rodger had left his car at a shopping mall parking lot around seven in the evening, half a block from their house. He did this because their garage had long since been converted to a guestroom for when Anna's mother visited, and because Rodger – never much of a hands-on guy – found it easier to walk five minutes in the cold than to shovel snow from the driveway every morning. He'd been taking his usual shortcut through the park when he ran into what the police believed was a single mugger. Rodger must've fought him, or tried to call for help, causing the mugger to panic and shoot him three times. The killer took his watch, his phone, his wedding ring, and all the cash from his wallet, before fleeing into the snowstorm.

By the time they took her home, well past midnight, Anna began to realize that everything had gone according to plan. Rodger was gone, the police didn't seem to suspect her, and she'd become the sole beneficiary of her husband's hefty life insurance, not to mention his savings and possibly his pension. Even her encounter with an already-dead Rodger could be explained as a guilt-induced hallucination. She'd spent the days prior to his demise wracked by doubt and paranoia, so nervous she hardly went anywhere without a cigarette in hand. Hell, she might've brought all that mud into the house herself, who knew? By all rights, she should've counted herself lucky. But she didn't.

Because, the very next night, Rodger came back.

Anna was home, drinking wine and trying to decide whether to redecorate the house or buy a new one, when the doorbell rang. The sight of his face on the other side of the peephole was like a hand tugging at her guts. She backed away from the door, muttering, "no, no, no," oblivious to the warmth running down her thighs. Black smudges bloomed at the corners of her vision. When she opened her eyes, she was on the floor, aching all over. Someone called her name.

Anna looked up and saw Rodger standing behind the living room window, his narrow shoulders covered with snow. The skin of his face looked like frozen paper, his lips peeled back in a pained snarl. His eyes had rolled back into his skull, but still she could feel his gaze. "Anna, please," he said, his voice a croak, "it's so cold here."

Anna ran, screaming, into the bedroom. She curled up in a corner and told herself this wasn't happening, the man outside was an impostor trying to drive her mad. Her mother's voice laughed at that and told her to cut the crap, because she knew full well that was Rodger's ghost outside. Anna pressed her hands against her ears, shrieking, "No! Fuck you! He's dead, he's *fucking dea–*"

Something struck the bedroom window hard enough to make her wince. It was Rodger. He was thumping his limp hand against the glass in slow–

Thump.

-weak-

Thump.

-strikes-

"Anna, help me," he said, his mouth so rigid, he had to mumble the words, his cheeks covered with frozen tears. "I can't tell which way to go."

Anna fled the bedroom, grabbed her cellphone from the coffee table, and ran into the bathroom, the one without windows. "Someone's trying to break into my house!" she screamed at the 9-1-1 Operator. Then she curled into a ball and waited for what felt like years, while Rodger rang the doorbell and knocked on the windows, calling her name. Eventually, a patrol car arrived.

The cops found plenty of footprints around the house, but no sign of Rodger, himself.

***

The moment the sky turned gray, Anna packed a bag, called a cab, and went to the Violet – a cheap hotel at the other side of the city, where, three years ago, she'd spent a few quality afternoons with a plumber Rodger had hired to fix the shower. She spent the day there, telling herself it wasn't the end of the world, that psychiatric hospitals didn't electrocute patients anymore and that she was just mentally exhausted. People would understand, what with her husband getting murdered and all. Even her mother's voice agreed things would probably turn out fine.

Rodger came to the Violet in the middle of the night. He rattled the knob and clawed at the door, telling her that he was cold and hungry and afraid. His stench slithered under the door and filled Anna's room, so thick, she could feel its stickiness on her skin. She opened the window and held a wet towel over her nose, but the smell still made her vomit.

Rodger vanished before the cops arrived. They found scratches on the door and frozen mud all over the parquet. The reek was so bad, one of them said a rat must've died beneath the floorboards.

The next morning, pale, tired, and disheveled, Anna called another taxi and told him to take her to a Serbian restaurant named *Konoba*. It was a cozy establishment, all dark wood and soft chairs and a big stone fireplace, that served the sort of high-cholesterol food she only dared eat during holidays. The owner, Danilo, saw her the moment she entered. Anna took a seat at an empty table. Fifteen minutes later, he joined her. He was fifty-something, with gray hair and deep-set eyes and a large, gold cross hanging from a gold chain around his neck.

"Is everything okay?" Danilo asked, his face impassive.

Her mouth twisted. "No."

"Cops giving you shit?"

She shook her head. "It's my husband."

"I heard it was taken care of."

"It was, but..."

"But, what?"

Anna looked him in the eye, swallowing. She'd met him almost twenty years ago, back when she was dating his nephew, a half-Serbian guy named Lazar. The first time they'd eaten at *Konoba*, Lazar had leaned close to her and whispered, "See those big guys my uncle's sitting with? They run this hood. He grew up with them in Belgrade. If someone fucks with him, all he does is make a call and *poof*, no more problem."

Lazar had gone on to explain that Danilo was *connected* and that Danilo sometimes did *business* with *the guys* and even *moved some stuff* when they asked him to. The next time they came to *Konoba*, Lazar introduced her to his uncle, and over the following couple of years Anna got to know Danilo well enough that, after Lazar and her broke up, she could keep coming to *Konoba* without risking discomfort.

Not that she went there often. Two or three times a year, and never in male company, just enough to keep in touch. Why? Anna asked herself that many times, and every time, her mother's voice gave the same answer: *Because men are beasts and this is their world, and you need someone with teeth to turn to if push comes to shove.*

And so, Danilo was the first person who came to her mind when, a week ago, Anna finally decided she'd had enough of her boring, passionless marriage. Rodger had been an accountant for almost ten years, and whatever ambition he'd once had to shoot for the stars had petered out long ago. Divorce wasn't an option as, without kids or a private business, the best she could hope to gain from it was a house in the suburbs.

So, she'd gone to *Konoba* and told Danilo she wanted to get rid of her husband. He asked a few questions, listened to the answers, then handed her the menu and said, "Come again tomorrow." Three nights later, Anna was microwaving fish sticks for Rodger's carcass.

"So?" Danilo asked.

She swallowed again. "He came home after...after it was taken care of. The next night, too. And the next. He'll probably come tonight, as well."

Danilo said nothing.

"He had, ah, *ice* on his face and he was pale and he *stank* like...well, like a corpse."

Danilo just stared at her.

"Other people complained of the smell, so I know I'm not crazy."

He stood up, said, "Come," and headed toward the toilets. Anna followed. They went through the door marked *M* and stood next to the urinals. "Who put you up to this?" he asked.

"Huh? Nobody, I–"

"Are you bugged? Take off your shirt."

"What, no, no, I'm–"

"Take off your shirt or get the hell out of my restaurant."

Do as the man says, Anna, her mother's voice told her. *Even if he rapes you, it won't be worse than what his mobster friends will do, if he thinks you're ratting them out to the cops.*

"O-Okay," Anna muttered, taking off her purse and jacket and placing them on one of the sinks.

As she unbuttoned her shirt, Danilo drew a handful of keys from his pocket and locked the door. He opened her purse and went through its contents, then took her jacket and checked every pocket. "Your pants, too," he said, his face locked in a frown.

Anna did as she was told.

Danilo waited, until she was standing in front of him in her socks and underwear, and then said, "Turn around."

She did.

"All right. Get dressed." He unlocked the door and walked out.

Breathing heavily, Anna put on her clothes and splashed water on her face. She found Danilo sitting at her table, sipping beer. She joined him. Without looking at her, he said, "Tell me everything." Anna did. When she was done, Danilo drew his fingers through his hair and sighed through his teeth.

"You think I'm crazy," she said.

"I do, but..." He shrugged, still not looking at her, then crossed himself and said something in a foreign language.

"I don't understand."

Danilo gave a dismissive wave. "I said, *zlu ne trebalo*. Serbian saying. Means *don't tempt fate*." He finished his beer. "There's this woman, I don't remember her name, but my sisters go to her to have their futures read. She can help you."

"I don't need a fortune teller, I need someone to ki–, I mean, to take care of him."

He shook his head. "Only a *mokosha* can take care of a ghost."

"*Moko*-what?"

"*Mokosha*. Witch. This woman's grandmother was one. I will tell her to help you."

"How much money?"

"Nothing."

"Oh? How come?"

"Well, the way I see it, you're *probably* mad, but...but if you're not, and your ghost becomes angry and decides to get vengeful, or something..." Danilo shrugged again. "*Zlu ne trebalo*."

***

The fortune teller was an old, diminutive woman; her wrinkled face so thin, Anna could actually see the outline of her skull. There were so many Orthodox Christian icons, tomes, and crucifixes in her apartment, Anna couldn't resist inquiring how someone could be both a devout Christian and a *mokosha*. The woman laughed, and asked, "Do you believe in God,

Mrs. Wilson?" When Anna shook her head, the woman said, "Then pray to whatever it is you do believe in that you never meet a true *mokosha*."

Anna described her problem. The not-*mokosha* told her there was a way to deal with it, but Anna would have to do it alone. The not-*mokosha* then turned on her laptop and printed out two pages. One showed a bunch of sentences handwritten in some language Anna had never seen before. The other displayed a drawing of a triangle filled with symbols that looked kind of like Chinese letters.

The woman tapped the triangle and said, "Draw this on the wall of your bedroom. Use something that's close to you. Blood is best, but lipstick or mascara will do, as long as they're your favorites. Draw it big. As wide as a TV. Shut the lights, kneel in front of it, and," she tapped the page with the writing, "read this in a whisper."

"Whisper?"

"Yes, whisper. It's *very* important."

"All right."

"Keep reading it. A hundred times, if need be. One or more of them will hear you."

"Them? Who are–"

"The less you know, the better."

Anna licked her lips. "Right. Then what?"

"You strike a bargain. No two deals are the same, so you must trust your judgment. Three things you have to remember: First, the terms of the deal must be *clear* and *precise*, because they *will* use whatever loopholes they find against you. Second: they should work through you, and you, alone. Do not, under *any circumstances,* help them get their own body. And third: no matter what they say, no matter what they offer you, no matter how scared you are, you *must not* look behind you."

Anna left the not-*mokosha*'s apartment around three in the afternoon. She went straight home, took Rodger's favorite painting – a huge reproduction of Dali's *Persistence of Memory* – off the bedroom wall, then spent two hours, and four lipsticks, drawing the triangle on the space the painting used to cover. As she stepped back to inspect her handiwork, Anna wondered if this was what insanity felt like.

By then, it was almost eight, and it had gotten dark outside. She lit a candle and placed it on the floor at the foot of the triangle, so that its glow would shine on the page with the incantation, then shut the door and switched off the lights.

Anna must've knelt in front of that triangle, facing it, for at least an hour. The words of the incantation were so long and convoluted and full of weird punctuation and vowel-less syllables, she doubted they were meant to be produced by a human throat, yet somehow, it felt right to read them in a certain way. It became hypnotizing after awhile, like a tune you hate but can't stop humming. At one point, she forgot herself and raised her voice a bit, and within moments her throat became numb and her gums began to burn like she'd downed a glass of hot water. She took great care to control her voice after that. Any moment now, she kept telling herself, they'd come and–

Xrai, Anna.

Anna gasped so loudly it was almost a cry. Something was behind her, breathing cold air against her neck. For an awful, endless instant, she thought she wouldn't resist the urge to look over her shoulder.

Ahhh, and here, old Acrion thought you'd be comfortable with the forbidden tongue, the thing said in her mind, its voice like slime swishing in a glass. *But, alas, you do not truly speak it; you merely mimic the expertise of others. No wonder, no wonder.*

When Anna did not reply, it leaned closer. It smelled like an abandoned basement, dry and stale and fetid with accumulated dust. *What, and was ancient Acrion summoned here to converse with himself and see his good will ignored? Come now, turn around and face me, so that we may be properly introduced.*

Anna swallowed, blinking rapidly. "No."

Acrion let out a deep hiss, his breath rustling her hair. *So rude,* he said, and then began sniffing at the air. *Ah, but, what's this? Another damned soul? Yes, yes, a scared little soul that clings to your warmth as a tick clings to a sow's hide, ignorant that it was you who murdered it. Poor, poor Rodger. Ha!*

"Y-Yes. I want you to...to..."

To make sure he does not torment you, anymore? But, of course, Anna, Acrion the Misbegotten will gladly grant you this little favor. There's just one, slight thing you need to know.

"Yeah?"

I will deal with Rodger as I see fit, and in doing so, I will exact the ultimate toll, and when I'm done, you will never, ever, ever, ever see Rodger again. His soul will be lost to this reality, taken to a place from which none return. He let out a long sigh, sounding almost sad. *Are you certain you wish to do this? To doom him never to lay eyes on his beloved wife again?*

Anna gave a shaky nod. "Yes. Take him. Do whatever you want with him."

Hah, not a shred of doubt in your heart. A rare thing, these days. Perhaps, someday, Acrion should take you down to ancient Abberon and set you loose in its windless streets. Your presence would bring joy everlasting to its denizens, oh, yes.

She shook her head. "No. No thanks."

He gave a chuckle that sounded like an ill dog clearing its throat. *So, so rude. But, no matter. Listen closely, for there are things you must know, rituals you must perform, so that old Acrion may be made manifest in your–*

"You're not getting a body."

He snorted. *And, what am I to do without a shape of my own, hmm? Spit insults at your dead husband until he leaves in vexation?*

"You can work through me."

A roundabout way to do what ought to be done with one's own hands? Pah! Why cripple old Acrion so, when we can accomplish so much more if–

"*No.* Either do as I say or get out."

Such arrogance. Very well, then, misbegotten Acrion will humor you.

Anna was opening her mouth to reply, when a gelid wind struck the back of her head. It cut like a dagger through hair, bone, and flesh, burrowing all the way to her eyes. She leaped to her feet, moaning, her hands clawing at her face. Her knees gave out and she stumbled against the triangle on the wall, smearing lipstick all over her shirt. She slid to the floor, and, for what felt like an hour in hell, she just lay there, groaning and beating at her head with her fists, trying to extinguish the chill in her skull.

Then, against her will, Anna's legs shifted and her arms propped her body up, helping it get back on its feet. Anna fought with all her might to control her own movements, but her limbs ignored her commands. She watched, a prisoner in her own eyes, as her body walked toward the door, turned the knob, and headed for the living room.

Why struggle against me, little Anna, Acrion said, inside her head, *when old Acrion is merely granting your wish? See how intimate we are, now? More intimate than you've ever been with poor, gullible Rodger, heh, heh. Here, gaze upon your magnificence, blessed now by Armenides of the Deep.*

Anna's body – even her *eyes* – turned to face a hallway mirror. She would've screamed, if only her mouth had been her own. The woman in the mirror was Anna, only that couldn't be, because Anna couldn't smile like that. This woman's lips were stretched halfway to her ears, revealing all of her teeth and gums and the insides of her cheeks. The eyes above that grin were so round, they looked ready to fall out of her head, the pupils shriveled to dots in a sea of white. Black mist spilled from her ears and nostrils, swirling around her head, her skin illuminated from within by a sickly, green glow.

Anna walked away from the mirror and entered the kitchen. Her hands turned on the stove, took ground beef from the freezer, threw it in the microwave, and thumbed the *Defrost* button. They went on to take food – eggs, milk, onions, mustard, ketchup – from the fridge and lay everything down on the counter, before taking a box of instant soup out of the drawer. For the next hour or so, Anna could do nothing but watch, baffled, as her possessed body cooked a spicy meatloaf and a bowl of chicken soup.

Enticing, isn't it? Acrion said, producing another one of those ill-dog chuckles. *Truly, Rodger is blessed to have a caring wife such as you.*

Acrion found Anna's finest cutlery – the thousand-dollar silverware set that saw the light of day only when her mother came visiting – and arranged the table for a single person. He even lit a candle. He laid the finished meatloaf on an ornate metal platter and covered it with a glass dome. Satisfied, he drove Anna's body back into the living room and sat on the couch. A quarter of an hour later, the doorbell rang.

Anna heard herself shout, "Come in."

The door opened. Anna looked at the visitor and realized she'd give anything to be able to slam the door in his face and run, *run, RUN,* until he wasn't even a speck on the horizon. But her body already walked toward him, her mouth forming the words, "Oh, honey, you're *freezing*."

"A-Anna," Rodger said, his rotten tongue turning it into *Ahhnnhhaaa.* "I am so, so cold." *Soh, soh, coooohhhld.*

"Oh, baby, we're gonna fix that right away. Come inside."

Anna watched in horror as her hand took his and led him into the house. His skin was so frigid it stuck to her fingers, making her insides squirm like a half-crushed bug. His gums and teeth were black, his eyes sunken and glazed, his pallid skin spotted with frostbite. The skin had peeled from his fingers, rendering his yellowing nails long and pointy, like a woman's.

"You must be starving," Acrion said with Anna's mouth. "Sit, sit. I prepared your favorite meal."

Rodger sat at the table, his empty eyes staring at nothing, until Acrion placed the bowl of steaming soup before him and poured some in his platter. He picked up a spoon and began eating, seemingly noticing the candle and the silverware for the first time. "Thank you, Anna," he whispered, between sips. "This is so nice. I love you."

"I love you, too, Rodger," Acrion said, then moved behind him and started rubbing his back. His jacket was so rigid with mud and frost, Anna doubted he could feel anything through it; yet, Rodger closed his eyes and sighed like a man receiving the massage of his life.

Afterward, his dead lips stretched back in a smile and he said, "You're so good to me, Anna. Thank you. I...I'm not so cold, now."

Her hands placed the big, metal platter before him and lifted the dome. "Voilà!"

"Meatloaf," he muttered, his widening smile causing chips of rime to break off from his cheeks. "My favorite." He finished his soup, and then cut himself a large slice of meatloaf. His movements seemed faster now, less rigid. By the time he finished eating, his skin had regained some of its color and his eyes had rolled back down. His irises were dry and murky, but there was liveliness to them now, almost as if his decomposing face was just a mask the old Rodger was hiding behind. "I feel so much better. I'm not afraid anymore."

Her index finger came to hover in front of her mouth, her pursed lips producing a *shhhh,* as her body went down on its knees before him. Anna did not understand what Acrion was about to do until she saw her hands working at Rodger's belt, pulling his pants down. She began to cry and scream, begging Acrion to stop, but all that got her was a mocking laugh.

"Oh, Anna," Rodger whispered. "It's been such a long time since you..."

He moaned as she took him in her mouth. Anna shrieked in her head, trying to puke, to spit, to bite down on the flesh that pressed against her tongue and made her throat feel like a rat den. To no avail. Acrion kept her lips wrapped around the shaft in her mouth as he moved her head back and forth, pushing her face into the damp, tangled shrub of Rodger's pubic hair. He wouldn't let her vomit or faint – not even after Rodger shot his viscous seed down her throat and she had to swallow it to keep from choking.

"Oh, God, oh, baby," Rodger said. "That...that felt so good. Thank you."

Acrion made her body stand up and slide her fingers through his thin hair. "I'm glad to hear that, darling. Are you ready now?"

"Yes. I am, honey. I...I'm running late, am I?"

"It's all right. You have all the time in the world."

Rodger pulled his pants up. He gave her hand a little squeeze and went to the door, hesitating for a moment before stepping out onto the veranda. The snow had stopped. The sky was black and devoid of moonlight. "I'll miss you," he said, looking at her. "It...it was all so sudden...I never had the chance to say goodbye." His mouth worked. "Goodbye, Anna. I love you."

"I love you, too, Rodger. Goodbye."

His lips formed a sad smile. Then, he stepped down into the garden and faded into the darkness. Anna's body approached the door and closed it.

The iciness behind her eyes shifted, pulling right through her flesh and bone and out the back of her skull. Anna screamed and stumbled against the wall, her fingers pressing over the nape of her neck, as if to cover a gaping wound. She slid to her knees; the tendons in her neck standing out in taut strings, her jaw clenched so tight, the tips of her teeth cracked from the pressure.

By the time the agony abated, Anna's clothes were so drenched in sweat, even her pants had dark spots on them. As she dragged herself to her feet, she became aware of the wetness on her crotch and the heaviness in her panties, and realized her body had done more than just perspire. Blood trickled from her ears and eyes and nostrils, her gums throbbing so hard, she thought her teeth were about to crumble. She wasn't aware of Acrion's presence, until he spoke, his dry breath brushing the hair at the back of her head.

A hot meal, a little tenderness, a selfless act of adoration...that was all it took to set Rodger's soul at ease. Yet, you needed old, misbegotten Acrion to do it for you. So, so foolish.

"What are you waiting for?" she said, her cracked teeth turning every word into a burning ember in her mouth. "Go after him. Take his soul."

*I never said it was **his** soul I intended to take.*

She froze, the pain forgotten. "What are you talking about? We agreed you'd take Rodger and–"

Old Acrion never agreed to such terms, little Anna. I said I would deal with Rodger as I see fit, and that when I was done, the two of you would never be together again. Now, it's–

"No, no, no, that's *not* what we agreed on! I obviously wouldn't make such a deal with *anyone*! I mean, for *Christ's sake*, I–"

Hands made of blackest ink, grabbed her shoulders, their talons digging into her flesh. A third hand caught a fistful of her hair, another grasped her crotch, and then, the many tendrils of Acrion wrapped themselves around her legs and belly and neck. Anna didn't struggle, didn't scream. She kept trying to speak, to reason with him, even as he seized her jaw and began turning her head around, laughing in her ear. *Oh, Anna, little Anna...*

*...It's **long** past time you looked at me.*

HUNGRY
Robert Stahl

The night Will Graves saw the meteor there was nothing unusual about him, biologically speaking. Nothing unremarkable about his emotions, except for the nagging sadness that came with the death of his father the previous year—from throat cancer, a terrible way to go. Other than that, there was nothing out of the ordinary about the teenage boy of medium build. Certainly there was nothing bizarre about his appetite.

He was trudging home from Otis's house, hoping he'd be able to put on a good face for his mother, when the ball of light came from behind, streaking through the cloudless night with a flash so bright he could make out the pinecones on the old trail floor, some beer cans, a few cigarette butts. A gasp stole its way out of his throat as the object zoomed off toward the horizon and disappeared behind a line of trees. Will stood there staring, realizing how lucky he was to be there in that exact moment, and it wasn't until he heard the impact that his heart started to race.

Otis's house was only five minutes away. Should he turn back for him? Otis wouldn't believe him, would laugh, thinking it was a joke. Otis wouldn't be convinced until Will dragged him out to the woods to show him the crater, the glowing red rock embedded there, smoke rising into the air like satin ribbons.

Or, he could make the discovery on his own.

If he did, things would surely be different at school tomorrow. There, he and Otis were outcasts. But after a discovery like this, the others would line up to be his friends. No more having to rely on Otis as his main source of companionship.

When he arrived in the field, there were no splintered trees, no smoking crater, and no signs of an impact anywhere. After an hour of searching, he gave up and headed home, his heart sagging with disappointment.

***

There was nothing about the incident on any of the stations, leaving Will to wonder if he was the only person who had seen it. The meteor had crashed nearby, he was certain. Two nights later, he headed out again after his mother had left for work. He hurried toward the trail with his gaze turned upward, hoping for more interstellar action. Which is why he didn't see the stranger at first. But he heard him soon enough, groaning in the woods near the ditch.

Will figured it was a drifter. Drunk, from the sound of it.

The man emerged under the yellowing glow of a streetlamp. He was stumbling about, his arms twitching and jerking like a marionette. *A druggie,* Will thought. *Or a lunatic.* Either way, Will crossed to the other side of the road for good measure. As the distance between them closed, he got a better look at the man. His eyes bulged out of their sockets, his tongue as gray as an earthworm and hanging out, and his emaciated flesh clung to his skeleton.

Will thought maybe he should call 9-1-1. He reached for his cellphone and remembered he'd left it at home.

The stranger charged in that moment, bringing with him an awful smell of death and decay. Before Will could scream, the man grabbed him. Powerful hands clamped down on his head, pulling him. The drifter's wild eyes fixed upon his, and his lips bared back to reveal bleeding gums and gnashing teeth. Will managed to jerk his face away as the man chomped down at the base of his skull. He felt skin tearing, felt the warm surge of blood on his neck and shoulders, and he kicked and struggled but the man held him fast. Before his consciousness slipped away, he saw a pair of headlights coming around the bend and a car door flinging open, a policeman stepping out. There was a gunshot. Bam! Then two more. Bam! Bam!

The stranger's head exploded in a spray of bone and blood.

Will surrendered to darkness.

***

"My miracle boy," sobbed his mother, on the day he finally woke up in the hospital. He listened drowsily as she sat at his bedside, explaining to him what the doctors had told her. He had lost a lot of blood that night after the paramedics had found him non-responsive, and the ER doctors had worked on him for over an hour. Her tears moistened his hospital gown. "Finally, your heart started beating again," she said, her hands shaking. "They don't know how you did it."

Intravenous fluids kept him sated while he recovered.

One day, his nurses brought him solid food, a few bland slices of turkey, a tasteless mound of mashed potatoes, before returning to their stations. He ate his meal in peace. But the food settled inside him like jagged bits of glass, and he staggered to the toilet to vomit.

Eager to get home, he never mentioned the incident to anyone.

The next morning, the doctors released him.

He couldn't bear to see his mother cry anymore, so he didn't bring it up when the same thing happened that night after dinner.

And breakfast the following day.

And lunch.

When his stomach finally settled again, Will realized—for the first time since the attack—he was working up an appetite.

***

Will was starving.

Worse, it hurt to move. And he had a throbbing headache.

He lay in bed—tossing and turning—when the idea first hit him.

Clenching his teeth against the pain, he eased open the window and snuck out. He moved quietly in the darkness, slipping through brambles and wet grass until he came to a stop near the ditch. The carcass of a dead squirrel lay at his feet, its hind quarters flattened by a passing car. Will stooped over, his hands moving as if possessed by an external force. Within seconds, he'd cracked the rodent's head open and was nibbling on the walnut-sized nugget of meat inside.

The next morning, he woke in his bed to find the squirrel's blood caked under his nails.

In the bathroom on his knees, he hoped the running bathwater would cover the sound of his sobbing.

***

Will made every attempt to hold off on his feedings for as long as he could, but the longer he waited, the worse the pain became. His head pounded, and his joints grew stiff, threatening to lock up. He didn't look so hot, either; his eyes protruded slightly from their sockets, and his skin grew sallow and smelled sour, like decay. *Just like the guy who attacked me,* Will thought. By the end of the third day, Will was unable to bear his hunger any longer. Sneaking out at night, he roamed the neighborhood until he found a rotting cat in a neighboring alley. Not far from that, he found a dead possum near the highway. Will sighed as he ate, each fetid morsel of rotting brains relieving him more and more of his agony.

The next morning, he scrubbed at his tongue with a toothbrush. When he finally dared to glance in the mirror, his complexion looked normal again.

***

Eventually, the brains of dead animals no longer satisfied him. His nighttime excursions led him to local graveyards, where he searched for fresh graves. Like a dog on all fours, he dug through yards of dirt with his bare hands, using strength he'd never possessed before, scratching and scooping until he reached the coffins below. Then, smashing through thin walls of pine and mahogany, he dragged corpses out of their eternal resting places, bashing their heads open to feast on the brains inside. He winced as he ate; decomposing brains were tough and had a coppery taste to them, like licking a dirty penny. But they made the buzzing stop and eased the pain in his aching limbs.

Later, in his room, Will held a photograph of his father, traced the outline of his likeness with his finger. The photo had been taken years ago, before the cancer had set in. In the glass, Will could see his own reflection, superimposed. How much the two looked alike: the flat blond hair, the solid jaw, the eyes set a little too close together.

"Something's happened to me, dad," he whispered. "Something terrible."

During the daytime, Will ate in front of his mother, regurgitating it later, in secret. At night, he stole out to sate his real hunger.

***

Will became well enough to go back to school, but he didn't want to go.

By now, the story of the attack had made it around town. The others would think he was a freak. He was thankful for Otis, who seemed to sense his unease, and promised to walk with him on his first day back. Stepping inside, a lump formed in Will's throat. The students who had gathered in the foyer stopped to stare at him. Will's mouth went dry, and he became mindful of the new scar at the base of his neck—the skin graft, still healing.

He turned back to the door. Maybe he should call his mom, convince her that he wasn't quite recovered…

When the first student started clapping, Will didn't understand what was going on, but then another student joined in, then another. Soon, the foyer filled with their applause. Will's cheeks flushed when he realized it was for him. Otis smiled, slowly guiding Will through the crowd.

"Graves, my man!" someone shouted.

Someone whistled, another patted him on the back.

But the best moment of all was when Becca Carlson approached him. He had admired her for years, but never had the nerve to approach her. She hugged him, and her chestnut-colored hair spilled onto his face. "Everyone's glad you made it," she said.

For Will, it ended up being the best school year ever.

*** *

May came. It was time for school to end and summer to begin.

With finals approaching, and with all the time he'd been spending with Becca, Will hadn't fed in four days. It was the longest he'd ever gone, and now he was ravenous. His head pounded; it felt like bees buzzing there, a terrible droning inside his skull. He sat in his bedroom pretending to study until his mother left for work. Through the open window, he could feel a late evening breeze pushing away the remaining heat of the day.

Soon, he heard his mother's car purring in the garage. He got up too quickly, his frozen knee joints popping like firecrackers. Making his way to the window, he watched her car's taillights disappear into the darkness. Back in his bedroom, he slipped into a black sweat suit and jerked a dark knit hat onto his head, and then made his way into the living room, his stomach gurgling and twitching all the way.

"Settle down," he said. "Dinner's coming."

He turned off the outside lights and opened the front door.

Otis was standing there, clutching a textbook and a ratty, three-ring binder.

Both boys jumped. The binder flopped open, spilling loose paper onto the doormat.

Will snatched the hat off his head and thrust it deep into his pocket. "What are you doing here?"

Otis gathered up the papers and stood again to look at Will. "Thought we could study for the history exam. I know, should have called first. But your grades have been lousy, lately. You know, since the . . . "

"You can say it, Otis. Since *the attack.*"

"Will, if you fail tomorrow, you'll have to repeat tenth grade. What's Becca going to think then?"

Will opened his mouth to protest, but the buzzing got louder. It was becoming difficult to think.

Otis squinted. "Why are you dressed like a ninja?"

"I'm, ah, going jogging."

"Right now? Do it tomorrow. Tonight, we exercise your brain." He pushed his way into the house. "You coming?"

An owl hooted from the woods nearby. Will wanted to scream at Otis. He wanted to say a million different things other than what he said next.

"Yeah," he offered meekly. He followed Otis inside and closed the door behind him.

***

In the kitchen, Otis was rummaging through the pantry. He seemed to always know where Mrs. Graves kept the good stuff. Grunting with pleasure, he emerged with a bag of potato chips and tore it open. "You hungry?" he asked.

The words hung in the air.

Had it been a harmless question, or…

Will crossed the kitchen and stared at his own reflection in the window. The buzzing ramped up while Otis munched another handful of chips. The noise sounded like a giant stomping through a gravel pit. Will grabbed at the counter to steady himself.

"You okay?" Otis asked.

Will lied. "Sure."

Otis shrugged and took a seat at the kitchen table.

"How about we get started?" he said, motioning for Will to sit next to him. "First question: Which tribe of warriors, fueled by starvation and natural disasters within their own walls, invaded and conquered most of Asia and Eastern Europe in the 13th Century?"

A pang of hunger erupted inside of Will, starting in his gut and radiating out to his nerve endings. His skin felt like it was on fire.

Otis, staring.

"I don't know," Will said.

"The Mongols, bro. That was an easy one." Otis looked around the room and crinkled his nose. "Dude, it reeks in here. Mind if I let some air in?"

Will shrugged.

Otis slid open a window, letting the muggy night air settle into the room. He sat down, took out a pen and started doodling on a piece of paper. Then he took a long look at Will and pushed the binder aside.

"We need to talk," Otis said.

"About?"

"You haven't been yourself, lately. Not since that night."

"People come back to life, man. It happens."

"Right," Otis said. "On TV shows, or in comic books." He looked down to find the ink had leaked on his fingers. Casually, he rubbed his fingers on his jeans.

"I don't know what to tell you," Will said. "Just got lucky, I guess."

"There's, like, a 0.5% chance of that actually happening in real life," Otis said.

Will stared back. Otis's cheeks had gone red.

"I'm sorry," Otis said. "I got carried away. Anyway, tell me what happened to the guy who attacked you."

"Not much to tell," Will said. "They weren't able to identify him. Just some bum, I guess. They don't know why he singled me out. Because I was there, probably."

Silence. Otis, glaring.

"Look, that's not all," Otis finally said. "I don't suppose you've heard about 'the brain snatcher'?"

Oh shit, Will thought.

"It's been all over the news. Someone, or some*thing*, has been digging up coffins all over town. Desecrating corpses. Stealing *brains*. Strange, huh? That it all started after you got out of the hospital?"

"Otis, this is—"

"Let me finish," Otis said, thumbing the pen into his shirt pocket. "You've been acting weird, lately. I can't remember the last time I've seen you eat something. And I've been watching you, Will. Over the course of a few days, you seem to go through a cycle. You start to get all thin and sickly-looking, and moody. And you smell bad sometimes, buddy. Sometimes you smell like death warmed over." He lifted his shirt to his nose.

"You smell bad right now."

Will didn't smell anything. "Your point?"

"So, over the course of a few days, your body gets all, *weird*. And wouldn't you know? These spells of yours coincide with the string of graveyard incidents. Every time this vandal strikes—well, the next day, the smell is gone and you're okay. Everything's back to normal. For a while. Until it starts all over."

Will felt like the walls were closing in. He gripped the edge of the table for balance and stood up.

Air. He needed some.

Otis stood up, too. A breeze filled the curtains and they billowed behind him like a shroud. "Dude," he said, "we don't know anything about the guy who attacked you. What if there was something wrong with that guy?" His voice trembled and he looked as if he were about to cry. "Will, what if he was a *zombie*?"

"Seriously?" Will huffed.

"Maybe you actually died that night. Maybe you came back to life as one of the undead, cursed to eat brains in order to survive."

"Jesus," Will interjected. "There's no such thing as—"

Otis would not be silenced. "I've been reading about it. Zombies have to eat brains to keep their own bodies from decomposing. I figured if it happened to you, then maybe you'd want to be a good zombie, you know, instead of an evil one. You'd probably hold off on the hunger as long as possible. But, eventually, you'd have to give in. And when you finally did, you'd never want to hurt anyone or anything. You'd probably force yourself to live off of things that were already dead. Brains from corpses, stuff like that."

"Man, there's no such thing as zombies, okay? If that guy were a zombie, where would he have come from?"

"I don't know. Terrorists, maybe. I don't have all the answers. But, I can't find any other way to explain it." Otis's face screwed up and tears trickled down his cheeks. "Something's happened to you," he said, his voice cracking. "You're different now, is all."

An ink spot had formed on Otis's shirt pocket. Will said nothing, only watched the stain expanding across the whiteness, slowly spreading outward.

"I want you to do something for me," Otis said, sniffling. "I want you to stand right there and tell me I'm wrong. Look me in the eyes and tell me you're not a zombie."

Will felt the world tilt under his feet. Sweat broke out on his forehead, liquid fire on his already hurting skin. His heart was beating in his head, causing the bees to buzz louder. He wanted to break something, wanted to run out into the night to feed.

Also, some part of him wanted to surrender. He was tired of being a freak, tired of foraging for rotting brains in the dark, like some kind of monster. Maybe he should come clean with Otis? Maybe then, the nightmare would end. On the other hand, who knew what the world would do to him? He might wind up in some hospital. Or a lab. He didn't want to be some scientist's guinea pig. What would they do, with their scalpels and saws, to find out the science behind his condition?

"Dude," Will said flatly, "Stop reading so many comic books."

For a moment, Otis seemed like an air mattress with a hole in it. After a moment, he looked up and offered a wan smile. "I guess I sound a little wacky right now," he said. "Sorry I brought it up."

The hunger inside Will settled into a dull ache. For the next few hours, he tried to ignore the dreadful droning of the bees.

***

In the morning, the hunger had intensified into a white-hot flame that tempered Will's every thought. He became vaguely aware of Otis's voice saying it was time to ready themselves for school. Otis grabbed some cookies from the kitchen and the boys set out, taking the trail through the woods, a shortcut. The sun shone like an angry god, sending hot needles of pain into Will's skull.

"Beautiful morning," Otis said, coming to a stop on an embankment overlooking a creek. He put his hands on his hips like some fat mountain adventurer. Sunlight peeped through the line of pine trees and glinted across his hair, crowning him in a halo of dirty gold. "What a view," he said.

Will could no longer hear Otis over the droning. The bees were furious. Someone had kicked up their nest.

Otis tossed a pebble into the creek. "I'm sorry about all of that stuff earlier, man. I shouldn't have doubted you."

Will couldn't hear him. Silent as a mouse, he removed his shirt, tossing it to the dirt. The same thing happened with his shoes, his pants. Otis turned in time to see Will, wild-eyed and naked, charging toward him.

"What—" Otis said.

Will's hands locked around Otis's neck, choking. Otis toppled backward, falling with a thud on a flattened boulder. Will landed on top of him, a growl forming in his throat. With terrible fury, he smashed Otis's head onto the rock below. There was a sound like ice cracking. Will repeated the action swiftly, once more, and Otis's leg twitched and then stopped moving.

Will's fingertips sunk into the broken skull, digging and prying, the bone snapping away like eggshell. His probing fingers found their mark, sinking deep into the fresh cranial matter. The gore glistened in the sunlight as his trembling hands lifted it to his hungry lips.

The taste was intoxicating.

The meat was warm, almost pulsing. And the texture was unlike anything he'd ever tasted. Fresh brains weren't tough, like dead animal

---

brains. They were spongy, melting against his quivering tongue. Already, he could feel the pain in his head and limbs subsiding.

When he had scraped out the last bits of his meal and licked his fingers clean, he dragged Otis's body into the bushes and made his way down to the creek. Covered in blood, he washed himself off and quickly got dressed.

***

Will made it to class just as the bell was ringing. He took his seat in the back row next to Otis's empty chair. Mr. Holladay handed out the exams. "Does anyone know where Mr. Collins is today?" he asked. Will glanced at the door and shrugged.

Mr. Holladay signaled for the final to begin. From two rows over, Becca winked at Will, curling her hair playfully around her finger. Soon, every student in the room was working on the test. Except for Will, who stared casually around the room. Mr. Holladay looked at him quizzically. Then, with a furrowed brow, he turned his attention to a stack of papers on his desk.

At that moment, Will couldn't have cared less about world history. School didn't matter, not anymore.

He was staring at all of the beautiful heads around him, carefully studying the perfect, bony craniums atop those young, unknowing shoulders. His mouth began to water as his eyes caressed every delicate indention, every line, every curve, thinking that only a bit of hair, skin, and a thin wall of bone separated him from the warm, savory meals inside.

A thread of drool dribbled onto his lap.

He was never going hungry again.

LOVE FEAST
Emilio DeGrazia

Meanwhile far off, life swelled and the court ladies glowed,
for by the riverside the black slaves pricked the bull
who stumbling, growling, turned his glazed and drunken eyes
on the packed massive crowd and roared with frantic rage.

–Nikos Kazantzakis, *The Odyssey: A Modern Sequel*

I still don't know how we got lost in a Louisiana swamp. Being away from home for the first time was weird enough, and Louisiana was like no place we'd ever been. Louisiana is like one of those Twin Cities city streets I've seen from the car—strange people walking around, some of them scary and weird. But it's the way Louisiana people talk that made us laugh. Rula, our camp leader, talked like them. "I a Delta girl," she said, "so don yo' worry yoself. I been 'round like the moon."

She was dark-skinned and tough looking when she stood hands-on-hips, and her hair was curly-wild black, like an animal's. When she smiled she showed her white teeth, and her lips were so pretty I had to look the other way. She was nothing like my mom, who has blonde hair that's almost white. I'd never seen it on a map, but I figured this part of Louisiana was like Africa. Rula was scary like Africa.

The highway sign pointing to the state forest preserve was obvious enough, and Stan, our driver, said not to worry, he'd been there a thousand times. "That ain't no woods you're going in," he said, like he was laughing at us. "It's a jungle in there. So, if you all want out, you gotta git out now." Then he laughed some more, showing us teeth that looked crooked, brown and small.

We started in okay, winding this way and that, but it didn't take long to seem like a jungle to me—the dirt road dead-ending into trees so thick and dark the sky looked like the blur you see when you're underwater looking up. I kept looking back to see where we were coming from, but all I saw was jungle closing behind us like thick, green fog. Right away I wondered

71

if camping in the wild was for me, and maybe I should've stayed home. We went bumping along for a long time before I asked Stan if he'd taken a wrong turn, but he just showed me his teeth and shook his head without saying no. We were in the middle of nowhere when he said it was *my* fault if we got lost, because I was talking to him, and then he said some bad words as he flung the van in reverse and started going backwards, the tires churning up mud when he laid on the gas. I knew we were headed for trouble when he stopped, got out of the van with Rula, and just stood there looking lost.

He got back in and took off between some trees, and we went this way and that between them. It was too hot for us to think about anything except how we'd be going back to school in two weeks, sitting there, bored silly in our seats, waiting for the teacher to let us out. We liked the way Stan gunned the van over the bushes and leaves, with Rula in back telling us to hang on. For a while it was fun seeing how far we could tilt the van every time he made another turn, but then the trees got so thick he had to go slow. By then Rula was sitting with her arms folded, glaring at Stan.

I know now it was wrong thinking Stan was there for me and the other four boys who signed up for the trip, while Rula was there for the two girls, Ashley the skinny one, and Britta, who thinks I'm cute. Ricky, going into seventh grade, was my best friend the whole time, maybe because he was from Bloomington. Hunter, Jason and Skyler were Cottage Grove boys, a year older than me.

We don't know where Stan made the worst wrong turn, but one turn led to another, until the jungle got so thick it was like going in and down rather than from here to there. Stan said we'd be fine as soon as he saw the highway, because he'd start all over from there, but Rula said it was too late to go back. He shut up because she was right. It was already dark and the van was going nowhere but axle-deep in mud. Somehow, he pulled out of the mud and backed up half-a-mile, before he finally found a space big enough to turn around. When I turned around to watch, I saw a big cloud of fog rolling in behind us. Then, he just started taking one turn after another in that fog, until he went too far and the front end of the van started sinking in mud again where the road turned into swamp. Those tires dug ruts in the mud so messy and deep my mind was spinning in them.

"Everybody out," he said. "We're camping in the van for the night. And watch where you walk. There's Cottonmouths in this swamp."

Rula, Ricky and I got out. I didn't know what a Cottonmouth was, maybe a rabbit or some creature white and soft, so I had nothing to say. But everybody else said, 'No thanks, we're staying put.' We looked around but everything was getting dark, and all we could see was ourselves standing there, alone. After she had a talk with Stan, Rula told us to get back in, but from inside the van we couldn't see a thing. And it was *hot*. With a real fire you move yourself away, but here the heat was *everywhere*, sticking to our skin and clothes, and you couldn't see it or wipe it off. Somebody said, 'Open the windows,' but they were already open. A critter stung me on the arm and I made a slap at it, but I didn't see what it was.

We heard Rula and Stan get into it. Stan wanted us in the van, but Rula said we should get out and camp on the ground. Stan stormed away, came back and turned the headlights of the van on, and then he went sloshing away again into the swamp. He was gone in a blink that left Ricky and me standing behind the van, wondering how he just disappeared.

"I don't like camping," Ricky said. "Do you smell what I smell? Hog breath. Something terrible."

Everything smelled weird, but I didn't mention why I was scared; something I had heard when the van was grinding away in the mud, like a *growling* sound. But maybe it was the van, something underneath churning the wheels in the mud. And I'll admit to another thing that made it worse: that van left no tire tracks. Maybe it was rain and mud, but I started thinking there was something in the fog following us that made them disappear so we couldn't follow them back – like maybe the fog had it in for us.

I felt better when Rula started telling us what to do. We found a patch of high ground and spread our sleeping bags there. The lights on the van were dimming, so Rula turned them off. That left us with nothing to do but lay back and stare up at blackness so thick there was no sign of tree limbs, leaves, or sky in it. Just when we were sleepy enough to close our eyes Ricky started to cry. Hunter asked him why.

"I'm hungry," he said.

Rula didn't say anything.

"Rula," said Ricky, "you got anything I can eat?"

"You bes chew the fat," she said, showing us her white smile as she got up. "Ain't no IGA here."

"I'll starve before we get back to the lodge. When we getting there?"

"Sometimes, if you be good 'nuff."

"Why not tonight?" Hunter asked.

"We ain't goin' nowheres tonight. Sometimes, is what I sed. Bite yo' tongue 'til sometimes."

"Ricky, are you scared?" I whispered.

"No, but I miss my mom."

"Scairdy-cat," said one of the girls.

73

"I think *you're* scared."

"This is the jungle. I ain't scared. There ain't ghosts in jungles, so why should I be scared?"

"When you're scared you're supposed to pray," said Ashley.

"I really hate leeches," said Britta. "You think there's leeches out there? And I haven't brushed in two days."

"Sure," I said. "It feels like leeches everywhere."

Rula flashed the lights on and off, and then laid on the horn so Stan would know where we were. It didn't take a genius to know the lights and the horn were running out of juice.

***

We got through the night but it was like being nowhere, nothing but darkness everywhere, with yesterday and today the same until the trees showed up and it was morning again, in the fog.

Now, I know what woke me up—the click, click of the engine, dead as road kill, with Rula slumped over the wheel trying to coax some juice out of it. Rula told us we couldn't just sit still waiting to be found. We had to find our way out. She asked me if I wanted to go with her and I said yes, even though everybody heard the thunder far away over the treetops. "I findin' us the road," she said as we sloshed away into the swamp.

Then it started to rain and Rula and I were ankle-deep in swamp, trying to find our way back to the van. It was rain thicker than Minnesota blizzard snow. I had a hard time seeing my feet, so there was no chance to find a dirt road. When I took a few steps and looked back, I couldn't find my own tracks. They were just gone, disappeared. It got me thinking about how maybe there was no getting ahead when there was nothing behind to show the way. I wanted to be home with my mom.

"I'm hungry," Ricky complained as soon as we got back.

"Me too," said Ashley, who was hanging onto Britta's arm. "Can we go home, now?"

We could see Ricky almost crying again.

"Why you crying?" we asked.

"Jason says I have worms in my shoes."

"You sure it don't *feel* like worms?" Jason said. "You want it to be leeches instead of worms?"

I shivered, but then laughed. "You still hungry, Ricky?"

"No."

"You still scared?"

"No."

"You believe in ghosts?"

"Ghosts? I never saw a ghost in the rain."

"But, look at all that fog. Looks like ghosts to me," said Britta.

"Too bad you can't eat fog," Jason said.

"Lot of good that would do."

"Ricky, you still hungry?"

"Yep."

"Then why don't you eat the leeches in your shoes?"

The rain kept coming down so hard you'd think it was slicing up the heat. But there was no letting up, sweat and rain and heat all mixed up in swirls of fog that kept curling away every time you tried to see through them. We laid low in the van, chattering and telling jokes that weren't funny anymore.

We asked Rula about Stan, and why he wasn't back.

"He ain't comin' back," Rula said. "He done quit."

"How's he going to get home?" we asked.

"Walkin'," she said, "to some mama who kin look afta him."

"What about us?"

Rula smiled. "Ain't no picnic today."

"Are they going to bring lunch to our van?" Ashley asked.

Rula laughed. "We dinin' out today."

"You mean, I'm not gonna get no breakfast or lunch?" Ricky said.

Rula said something back to him, but it was raining so hard we didn't hear what it was.

***

The van was no Noah's ark. The rain sounded like a steady load of nails dumped on the roof, with us inside not knowing if it was night or day. Would the roof collapse, or would the rain just keep pounding away until the van sank in the mud with us inside?

"Shuck yo' wet clothes and throw 'em in back," Rula said.

"My underwear's soaked," I said.

"Then shuck it."

Nobody giggled or said anything and pretty soon all of us changed into dry clothes.

"Rula, what are we going to do?" Hunter asked.

"For now," Rula said, "we in the rain. Then, we do what we gotta do."

Britta was quietly crying. "I want to go home."

Ashley nudged me. "Hold her hand. Say something nice. She likes you."

Rula was looking at me with that smile.

"No. Tell her I like somebody else."

"I wish we had Stan," Skyler said.

Rula laughed her friendly laugh. "Oh, dat Stan's lon' gone by now, sittin' in front of his mama's TV."

"Eating a hamburger and fries," Ricky said.

"With leeches inside," I said, to make people laugh.

Nobody laughed.

"We sleepin' in the van tonight," Rula said, "so, you all hush up."

We hunkered down in the dark, with Rula flashing her light to see if we were okay. For a long time nobody said a word, the silence thicker than the noisy rain falling on us. We couldn't see, and the van windows were all fogged up. I hope I'm never blind. I know Ashley was next to me because her hair brushed my arm, and Hunter had a certain stink that got me thinking about that hog breath smell. I knew Rula was next to the driver's seat, because I could smell her too, not a fake smell like perfume, but like cedar trees.

"I can't go to sleep," Skyler said.

Ashley slumped down and pushed my foot away. "And I can't sleep sitting up, so stay on your own side."

Nobody said nothing for a long time, all of us looking out at the fog curling up against the windows like it was trying to get in. The worst thing is that it had no face or eyes, just gray-white blind, like the dark. Then Rula, as if she could see in the dark, began telling us a story about an old man who lived in a lighthouse on an island surrounded by crashing waves and dangerous rocks, alone except for a faithful cat he'd found on the island years ago when he landed there after being shipwrecked and lost at sea for eleven days. For many years everything went well for the man and cat. As they grew older together the cat learned to understand everything the old man said to her, and when the cat wanted to go somewhere— maybe to a favorite rock where the two of them could watch the sunset, or to the woods where the cat liked to hunt for field mice—the old man understood the cat's eyes and its purring sounds and the movements of its tail. And they lived happily together, until one night there was a terrible storm, and the two of them saw a sailing ship heading straight for the rocks. The clouds that night were huge, dark as mountains of smoke, so the lighthouse lantern was too faint for the ship to avoid the rocks. All the old man and cat could do was wait for lightning flashes bright enough to show the ship its broken mainmast and dragging sail, and the black silhouette of one man standing on the ship's prow. Just as the ship crashed on the rocks, the cat's tail stood up in a way it never had before, and its eyes blazed with an eerie light. And suddenly the cat disappeared. The old man didn't believe it could move so lightning fast. He saw the ship sinking behind the rocks, but there was a glow, like a halo, around the man on board, and surrounding the broken mast and sail. And, as the ship slowly sank into the sea behind the wall of rocks, the glow sank into the waters. In his rowboat the old man braved the storm to get to the ship, but the high seas kept pushing him back to the shore. As dawn came on with its green and yellow sky he saw nothing but calm surrounding the rocks. Sadly, he gave up on the sunken ship, and when he returned to the lighthouse the cat was gone too. He spent days looking for his good friend, the cat, wandered the island calling for her, but all he saw was the picture of the sinking ship, its black skeleton lit up by lightning, and the man standing at the prow of the ship in the glow that was the same color as his cat's eyes.

We don't know what happened next because we were all asleep.

***

I found the cat in my dreams that night. She was standing with the old man on a big rock, staring at a sunset sea so beautiful you wanted to float away in it. But the cat was young again, just the same kitten she was when the lighthouse man called her out of her hiding place inside the knothole of a big old tree.

It wasn't the kind of dream that wakes you up. So when Rula slapped me on the butt I didn't know where I was.

"Get yo' stuff," she said. "We sinkin'."

It still looked like night outside, but I could see there had been no letup in the rain and the wheels of the van were long-gone in the swamp. Worse, the van was listing so far left I had to hang onto the seat to stay up. We piled out fast, and landed knee-deep in the muck. Rula led the way to a fallen log big enough to hold us all. "Git on board," she said as she pulled us and our backpacks up one-by-one. "And don't you dangle your feet in the water. Ain't no tellin' if some critter down there be lookin' for a bite to eat."

So, we squatted, hunched over like fat birds. We waited half-a-day for a let-up in the monsoon that just wouldn't move on to some other country where people are hungry and poor and used to it. And with the rain coming down there was no way to tell if Skyler and Ashley and Britta and Hunter were almost crying most of the time: their faces had that sad, hanging look, but they were so rain-streaked no tears would show.

Nobody said it, but everybody was thinking it: we haven't eaten in almost two days. The thought of food came on in our guts like the deep rumble of thunder we heard now and then. Secretly I was wishing for sharp blasts and lighting, so we could run and scream. But it just rained and rained, and the swamp just kept filling up.

Then it was almost dark again.

"Rula," we said, "what are we going to do?"

"Tonight, we do our campin' on the ground."

"Rula, we want to go home," Britta said. "Can we go home?"

"No."

"Rula, are you afraid?"

"No."

Ricky asked if I was afraid.

"A little, maybe, but not really." What bothered me was those tire tracks that disappeared without a trace.

"Do you pray when you're afraid?"

"Sure, sometimes."

"What do you say?"

"In my religion, we say, 'In the name of the Father, Son, and Holy Ghost.'" I made the Sign of the Cross.

"Show me how to do that again," Ricky said. "I never go to church."

"Just use your own words," I replied, turning the other way when I saw Rula looking at us. "Don't be afraid to use your own words."

Rula was too young to be my mom, but I couldn't get over the way she smiled, her high cheekbones and her dark skin and lips. She was making the rounds again, wiping our faces with her hand and telling us everything would be okay. Her hand was cool, and I didn't want her to take it away. She looked me right in the eye and said the rain would let up by morning and we'd find our way out. But now we had to camp out, find a nice piece of ground to spend the night on.

"But what are we going to eat?" Ricky asked.

"The fat o' the land," Rula said, with one of her soft smiles.

But she had a worried look on her face. She'd get us through this mess, but she wasn't sure how. When Britta broke down, just bent over all doubled up with a pain in her gut, we were relieved to hear Rula raise her voice for the first time.

"All you li'l buzzard birds! Grab yo' stuff and come wit me!"

She half-carried Britta, hoisting her up one-handed on her hip, when the swamp water rose up past the knees. Rula took long steps, slashing away at the brush with a long knife, and it was hard keeping up. Once she got so far ahead she stopped to wait, saying something to Britta that had her laughing in her tears. Then suddenly the rain let up a little and we saw a beautiful sight—sunset colors showing through the trees. We sloshed along another hour, trying to make a game of it. It was good just to be going and working hard at it, even after the rain started in again and the sky went out. God only knows what time it was when Rula pointed to a clearing up ahead. There the ground swelled into a grassy mound with some boulders looking like they were sitting around a campfire. It was an island of sorts, hid in the jungle where we were lost.

We started making a mad dash for the place, shouting and splashing our way. But Rula put a halt to us. "No," she said, "yo' all wait here. I check it out."

Without saying it we figured she knew there might be something there, especially after we saw her take out her long knife as she walked closer to the mound.

I wondered if Cottonmouths could walk on land.

***

The ground was soggy, but it *was* ground. Rula told us things to do—clear the brush and lug stones to the circle of boulders near the top of the mound. That night we'd have a campfire inside that circle of stones, she said. We had to haul logs out of the swamp to set around the stones–somewhere to sit–get ourselves off the wet ground. Then we hacked away until we had six poles long enough to make a teepee frame. She showed us how to notch the poles and let us use her knife to cut some hanging vines to tie the poles together on top. Next, we hacked the branches off some small trees, threw them over the teepee skeleton, and tied them down with smaller vines. By that time it was so dark we were nothing but shades going bump in the night. And then the rain suddenly stopped and we had a house on that mound big enough for all of us.

"Now we need a fire," Rula said, "and somethin' to eat."

"I could eat a bear," Ashley said.

"Raw."

"I heard something out there last night," Ricky said. "It was big."

"I saw it too," said Skyler. "I saw its eyes. And it had teeth big as saws. It was watching you."

"Don't try to scare us," said Britta. "Just tell the truth. I hate people who try to scare us."

"Eyes big as fried eggs," said Skyler, making circles around his eyes with his fingers.

"Git sum sticks," Rula said, "and bring me sum log that ain't been sittin' on the ground."

She hacked away at the bark of a big branch we brought her until she got to the smooth core of the wood.

"Now," she said, with that white smile of hers, "yo' all give the fire somethin' to eat."

"What?"

"Somethin' dry's a bone."

"The only dry thing I've got," said Jason, "is my underwear."

We all tried not to laugh.

"Not me," Hunter said. "No way."

"But I bet you got leeches in there," Skyler said without cracking a smile.

Rula tore a few pages out of a book she had in her backpack.

"Here, now yo' make a pile that has got lots o' air to breathe. We get these sticks hot 'nuff to burn."

She tore up Jason's t-shirt and laid the pieces over the crumpled paper. The twigs and sticks went on top. Rula's match flickered and the paper caught. A little cheer went up when the pile glowed and began to smoke. We all got on our knees and blew.

Then the fire flared. As we looked up to watch the smoke curling away, we saw the clouds were gone. We had a sky full of stars. And here we all were, camping out.

"I don't know if I'm hungry anymore," Ricky said. "But I think I am."

"Ricky better eat tonight," Hunter said. "He looks like a ghost."

"No, I don't!" Ricky shot back. "You ever seen a ghost before? So how do you know? I heard something out there growling at us."

"Ghosts don't growl," said Skyler. "You ever see a movie with a ghost growling in it?"

"Never yo' mind 'bout ghosts. Tonight, nobody gonna eat in this here dark," Rula said. "Git dry and get yoself a snooze. Tomorrow mornin' we dig 'round and find somethin' to eat."

***

The air was hot and dead, and the campfire smoke had a sweet cedar smell that made it hard to breathe. So there was no sleeping for me, no getting dry, even with the moon shining full blast overhead. I could see Rula next to the fire, her back turned to me. Now and then, she stirred it up and threw on another hunk of wood. Then both of us watched the wet wood sizzle and smolder, wondering when it would flame out.

I didn't know what to think about Rula—hadn't thought much about her when she and Stan pulled up in the van to load us and our backpacks in for the trip, me just staring at her fuzzy black hair and brown skin that made her pretty in a way I can't explain, especially the something about her smile and eyes, the way the eyes were so black inside, I wanted to go looking for them in the dark. When those eyes and her big smile found you, they took you in and wouldn't let you go. I could see her arms and legs were strong. She could lift more than a grown man. I couldn't help thinking my mother was like us, the kids, compared to Rula.

Once she had the fire blazing she finally lay down on the ground. I wanted to be next to her, thinking, *I want to sleep with her arm around me.* It wasn't just because I was scared, but I knew enough to stay put. So I just lay there, watching her, the moon and fire, thinking this is how maybe it was for people before they had cars and TV. And I was thinking how, when I got back home, I would do things different from now on.

Sleep was coming on, so I turned on my side. And just then I saw a glimmer of light just to the left of the fire. I lifted my head, the sleep in me suddenly all ears and eyes. Then I saw it again, the glimmer surging ahead a few feet more—toward Rula. There, in the grass, pale as the moon. And it had big yellow eyes staring straight at me.

"Rula," I whispered, my heart suddenly pounding in my chest.

"Shush," she hissed back. "I seen it."

The alligator was longer than a full-grown man, and fat enough to swallow Ashley whole. It made another quiet surge toward Rula, and then lay still again, just out of reach in the grass.

I saw her shadow first, Rula slowly lifting herself up on an elbow, and then the gleam of her big knife in the moonlight. And I dared not breathe.

The beast lunged but Rula was too quick, her knife plunging down just as its head came up. There was a terrible dragon noise, and then I saw them wrestling in the dark, Rula grasping the creature under the neck with one arm, lifting it right off the ground, hanging on for dear life and doing a crazy dance while she churned the knife in under the creature's jaw with her other hand. Then they both went down together, twisting in the grass, Rula never letting go as they rolled over and over, with her finally wrestling herself on top of it, her knife hand still twisting and turning underneath, digging for the one spot where the creature's life was trying to hide, deep behind its eyes.

Then suddenly the beast quit, went limp and lay there, still, except for small quivers that sent cold shivers up and down my back. I couldn't help myself from feeling sorry for it right then. I was looking at its eyes, seeing them thinking about itself, asking, 'why was I born this way, ugly and terrible, when everybody else is somebody else'?

One-by-one, the other kids came out of the teepee, terrible dreams inside eyes full of sleep.

"Oh my God," said Hunter when he saw Rula all bloody on her knees, already slicing the poor creature right down the middle of the belly, with her knife more than six inches in, sawing away to get through the hide.

"Git some mo' wood on the fire," Rula said to me. "Git it goin' real hot."

I knew I'd never tell Rula what I felt: I was in love with her, even as she kept slicing away right down the whole length, turning the knife underneath the hide, sliding it back-and-forth as she pulled it apart. And while I stood there watching she began peeling the hide away, pulling and cutting so big sections came loose all at once. Pretty soon, she had the whole hide loose in one piece all the way to the claws, and there was a lot of blood all over both of them.

We just stood there and watched.

I won't tell you what happened next, how she gutted it and hauled handfuls away, leaving the flesh to lie there naked on the grass. I wasn't sick but I was sad, the alligator suddenly nothing but a sleek mound of something else I'd never seen before, yellow in moonlight, with its hide in a heap next to it like a winter coat you drop on the floor when you come in from outside. It didn't seem right, what Rula did to the creature, even if she saved her life or mine. I felt sorry for the thing because that's what it was now: not an animal or even a thing I could name. It wasn't its fault, being born what it was. I didn't have a word for it. Where did it go when Rula sent it away with her knife? Did it disappear out of its skin and go hiding somewhere out there in the dark again?

Something made me want to run away and howl. But what I did was strange. I didn't want to see the hide all crumpled on the ground. I didn't want it dirty and spoiled. So I went splashing away into the marsh and trees, and then came back, hauling two thick poles with me.

"Here, Rula," I said as she was cutting into the meat. "I need some help. I need to make a crossbeam of these poles. Can you tie them together for me?"

Without using words she showed me how to twist the vines under and over so they didn't slip. Then she got busy and already was putting meat on the fire, when I stretched the hide over the poles and tied it tight. Pretty soon I could smell the meat roasting, hunger coming to my mouth every time I swallowed empty and hard. First, I dug a hole just big enough for the pole to sink in plenty deep, and then I lifted it up, the hide hanging like a scarecrow on it. The mainmast tilted a little until I packed stones and mud in the hole, but pretty soon I was sure it would hold. That's when I stepped back to see how far its claw feet stretched out, with everyone sitting around the fire and Rula passing out chunks of meat.

"Yo' all wait," Rula said. "Don't nobody eat. We got to give thanks."

"I can't believe it!" Ashley said. "I'm going to eat this! Alligator meat!"

"I don't care what it is," Hunter said. "I just won't look at it."

"I'm not gonna say Grace," Britta said, "not 'til I get home."

But I said Grace that night, thanked Rula and the thing for everything they did for us. Then we ate and ate some more, Rula smiling her smile as she put more meat on to roast, all of us so belly-full we fell asleep right there next to the fire, with that scarecrow hide, its jaw limp to one side, hanging over us from that cross.

A STORY FOR THE BOYS
John Teel

"Tell us a story, Mom," Paul said, his sleeping bag already rolled out beneath him as he threw another stick into the fire. "Dad always comes up with some really scary ones."

"I wish he was here," Danny Junior said, his sulking face reflecting a look of someone who had sucked a lemon and sniffed a turd both at the same time.

Jackie had tried all day to get him out of his slump, but Danny was almost a teenager now and he knew that his parents weren't getting along. He could hear the fights and he was angry about it. He was afraid, too. He didn't want to be one of those kids alternating weekends with his divorced parents and pretending to like their new significant others. The double Christmas presents wouldn't be so bad, though.

The campground was always the boys and Daniel's favorite vacation, filled with fishing, farting and pissing on trees. Jackie, on the other hand, was never a big fan. The bugs, the inconvenience of going to the bathroom, sleeping in a tent on the hard ground. But she knew how much the boys loved it and she wanted to spend some time, just the three of them, but mostly, she wanted to take Danny's mind off of his worries for the weekend. So far, it had been a total failure.

Jackie smiled at Danny and said, "You know your father is on a work trip. You'll see him soon."

"He's always working," Danny said. "I guess work's more important than us."

"Danny," Jackie said, "you know that's not—"

"Come on, Mom. Story," Paul blurted out.

Jackie sighed. She wished there was more she could say to Danny, but she knew it was pointless. He was pissed at both of them and there wasn't much she could do to change his mind. "All right, you little pain. You want a scary story? I got one."

Paul smiled wide and tucked his knees to his chest. Danny stared off at the trees.

"When I was a little girl, Pop-Pop used to take me out here. This campground is where I met your Dad. That lake we always take you guys to, well that's where we, uh, decided to have you, Danny." The memory of Daniel taking her there, on the grass beside the lake, made her smile.

"Come on, man," Danny said, disgusted.

"What?" Paul asked.

"Anyway," Jackie said, moving on, "There was always talk of these woods being haunted. People said they saw things. Ghosts. But that was all crap. It wasn't a ghost that haunted these woods. It was something else." She paused and, on cue, the wind picked up and the branches overhead rustled and swayed. When the wind stopped blowing, Paul spoke. "What was it?"

Jackie grinned. The orange of the campfire, mixed with the shadows, gave her face an eerie glow.

"Not that long ago, there was a couple who lived around here, named Robert and Sheila Kissel. They were pretty wealthy, owned a few businesses. That diner we used to go to was theirs. They had the biggest general store in the county, when there were still general stores. He and his wife had a daughter named Abby, about your age, Paul. She was the best thing in their lives and they loved her, loved her so much. She was smart and beautiful and caring. Just a really good kid, like you two boys. Everything was perfect and things looked even better when Sheila became pregnant with their second child. Abby was beside herself with happiness at the thought of having a little brother or sister, the one thing she'd always wanted.

"As the months rolled on, Sheila began having a hard time. There were complications with the pregnancy. The contractions were so bad, she thought the baby was gonna burst through her stomach, like the dinner scene in *Alien*. When the doctor did the ultrasound, the baby's hands were all wrong. Instead of fingers, it had three, long, curved claws, like tiny meat hooks. The head was big and misshapen and it had a long tail that curled and uncurled around the thing's crooked legs. The doctor told them to abort it; said he'd never seen anything like it before. Later that night, when Abby heard her parents discussing this, she talked them out of it. She told them: all things deserved a chance, even if they're different. And so, they decided to have the baby."

Danny's arms were uncrossed and he was hanging on every word.

Gotcha, Jackie thought with triumph.

"This is great," Paul said, "But how about some S'mores?"

"Got the stuff right here," Jackie said, handing him a marshmallow and a stick. "Got some of my homemade chocolate bars, too."

Paul's marshmallow was already engulfed in flame on the end of his stick. "This is the best camping trip ever."

Jackie offered Danny a stick and a marshmallow. "Come on, you gotta have one."

He flashed his handsome smile, that made him look so much like his father, and took the stick; holding his marshmallow above the fire, turning it over and over, evenly distributing the char. She gave them each a square of chocolate and two graham crackers and got on with the story.

"Where was I?" Jackie asked.

"The mutant baby was being born," Paul said as he chomped down on his S'more, white goo sticking to his chin.

"Right. The Kissel's had the baby at home instead of the hospital. They didn't want anyone to know that they had birthed a monstrosity, for fear of their businesses losing money."

"Jerks," Paul said.

"What did they do with it?" Danny asked, between bites.

"It wouldn't take milk from a bottle. It would make high-pitched animal sounds, day and night, and whip its tail at them and hiss like a cat; a trail of thick, green drool pouring down its chin. Sheila tried breastfeeding, but the thing had these razor sharp teeth and when she pulled its face away, she had cuts all over her breast; the thing licking its lips and wailing because it wanted more."

"More what? Blood?" Paul asked.

Jackie nodded.

"Gross," Paul said.

"So, after that, they decided to lock it in the attic without food or water. Kissel took an old chain and collared it to the thing's neck and padlocked the other end to a thick, wooden support post. They decided to let it die up there and bury it in the backyard like it'd never existed.

"But Abby couldn't let that happen. She would sneak up to the attic and unlock the door and pet its long head or the place on its neck, where the chain prevented it from scratching itself. Sometimes, she would sing to it, its body swaying and moving to the gentle sound of her voice. It would let her hold it, falling asleep in her arms as she serenaded it. Abby could tell it was hungry. She tried giving it raw meat, but it wouldn't take it. It whipped a bottle of milk out of her hands. She thought it was hopeless."

The wind blew in again, rustling up some leaves and making the boys jump. Jackie giggled.

"I can stop, if it's too scary for you guys," she said.

Paul's eyes scanned the woods for any mutant babies. Nothing.

"I gotta hear how this ends," Danny said. He yawned and then popped the rest of his S'more into his mouth.

Jackie could tell the boys were getting tired. *Have to wrap this up*, she thought.

"One night, while she sang to the thing, a tiny mouse darted across the floor. It saw the mouse and it stood, its tail shooting straight out like a lance and spearing the mouse into the floor. It went into a frenzy when it saw the blood, tearing at the mouse and swallowing every bit, lapping at the tiny droplets of blood on the floor. Abby stroked its head. And then she had an idea. In her bedroom were the gerbils she'd gotten for Christmas. She brought the cage up to the baby and it started growling – a deep, guttural sound bubbling out of its throat. It threw itself at the cage, the chain around its neck jerking it to the floor. It jumped back up, the tail whipping back and forth like a cat ready to pounce. Abby shushed its growling and placed the gerbils in front of the baby. In the blink of an eye, it tore through the wire cage with its claws, grasping the gerbils and ripping their bodies apart with its jaws, holding them high and letting the warm blood drip down its gullet."

Paul's mouth was agape, mid-chew, his eyes wide, like he'd just seen a naked girl for the first time.

"From that moment on, she vowed to keep her brother alive. To take care of him. No matter what."

"This is sick, Mom," Danny said, smiling in spite of himself and finally enjoying their time together. "Can I have another S'more?"

"Have as many as you want, kid," Jackie said, handing him another piece of chocolate and the bag of marshmallows.

"This is way better than any of Dad's stories," Paul said.

Jackie laughed. Paul took another marshmallow from his brother and stabbed it onto his stick. "There's one thing I don't understand. You said that it haunted these woods," Paul said, yawning loud, exhaustion creeping in. "But how did it get out of the house?"

Jackie lowered her voice and moved closer to the campfire.

"Abby was only a little girl and she only had so many things to feed it. The gerbils. A stray cat here and there, but after a while she had nothing for him and he would wail and moan and thrash about on the attic floor in agony. Seeing the poor thing in such pain finally sent her over the edge. Abby knew what she had to do.

"When her parents were asleep, she swiped her father's keys and unlocked the chain from around her brother's neck. She emptied out her book-bag, stuffed him gently inside and zipped it up. She crept out of the house and hopped on her bike, pedaling as fast as her little legs would take her, not stopping until she made it out here, taking the winding road down to the lake, past that and into the trees, stopping where the old caves are.

She took the bag from her shoulders and placed it on the leaf-covered ground. She unzipped it and the baby popped out, wide-eyed and excited. It was the first time he'd ever been outside.

" *'There will be plenty for you to eat out here. But I want you to stay in there,'* she said, pointing at the cave. *'And you're not to come out until it's dark, you understand?'*

"The baby cocked its head and smiled, showing every one of its razor sharp teeth. It reached up with those hooks and gently touched her face. She closed her eyes, holding back the tears.

" *'I'll come back. No matter what, I'll always come back. I promise,'* she said, and then the creature picked up the scent of some animal and it disappeared into the mouth of the cave. The next morning, her father was waiting for her and he was furious.

" *'Where the hell did you take it?'* he asked.

" *'Far away from you,'* she said.

"Children started going missing not long after that. They tended to be the kind that bullied other kids. They were never found. People thought it was the work of a serial killer or a cult or something."

"It was the baby, wasn't it?" Danny said.

Jackie nodded. "With some help from his sister."

Danny was shocked. "She brought him the kids?"

Jackie nodded again. "Abby's father knew who was behind the disappearances, but he would never turn his little girl in. One morning, he asked her flat out if she had anything to do with the missing kids and her response was, *'If you won't take care of him, then I will.'*

"Her father looked at her, realizing he no longer knew this cold-hearted little person standing in front of him. *'You're more of a monster than he is,'* he said.

"When confronted with what their daughter had become, Sheila took to staying in her room, most days, and Robert began to drink a lot. He stopped running the general store and soon after, had to close it down. He had to sell the diner, too. The burden of what he knew became too much for him and the gun he sometimes dreamt of using on his son, he eventually stuck in his mouth. Sheila never recovered and she ended up in an institution. Abby was put into foster care, far away from here. After that, the disappearances stopped and things seemed to go back to normal."

"What about the baby?" Danny asked.

"Well, he had to learn to fend for himself. She would think about him all the time, but she wasn't worried about him anymore. Somehow, she could sense him and she knew he was all right. He had grown strong. Abby brought him up right."

"Did she ever see him again?" Danny asked, his voice drowsy and far away. Paul was already fast asleep, sprawled out on his sleeping bag.

"That's another story, kid. But, yeah. She did. She promised she'd be back. And she always kept her promises."

Through the trees, the black sky was dotted with stars, like whiteheads on the devil's ass.

"Not everyone can keep their promises, though. It seems like such an easy thing to do. Your father, for example. He broke the promise he made to me on our wedding day, when he decided that girl he'd been going on his 'work trips' with was worth breaking our family up over. And I just can't accept that."

Jackie looked at her two boys, slumped over in the dry, autumn leaves, and wiped the tears from her cheeks. "Anyway, it's over now."

The crushed up sleeping pills she mixed into the chocolate bars took effect a lot faster than she thought they would. She carried her sons, one at a time, to the tent and covered them up with their down blankets. She zipped the tent up good and tight and took a few bottles of water to douse the campfire. She got in the car and started it up, but kept the lights off, slowly following the trail down to the lake. When she got there, Jackie killed the motor and stepped out onto the grass, leaning against the car and watching the water ripple and dance to the breeze, the moon reflecting off of the water like a milky disco ball.

And then, she began to sing.

Low at first, her voice soft and sweet, the wind carried it out into the trees. She went around to the back of her car and popped the trunk. Daniel's eyes were open, dry blood staining the skin around the slash in his throat. He was wrapped in a tarp and she pulled him out, his body hitting the ground with a loud thud. He had a smudge of grease on his cheek, probably from the spare, and she wet her shirt with her mouth and wiped it off. She stopped singing.

"I forgive you," she said.

Jackie smiled when she heard the leaves rustle just past the car, the familiar patter of tiny feet in tandem with the dragging of his tail. It'd been a year since she saw him, but he looked the same as always. He was maybe a foot taller and a tad bit dirtier, with a little pouch of a belly, but her brother was exactly as she remembered him. His claws were caked with dirt and dry blood, his pale skin almost translucent under the light of the moon. His tail cracked back and forth excitedly as they embraced.

"I missed you, little brother," Jackie said. "I brought you something, just like the old days."

He had already caught the scent of the gash in Daniel's throat, and he was on him like a voracious jackal, sinking his claws into the wound and opening him from throat to groin, like a body on an autopsy table. In a flash, he was burying those razor sharp teeth into the soft flesh of Daniel's organs. He ate until he could barely move, all the while, Jackie knelt beside him, stroking his back and neck. When he was done, he smiled at her, his face stained red like a contestant at a pie-eating contest.

"Don't worry about the mess," she said, gesturing at what was left of her husband, "I'll clean it up."

Her brother wobbled over to her and settled in her lap, his little black eyes pleading with her and she knew what he wanted, even though he couldn't speak.

"Ok," she said, "but after this, I have to get back to the boys."

He snuggled close to her and Jackie sang to him, just like she would in the attic, and before long, he was sleeping, blood-stained and calm, cuddled up in Jackie's lap – the only place he ever felt safe.

PIECES OF ME
Craig Steven

Bobby's parents sat in the front seat of the Honda, talking about how much fun they were all going to have at the circus. He looked out of the back window at the passing city lights. He was as bored as he'd ever been without his cell phone, and he knew that the rest of the night would follow through with the standard of entertainment he'd been subject to since getting himself grounded just days prior.

His parents were laughing it up about something one of his father's co-workers had said. Bobby understood the joke, but by no means did he think it was funny. He sighed loud enough to be heard over the raucous, sure to let them know of his displeasure thus far.

His father looked back at him with a furrowed brow. "What's your issue *now*, Bobby?" he asked.

"You know I don't want to go to this stupid circus," he answered, pouting. "What am I, six?"

"Yeah, well, you could have sat it out, but being grounded means not being allowed to stay home by yourself, if I remember correctly."

"Can I at least have my cell phone? *Please*? I'm gonna be bored out of my mind."

"Then you should have brought home a better report card, young man," his mother chimed in. "You think you can get away with whatever you want and we're not going to punish you for it? You were on the honor roll last year, for Pete's sake! I don't care who your friends are or if you want to look cool in front of them. Until your grades get back up, you're not going to know what the outside of your room looks like."

"I'd rather be inside that room than going to this damn place," he muttered, resigning the argument. He'd lost, like he knew he would. He envied the kids who'd been raised by single parents; it must've been so much easier to win inter-family arguments when it wasn't two against one. They acted as if he'd failed every class. By the time the end of the semester rolled around and Bobby was handed a sheet with a few low C's and high D's on it, he'd been content. Apparently, however, his was not the attitude to have.

Bobby laid his head against his seat, coming to terms with the fact that his Friday night was ruined. He could only hope that the circus turned out to be more exciting than he'd give it credit for.

***

Bobby's family arrived at the circus shortly after their spat. His father pulled the car expertly into a spot between two others in the lot, next to the large field that'd been reserved for the festivities. It was usually where the local high school's baseball team played their home games, and as baseball was out of season, the field was open for business to the highest bidder. That particular week, it'd been reserved for the circus that'd rolled into town.

The flashing bulbs, reminiscent of Christmas decorations, lit up the night sky. Children and adults alike, cried for joy as they rode the miniature roller coasters, the merry-go-round, and the twirler. Balloons popped in the distance – victims to the darts that'd been hurled at them – and the sound of water guns as they knocked down plastic clowns filled in the blanks. The smell of cotton candy, cool summer air, and funnel cake filled the night. Kids whined as they waited in line for the rides or to play their game of choice, while their parents stood idly by, wondering why the circus had seemed like such a good idea in the first place.

Bobby's parents were on another tier altogether, by far the two most excited chaperones on hand. They held each other's hand, pointing at the rides and the games, asking what they should do first. Bobby was secretly delighted to see them acting as such, since their careers often left them stressed out. Though they'd disciplined him by bringing him along in the first place, he still liked seeing them having a good time. A red-and-white striped tent near the center of the field caught their attention first.

"What's over here, honey?" Bobby's mother asked, steering Robert Sr. toward the tent. As they approached it, they noted the large wooden sign positioned just above the entrance flap. It read 'The Freak Show! Enter at your peril! You've been warned!' It was written sloppily in red paint to give children the idea that it'd been written in blood. As if on cue, a girl no older than six years old ran out screaming, tears streaking her face. Her father followed close by, irritated. *She's six years old and you thought it'd be a good idea to take her to a freak show?* Bobby thought to himself, shaking his head. *Dumbass.*

"Let's go check it out," Bobby said. If anything there would pique his interest, it'd be whatever lay in that tent. Everything else was too childish for his tastes, regardless of his parents' enthusiasm for it all.

"Sounds good to me," his father answered, leading the way.

A carnie, who looked less than thrilled to be on usher duty, outstretched his hand as they neared the entrance. "Five bucks each," he mumbled in a monotone voice. This was a steep price just to get into a tent, especially when they'd already paid general admission, but Robert, being the gentleman he was, paid the fee with a smile. The Butcher family walked into the tent to witness the horrors that awaited them.

Bobby was instantly displeased. He'd been hoping for real live freaks: bearded ladies, strong men, Siamese twins. Even a little person or two would have satisfied him. What confronted him, instead, was someone's twisted and stationary art. Here was a plaster of a human torso, glued to the lower half of a fish to make it a merman. It was hung in the air, supported by the wooden beams above it, as with the rest of the exhibits in the tent. A child, nude but for his jeans, his eyes glazed over and an enormous pair of antlers glued to his bald head, sat behind a glass case in the middle of the floor. A woman's head had been placed on the body of a tiger, and the exhibit was on display from on top of a high pedestal.

Well, this is disappointing, Bobby thought. He couldn't argue that the pieces didn't at least *look* authentic. His mind worked in circles asking how the creator of these sculptures could have gotten them to look so realistic. He'd been hoping for something more interactive, though; something, or someone, that could have walked up behind and scared the bejesus out of him when he turned around – a guy swallowing swords – while the crowd ooh'd and ahh'd. Instead, he was stuck with this; more of an art exhibit than a freak show.

He knew his father wouldn't demand his money back. Not because he was a classy man that wouldn't stoop so low, no, but because everything inside the tent excited him to no end. His parents were still on the first exhibit – the merman – pointing and gaping at it as if it were the second coming of Christ and not a crudely-imagined fish man attached to some rope.

"I'm going to take a walk," he told them. "This is super lame."

"Suit yourself, kiddo," Robert said behind him. "Don't be gone too long. Meet us back here in ten minutes."

"And don't go too far," his mother said. "Don't forget; I've got your cell phone."

"Yeah, yeah." Bobby walked out of the stuffy tent, happy to be rid of that waste of time. The carnie that'd allowed him entrance smiled at him with rotted teeth and thanked him for coming. Bobby nodded, cringing back. The man's breath smelled strongly of bourbon and cheap cigars. *This night can't be over soon enough.*

With no clear destination in mind, he walked away from the tent. He walked past the screaming kids, nearly knocking over several who ran right in front of his path more than once as they played a game of tag that'd nearly gotten them trampled. The flashing lights, the yelling, the loud carnies trying to persuade the adults to spend money on their rigged games; the commotion was giving him a headache. He walked clear from the swinging pendulum ride. Knowing his luck, he thought, it'd smash into him and send him 100 feet into the air. Once past it, he was officially out of the carnival, arriving in the large field between the festivities and the dark woods just a hundred yards away.

I remember those woods, he thought, smiling. It'd only been a year ago when he went there with his friends, Travis and Shane, to hang out and get high away from the ever-watchful eyes of their parents. Of course, he'd chickened out in the end, knowing that his mother, with the nose of a bloodhound, would smell it on him, had he partaken. The other boys mocked him before indulging in it themselves, but they'd all had fun that night in the woods as more and more people steadily joined them. They eventually had a full-fledged party on their hands. It was almost dawn when the last person went home that night. It'd also been the first time he'd made out with a girl. Yes, Bobby remembered that night perfectly.

As he reminisced, he let his feet guide him toward those woods once again, trying to remember exactly where it'd all taken place. The moon shone down on the abundant grass, freshly cut just the day before. The wind, heavier than usual due to the storm they were calling for the next day, blew through the trees, their branches cracking together like percussion instruments. The noise from the circus had died down to a minimum, the occasional over-the-top screech reaching him, even still. *Finally*, he thought as he leaned back against the first tree he reached. *Some peace and quiet.*

***

A woman screamed behind him. She was far away, deep in the woods, maybe as far away as the circus, but in the wrong direction; a blood-curdling scream of someone experiencing terror beyond their most horrific nightmares.

Bobby turned toward the noise, his heart thumping hard against his ribs. His breath came in short, shuddering spurts, every hair on the back of his neck on end. Hoping against hope, shunning logic as best he could, he told himself that he'd gone bananas for a moment; that the scream actually *had*

94

come from the circus, that he had nothing to worry about; though he really should be heading back, if he wanted to meet up with his parents on time.

The woman screamed again, louder this time, only for a few seconds, before something abruptly cut her off. Bobby cried out himself, jumping a foot into the air and turning around in the process. She'd sounded closer, though he knew that wasn't the case. There was nothing to be seen behind him. But if he strained his eyes, he could see the smallest resemblance of what looked like a light in the middle of the woods. And being exhibited by this light, in all of its glory, was another circus tent, far from the field its kin had been set up in.

What the fuck is going on out there? Bobby thought. *Surely that can't be a part of the circus, being all the way out there. But, what if it is? What if that's the **actual** freak show? I should go get Mom and Dad.*

That'd been the initial plan, but that would have been such a far walk. And if it ended up being something far more sinister than a freak show (which Bobby highly doubted at this point; why would someone be in the process of being murdered in a circus tent in the middle of the woods?), he stood a far better chance of high-tailing it out of there by himself, without his parents slowing him down. Hoping he was making the right decision, Bobby began walking through the trees.

***

The sound from the circus had now completely died, and the only noise came from the grass crunching beneath Bobby's sneakers. Birds and crickets rotated chirps through the woods, and the occasional shuffle of underbrush drew attention to the rest of the critters roaming around. Though the interstate had been built over these woods a mile to the east, they remained virtually untouched here, one of the few places left in the country where nature was allowed to just be nature. The moon and the stars shone overhead, joining the light cast from Bobby's outstretched, miniature key-chain flashlight, as he made his way to the out-of-place shelter.

Blinding light from inside lit it like a torch, revealing every stain, rip, and tear in the old tent. Still, it was a nicer quality than those few Bobby'd seen at the circus behind him. Why they would reserve the best one for the middle of the woods, where surely not many people would notice, Bobby could only guess. It didn't seem like good business. Then again, everything about the situation seemed odd, and though the urge to turn and run back was almost overwhelming, his curiosity was piqued. He was alone in the middle of the woods with the mysterious circus tent and he was bound and determined to discover what secrets were hidden within.

He arrived at the flap that would grant him entrance. It was slightly open, and the light from inside poured onto the grass at his feet. Unlike the other tents, surrounded by excited carnies, playful children, and agitated parents – the atmosphere full of delicious smells and annoying music – this one was alone. No one was out here with him. The only smell came from the natural scent the greenery carried. And the only sound was that of a man inside the tent, grunting while others moaned. He gulped. *I need to go back to the circus, now*, he thought, fully aware that what he'd discovered was far from being the main attraction. However, since he couldn't answer any of the hundred questions racing around in his mind, he set his qualms aside and stepped inside.

* * *

Corpses of men, women, and a few children, littered the floor inside. Their bodies were nude and mutilated, most of them dismembered in some form or another. There was an older man whose arms had been cut off at the elbow; a younger lady, with her hands and feet crudely hacked off; another man that looked strikingly similar to the person beside him, maybe brothers – twins, even – both of them sewn together at the torso; arms and legs cut off of the opposite sides to make room for such a procedure. An infant's body lay just a few feet away from Bobby, and he stared in horror at it, wondering why it had no face, before realizing that its head had simply been twisted backwards. A man groaned amongst the mess of carcasses, and Bobby saw that, though his body had been separated at the waist, his legs had been replaced with those of a goat. He hung, bleeding, crucified by hooks that suspended him between two poles.

The grunting that he'd heard before continued, and shell-shocked as he was, Bobby looked for the disturbance in the tent of the dead. A man – short and balding – with a curled mustache, was having sex with a woman. A *dead* woman, from the looks of it – decapitated – her head replaced with that of either a mule or a young horse.

"What...the...fuck..." Bobby whispered. It felt as if his heart had stopped beating. He'd gone into a state of shock so severe that he nearly forgot how to breathe. His head swam with a migraine and his stomach lurched as he stared unblinking at the images before him. As he whispered, however, the man stood from his spot on the ground, pants around his ankles, the sleeves and collar of his red suit jacket ruffled and out of place.

"*Get him*!" he yelled. Bobby wanted to run, but could only stare, sure that he was experiencing a nightmare more realistic than it had any right to be. None of this could be real, could it? "I said, *get him!*" the ringleader yelled again, raising his arms to the air. "Get up and get him, now!"

Slowly, piles of bodies around the room began moving. Only inches at first, but further on, until arms and legs poked themselves through the masses of the dead and worked toward becoming fully erect. Though the bodies he'd seen up until then had been failed experiments, prototypes, and works in progress, those that stood were much worse to look upon; the successes, the perfect creations to carry out their master's will. As it was, their will, at that moment, was to catch and murder Bobby. They acted swiftly to obey that command.

***

Bobby only absorbed the bare bones of the threat he faced before he turned and ran from the tent. A bulky man, with the head of a bull; a tiger, with the face of a man; a woman, with the head of a vulture and wings spreading from her back, conjoined from many different aviary predators. These things stared at him with dead eyes, while he stood in the tent, and when he began to run away from them, they quickly followed suit.

His feet pounded the earth beneath him as he raced, panting, back toward the illuminated skyline above the circus. Goose bumps spread across his body, and though he knew not how close they were to gaining on him, he swore he could feel the beasts breathing down his neck. He could hear them grunting, hissing, roaring, and screeching as they closed in – ready to devour him on the spot.

Any hope of reuniting with his family had evaporated. This was where he would die, he was certain. He found some solace in the fact that the man's creations would likely kill him before dragging his body back to the tent, so he wouldn't have to suffer the agony and humiliation of being transformed into one of his experiments, failed or no. A branch behind him snapped as one of the creatures' weight pulled it down while swinging after him. The bushes rattled with the impact as they trampled through them. A clawed hand swiped at the back of his neck, drawing blood. With a burst, an effort that'd nearly killed him, Bobby exploded from the cover of the trees, tripping over his own feet in the process. He covered his head with his arms, bringing his knees to his chest, ready to be ravaged.

***

Nothing happened. After a few seconds, he dared to let his eyes open, searching for the reason he was still breathing.

The beasts had stopped just beneath the final tree between the tent and the field. They stared out at him, their faces indifferent. The Minotaur's body flexed as he breathed hard. The man-tiger looked out at the circus, uninterested, its tail lolling lazily behind it, as if it hadn't just been in a race to the death. They stood only a few feet away from where he'd fallen; yet they made no move to advance.

The trees, Bobby thought. *They can't leave the woods, or they'll risk being seen. That's gotta be it.* As if they could read his thoughts, they slowly began to dissipate into nothing, as their forms disappeared back into the trees, and soon, Bobby was alone in the field once again, far from the tent that'd very nearly cost him his life.

Without hesitating, he ran back toward the flashing lights, the screaming children, the parents that couldn't wait to get home, and his own parents, wondering why he'd left their side in the first place.

He dashed the length to the circus as quickly as he could, running through the crowds, dodging passersby and carnies, alike.

My God, are they in on it, too?

In front of the original freak show tent, the one whose authenticity had proved very worthy, Bobby's parents waited for him, hands over their eyes as they scanned the crowds for him. He arrived at a full sprint, nearly crashing into them. Robert steadied him, grabbing him by the shoulders and stared into his eyes as he stammered away, uselessly.

"Bobby?" he asked loudly, trying to put an end to his incessant and nonsensical gibberish. "Bobby! What's wrong, son!?"

His mother began yelling for help, but Bobby had no idea why. Slowly, and much too late, it occurred to him that he was falling to the ground, his vision fading to black.

***

When Bobby awoke the next morning, he stared up at the ceiling of his bedroom, wondering vaguely, how he'd gotten there. His head hurt something awful, and though he could tell by the sun's position through the window that it was early in the morning, he felt as if he'd been sleeping for days. The events of the dream he'd had the night before came back to him as he sat up and rubbed his eyes.

He immediately remembered that there *was* no dream.

Throwing the blankets off of himself, he ran out of his bedroom and to the kitchen, where he knew his parents would be up, early risers that they were. *I don't even remember coming home. What the hell happened last night? All I can remember are those **things***. His parents were there, just as he'd thought; he wasn't, however, expecting an officer of the law sharing their dining room table with them.

All three of them stood upon his appearance, staring at him, carefully.

"Bobby," his father started, slowly. "Good to see you up, son. Why don't you come sit down with us for a second? Officer...?"

"Franklin, Sir," the man in the uniform reminded him with a small smile. "Officer Franklin. How are you feeling, Bobby?"

"Uhh..." He didn't know how to answer. He didn't know how much he'd divulged the night before to his parents, and the fact that this man was staring at him so intently made his courage waver just a tad. "I'm okay. Thank you."

"Good, that's good. I'm just here to ask you a few follow-up questions. Your parents called the station last night and told us of some pretty serious accusations you made before you fainted."

That's what happened. *No wonder I can't remember a Goddamn thing.*

"You mind reiterating some of what you told them last night, anything you can remember before losing consciousness?"

Bobby knew that telling him wouldn't be the problem. Being able to claim his sanity as his own afterward was a completely different story. He looked to both parents, who nodded at him, telling him to go on, this man could be trusted. And so, he spilled the beans.

Bobby told Officer Franklin about how he'd wandered away from the main attractions, walked toward the woods and saw the glow of the tent through the trees. He painstakingly remembered the images that greeted him, once walking through its entrance; the sights he'd seen, the amount of death that awaited him; about the man having sex with a woman's carcass, whose head he'd replaced with that of a barn animal. Lastly, he reiterated the chase through the woods, unrelenting in his recollection of the events and the exact nature of the beasts he'd been running from.

Once he was finished, and Officer Franklin had just put the cap back on his pen, after taking a few notes during Bobby's rambling, he stared at the notepad in his hand for a moment, before shutting it. He looked to both of Bobby's parents, his face grim.

"Do you two mind if I talk to Bobby alone?" he asked, his blue eyes unwavering. "I just need to ask him a few more questions."

Though they looked unhappy to be leaving their son by himself, with a man they'd known for only a few minutes, they did as asked. Robert pulled out his wife's chair and the two of them made their way to the backyard. Officer Franklin stared a hole through Bobby, smiling, calm, and smug. He scratched his head, the fifth or sixth time he'd done so since Bobby'd arrived in the kitchen.

"Son," he started, leaning forward and speaking in a low voice. "I'm only going to say this once. I was your age, once. I get it, man. Your parents drag you out of the house because you're grounded, and you retaliate by wandering off into the woods and smoking a little *somethin'-somethin'*, right? I've been there before, my friend.

"My folks were horrible people, kept me sheltered my whole life. But, guess what? I never went dragging the police into anything that could be traced back to a bad trip. None of what you're telling me makes a lick of Goddamn sense, and you know that.

"I'm going to get out of here, and give your parents a call back, saying that I investigated and that everything looks fine. But all I'm going to do is go back to the station and forget that this little conversation ever happened, all right? For *your* benefit."

Officer Franklin scratched his head again and wiped a light sheen of sweat from his forehead, though the central air in the house was set at 64 degrees year round. "Are we crystal clear on all of this, Bobby?"

"Uhh, no," Bobby answered, his confusion turning to anger. "I didn't go out to those woods to get *high*. You can give me a drug test, right now. I'd consent to one. What I saw, everything that I told you I saw, is one hundred percent true. I didn't embellish anything. If you would just ride out to that tent–"

"Impossible, even if I wanted to. They packed up last night and were gone this morning. Headed for another show, probably a few states over. No can do."

"And you're telling me you don't find that the least bit *fucking* suspicious?!"

"Son, listen *real close*."

The cop leaned in close across the circular table. His breath reeked of scotch, though the clock on the wall said it was barely 7:30 in the morning.

"I'm getting out of here. Get sassy with me one more time, or waste my time with any more of this *bullshit*, or even think about calling the station, and your ass will be in a juvenile detention center by the end of the day for obstructing justice. Like I said, I don't got time for your bullshit."

He stood up, hitching his belt.

"Now, tell your folks I said to have a good day. You do the same, boy, and mind you watch how you're spending your time. And where, for that matter." With that, Officer Franklin turned around and was out the front door before Bobby could say another word.

He sat there, dumbfounded. He couldn't believe the officer had just played him like a fool.

It took a lot of fucking guts for me to tell him all of that and he's going to laugh in my face and call me a doped out liar? Well, juvenile detention center or not, I'm going to give that motherfucker a piece of my mind.

Kicking the wicker chair from beneath him, he stormed to the front door himself, opening it to hurl insults at the officer, but what he saw, instead, stopped him cold.

The man that'd just interrogated him had his driver's side door open, one foot on the pavement and one inside the car, staring ahead. He reached up and pulled at his black, combed hair, hard as he could, before it fell off. It'd been a wig the whole time, so it would seem. The hair beneath it – his *real* hair – was a bright cherry red. He shook it out, after throwing the wig in the passenger seat, happy to be free of its stifling constrictions and constant sweat it'd caused.

Bobby could only stare, as the fake cop-cum-clown, started the mock police cruiser and drove off down the street – the sleeve of a red, polka-dotted costume hanging out of the trunk.

A SLIPPERY CUSTOMER
Marlena Frank

He wasn't the most attractive man at the bar, but the brand of his bulky leather jacket meant he either had money or he knew how to find it. Carolyn unbuttoned the top three eyelets of her blouse, just enough to reveal the push-up bra underneath. She flattened out her skirt that barely covered her butt and sauntered over. Jimmy glanced at her from behind the bar, his blond, scruffy hair always getting in his eyes. He smirked and nodded to her, but arched an eyebrow when he saw her target.

She trailed her nails over the back of Mr. Moneybags' neck and dragged her fingertips along the leather of his shoulder. Just as she thought: real leather, none of that fake crap. "Hey sugar, you got a light?"

"Um," his breath smelled of the top shelf beer he was nursing, the foamy remnants of which still clung to his mustache and beard as he gaped at her. His eyes met her face, briefly, before descending to her chest, her legs, then back to her chest again. That confused expression slowly turned into a grin. *Bingo*. "Absolutely."

He fumbled at his inner breast pocket for a minute before he produced the lighter. Most probably assumed it was your typical dollar store variety, but Carolyn spotted the engraved initials at the base. She leaned in so he could light her cigarette, and spotted the billfold in his breast pocket, stuffed near to busting. There were even a few bills poking out along the top. The man was loaded. She pulled herself into a stool beside him, blowing smoke off to the side, but studied him carefully this time. Beads of perspiration were pooled on his forehead and the hand that clung to the bar's edge was moist with sweat.

She smiled and crossed her legs so he could see just how far up the skirt went. "You don't look at all familiar. New to these parts?"

He grabbed a napkin off the table and wiped at his face. "Just passing through, really. My last job didn't pan out so well, so I decided to get away from it all."

She smiled, "Well, you nailed that then, sugar! Nobody comes around these parts on purpose. The biggest events are the Bingo competitions at the retirement home, or maybe the occasional estate sale."

He grinned, "Sounds like you're experienced."

She flashed a grin at him, "Excuse me?"

"At Bingo. Sounds like you've spent a night or two down there."

She nodded, taking a moment to pull on her cigarette. For all the nerve this guy had, he didn't shy away at her comment. Most men would have fumbled at a slip like that. Maybe laughed it off, backtracked, or at least apologized. On top of that, he was watching her a bit too close for comfort. She'd have to watch herself around this one. The vibes he gave off reminded her of a guy into freaky sex games or worse.

He dabbed at his face again before asking, "So, you busy tonight?"

"Hmm, I don't know, sugar. I'm an expensive girl. You might not be able to afford me."

He swiveled around to face her fully, the stool squeaking under his weight. "Try me. I may be out of work, but I've got enough to spare on a sweet set like you." His eyes drifted, then settled onto her gaze fully. Carolyn had to look away.

She thought of the fat wallet stuck deep in his chest pocket, and the feel of the leather on her fingertips. "Five hundred to start."

He whistled and slurped some of his beer, his eyes only momentarily flicking away from her. "Damn, woman! You weren't joking, were you? I thought you said this place was boring?"

"All the more reason for a girl to not back down." He grinned, but Carolyn continued. "Besides, I never joke where money's involved. The best of us don't go for pocket change. Thanks for the light, anyway." She stood to leave, but he caught her wrist. She couldn't repress the shudder that went through her, even though he let go almost immediately.

"Wait, I never said I couldn't pay." He lowered his voice, "I've even got cash." His eyes were searching, desperate. Carolyn relaxed a little. Perhaps his creepy vibes were born from plain loneliness. Likely, the man hadn't had a lay in ages, on his long trip, which made him all the more insistent to take even such an expensive night.

"If you can pay," Carolyn said. "Then we've got ourselves a deal."

***

She fetched the keys for her regular room from Jimmy, who was still smiling at her as he dropped the keys in her hand.

"It's clean this time, right?" she asked.

"As a whistle. Just be done before dawn, all right? I've got some folks who reserved it for tomorrow, so we'll need to make sure everything's clean."

"Really? Someone's actually booking your rooms?"

He grinned, "Yep, and paid up front, too."

She sighed and glanced up at the clock. Already, it was nearly midnight. "Guess I'd better get to work, then."

"Hey," he leaned over the counter. His white sleeves were rolled up around his elbows and the lamps above them revealed the red tattoos trailing upwards from his forearms. "How much did you ask for, anyway? I thought you might lose him, for a minute."

She bit her lip. "Five hundred. We'll see how much more I can get out of him."

He shook his head. "You're lucky he didn't just up and walk out." He glanced over to the man at the other end of the bar, smiling to himself and eying Carolyn, despite her distance, and lowered his voice. "He gives you any trouble, just let me know, okay?"

"I'll be fine, Jimmy. How many times have we done this, again?"

He shrugged, "You're my little sister. I think I'm entitled to worry a little about you."

Carolyn rolled her eyes and turned around. "Bye, Jimmy!"

***

The room was hideous, even by the bar's standards. It still amazed her that anyone would want to reserve it, though she guessed the unlucky patron just hadn't looked at it in advance. The paint was peeling, and spiders had claimed almost every corner. Not that Jimmy or she did much to keep the place clean, really. It wasn't a room for relaxing with the family or for getting away from the world, or really even where a proper girl ought to take her client for time alone, but it fit her needs. Besides, if the man was drunk enough, he wouldn't give a shit.

"What's your name, anyway?" He closed the door behind him and propped his hat up on the closet doorknob.

"Rosie. And yours?" Carolyn had three different names she would alternate between. He looked like the Rosie type.

"Dylan," he unbuttoned his shirt, furrowing his eyebrows as he looked around the room. "What a dump. For this price, I ought to at least have a clean place for the night."

Maybe drink alone wasn't enough for Dylan. She sat on the edge of the bed and pulled off her top, allowing a single bra strap to slide down her shoulder. "I guess you could always cancel, if you're not happy. I'm not trying to rip you off, here."

He had been unbuckling his belt, but paused at the show as his cheeks turned red, "No, no this is good. This is fine."

A Slippery Customer

She smiled and got to her feet. "Give me a moment. A girl has to clean up, you know," she winked before slipping into the bathroom. With the door safely closed behind her, she slid off her skirt and removed the concealed dagger from her left boot. She clutched the blade in her teeth as she slid aside her discarded clothes.

"You all right in there?" Dylan called. *Did he think she was Wonder Woman?* She imagined carrying that much money around in his pocket made him bossy, but that wouldn't last much longer. She removed the blade from her teeth and pulled back her hair.

"Hold your horses, sugar! I promise, I won't leave you hanging."

If Carolyn had her way, he wouldn't last the night.

***

She turned off the bathroom light and creaked open the door, her dagger clutched behind her back. All she wore now was her bra and underwear, just enough to make him feel like he had a present to unwrap. "You think this is worth the money now, sweetheart?"

The bed was empty. She glanced around the room and saw Dylan's shirt and shoes tossed in a pile in the corner. Unless he was running around the bar half-naked, he couldn't have gotten far. The closet door creaked. *Had that been open before?* She couldn't recall. She took a deep breath, but kept her smile and held the dagger firm.

She slinked over to the closet, noticing how the room felt darker than it had. Though, that could have been because she'd just left the glare of the bathroom light. Downstairs, she could hear the vague murmuring of patrons and the occasional chinking of glasses. Nothing out of the ordinary, at least. "Dylan, sugar? Are you hiding from me?"

Something thumped inside the closet and Carolyn dropped the dagger down to her side. Her heart was beating in her chest, but she kept herself focused. Maybe Dylan was terrified of women; maybe that was why he seemed so nervous downstairs. Perhaps he'd gotten cold feet and hid in the closet. Men had strange ways, sometimes.

With her free hand, she had only barely touched the doorknob, when the door was flung open. Carolyn jumped back, but the edge of the door slammed into her arm that still held the dagger tight. Something dark leaped out from within and sprinted across the room. Carolyn spun toward it, her knife outstretched before her.

Standing on the opposite side of the bed was a man she didn't recognize. He was so tall that he would have had to hunch if he'd come in through the doorway. His face was gaunt and angular, as though he'd been

105

without food for weeks, and his pale skin gleamed against the dim lamplight. He wore no shirt, only a pair of blue jeans that seemed far too big for his bony hips.

"Who the hell are you?" she asked.

He smiled, but it looked more like a poor imitation. "I am very sorry." His voice slithered across the room in waves, as though it was traveling over water instead of air, and it took a moment for Carolyn to realize that his lips hadn't moved. Carolyn felt a shudder go down her spine. "I'm afraid that will be no good here." He pointed a bony finger at the blade in her hands, and suddenly, it increased in weight. It felt as though she was carrying an entire table instead of an 8-ounce dagger in her hand, and despite her attempt to keep it raised, her fingers couldn't take it. The dagger fell to the ground with a dull thud.

"What are you?" she whispered, her throat not working right. "What did you do with–"

"With Dylan? Oh, my dear child, please don't tell me you fell for such a farce. A talented killer like yourself should sense when she is the prey." His face shifted, melted in places, and rose in others, like a time elapsed landscape. His body hadn't morphed, but his face now resembled the man she'd brought up here just minutes before. "I am Dylan."

She backed away, shaking her head in disbelief. "No, no, that's not possible."

"I am a shifter." His face changed back almost instantly, like a folded balloon that's been released. Carolyn felt a few hangers hit her head and realized she had backed almost into the closet. That meant the door to the room was only a few feet away. She wasn't sure if she'd be able to make it, but she had to try. "I've been traveling for quite some time, you know," Dylan said. "I knew a vicious, young woman like yourself was just the boost I needed."

She had no idea what it meant by a boost, but Carolyn had no intention of being eaten or absorbed or whatever entailed being this thing's prey. She darted for the door, her hand wrapping around the doorknob. She expected it to be locked, but the knob turned without complaint. She wrenched the door back and then felt hands clasp down on either side of her head, covering her ears. What felt like freezing ice picks, jabbed into her skull, and the pain reverberated down her shoulders and spine. All she could manage was a gasp as she collapsed to her knees.

His voice seemed distant and faded by the moment. "So much energy. I promise not to waste it as you have, my dear."

***

Jimmy cleared away a couple more empty bottles from the countertop. His last remaining patrons were slow to leave and he'd watched the hands tick by on the clock with increasing annoyance. The first rays of sunlight were creeping in through the grimy windows when his remaining visitors finally headed home. He wished them well and was pleased to see the generous tip one had left behind. After the door to the bar swung closed, he headed upstairs. Carolyn never took this long, unless she was having trouble. Had she offed him already, or had she fallen asleep again?

He reached the closed door and tried the handle. Locked. Now, this was just too much. Did she want his help or didn't she? He banged a fist on the door, "Carolyn? Wake up. That room has to be cleaned, remember?"

Silence. Not even the rustle of covers or the creaking of floors.

He sighed, slightly dismayed that it was so quiet. "Carolyn? Are you all right? The bar's closed. Come on, open up, will you?"

The knob clicked and the door swung back. Carolyn's eyes were dilated, and her clothes were haphazard, hanging at odd angles. She looked heavily drugged, though that couldn't be right. Neither of them had taken drugs in years, ever since they started their murderous racket.

"What the hell? Are you on something?"

She shrugged and smiled. "Guess it's a hard habit to kick."

He sighed and flattened down a portion of her hair. "Looks like you had a rough one this time. Did he hurt you?"

She bit her lip, holding back laughter. "Nothing I couldn't handle, but I can't move him. He's too damn heavy."

"So, you were waiting for me to come take care of it, then? Damn, couldn't you have come and let me know? They sit too long and they start to smell!"

"I've got to make you feel useful somehow, right?" She pulled him down and kissed him on the forehead, her lips hot and feverish. He felt strangely dazed as she pulled away. "You don't mind, do you? I'm going to head home and get some rest."

He blinked to clear the haze, "Sure, sure. Just get some rest, okay?"

"Will do, sweetie."

She must be tired, he thought. She never called him sweetie.

***

Carolyn wasn't exaggerating. His body was heavier than he had expected, and on top of that, Carolyn had made a mess with the dagger in his chest. Jimmy wrapped the body in sheets, frowning as his fingers met with the man's spongy skin. Even in death, the man felt like he sweated buckets. It took a while to drag him outside and Jimmy had to pull out a spare piece of plywood to get the man into the trunk of his car.

It was costly having to buy sheets so frequently for that room, but the money Carolyn brought in more than made up for it. The drive out to the swamp was long, with winding country dirt roads that were completely empty so early in the morning. The sun was just poking its head up over the magnolias, and as he shut the car off, a chorus of frogs and crickets filled his ears.

He went to the trunk and pulled the body out. He sure as hell wished Carolyn had stuck around to help him carry this one, especially since she was the one who picked him out. Jimmy hooked his arms under the man's underarms and dragged him across the mud until his own legs were ankle deep in the swampy marsh. He dropped the man's upper body so that his head was just barely touching the water, and went to work on the legs. He would spin the body around until it was horizontal, then he could just kick it into the green soup.

Just as Jimmy lifted the legs up, his feet slipped and he fell backwards up the slope and heard a popping sound, like a water balloon that got busted. The feet that he'd been holding suddenly shriveled down to nothing, and he looked down to see the thin skin that had been the man's feet hung on his fingertips. His eyes moved up the body: there was a large lump within the thin skin around the upper shoulders and head, making the face grotesquely large and disfigured, like a badly molded mask. The skin at the crown of the head was shredded, and must have been where the popping sound had come from. Above the head was Carolyn's sleek midsection and breasts still cupped in an attractive pushup bra. Her eyes were wide and her skin shone pale-grey beneath the thick green water.

Jimmy wouldn't remember puking, but he did remember the look of the magnolia leaves against the grey morning sky just before he passed out.

ONE GOOD DEED
David J. Gibbs

The disjointed finger of road cut a path across the darkened countryside. My headlights were the only ones on the road at this hour, twin pools of light hungrily chewing up the darkness. The sleepy van's tires bounced on the uneven pavement, the double yellow line having long ago faded to almost an afterthought. A bright green mile marker, drunkenly leaning to one side, leered at me for a brief moment before being swallowed whole by the dark country night that pressed in on me.

I rubbed my eyes again, tired, more so than usual. The fact that I still had an hour to go didn't help, either. I felt in my shirt pockets for my cigarettes and found them already on the console. The lighter tucked into the almost empty pack was a treasure handed down from my grandfather who had traveled with it all over the world while in the army. It had quite a few miles on it, much like I did. I moved my head quickly to the left and felt my neck cracking loudly, giving a brief respite from my pain. My back and shoulders always ached after playing a show.

I was really tired. It'd been a long week and I wasn't looking forward to getting up earlier than usual tomorrow morning. I actually had to get up in four hours and be chipper at my son's soccer game. He loved to play and I loved to watch him, but I was going to need some serious coffee to kick the sandman's butt.

I got stuck hauling all the gear, because I was the only idiot in the band that actually had a vehicle that made sense to someone with a family. Everybody else was still holding onto two-seaters, except Jimmy, who had a Harley. He always showed up with just a zipper pouch carrying his microphone.

Thanks, Jimmy, for helping haul gear.

We were a group of friends from high school, four of us in all. We'd played in a lot of different bands over the years but always seemed to gravitate back toward one another. This particular reincarnation of our coven was called Beautiful Envy. It sounded a little heavy for the kind of music we played but it was what we had all agreed the name would be.

We'd tried writing and playing our own music, which was great when we were still in college, all four of us living in a small, one-room apartment. But when you're closing in on fifty and you have a mortgage, two kids in braces, and one heading to college in another year, you had to change some things. So, we would sneak in an original tune or two each set, but for the most part, we were stuck playing covers. That's what the clubs wanted to hear and besides that, it paid the bills.

The gig had gone well. Granted, it was in Milford, so it wasn't anything big. The small burgh was nestled in cleared farmland, thirty miles northeast of Cincinnati. And when I say small, I mean *small*. Three traffic lights were all that was needed to manage the traffic load through the town. The biggest attraction used to be a first-run movie theatre that closed sometime in the late 80's. The space had been taken over by the Lord, converted into some new age church, complete with huge, lighted signs, to call out to the masses from the highway.

The club we played was off the beaten path a bit. How we ever landed the gig was still somewhat of a mystery. But hey, if they're paying then we're playing. They booked us a string of dates out through summer, which was a good feeling when I was living week-to-week off of what I made.

The sky held the moon hostage behind thick, dark clouds, so it was much darker than usual tonight. Between that and being so tired, I was struggling to see the road and to keep the van's tires from gnawing on the edge of the pavement on my way back home. She always rode heavy in the ass end with the band gear weighing her down. And she was barking a little bit, managing the hilly back-country roads, rising and falling beneath the moonless night.

I snapped the lighter closed as I inhaled the harsh smoke, lightly spitting away a stray piece of tobacco sticking to my tongue. The exhaled smoke was whisked out the courtesy window I had cracked open. The small triangle of glass was the only window I could open on this side of the van, the larger window was duct taped shut across the top edge. A few years ago, it had come off the track inside the door and I couldn't figure out how to fix it, so I did what my dad would've done and taped the damn thing shut. At least it kept closed when it rained.

The radio signal was growing weaker and more fuzzy, spilling over the music, as I continued working my way east. I noticed the hazard lights, sleepily winking at me along the edge of the road, when I reached toward the radio in hopes of finding a decent station to keep me company for the drive. It made me put both hands on the wheel, watching for anyone standing in the roadway, flagging me down. I blinked my eyes rapidly to try and clear my vision a little more.

That'd be all I need. Hit some kid that ran his mommy's car off into a ditch.

I realized the hood was propped up and that it was some kind of newer model SUV, dark in color. I couldn't tell if anyone was sitting inside or not. The dual-eyed hazard lights hypnotically continued blinking as I closed the distance, my foot lifting off the accelerator to slow just a bit. Passing by, I saw someone moving across the front of the vehicle, the headlights cutting across their legs.

And that's when I swerved a bit, though I didn't mean to.

The legs were poking out of a shorter-than-most skirt, the tights or hose or whatever they were, tightly embracing their length. They ended in heels, the distinct line of her calf visible as I passed. She had long, dark curls of hair that were being pulled by the wind, her jacket open, revealing several lengths of silver around her neck, and a glittery-looking top.

I'm a sucker for legs, always have been. But I knew I wasn't going to be able to help her. I didn't even own a cell phone and I knew next to nothing about cars. If duct tape couldn't fix it, then I was outta luck. And besides, how creepy would I seem, some long-haired guy, stumbling out of a beater-of-a-van, smelling of cigarettes and booze, to ask if she needed help? With my luck, I'd end up arrested, or even better, Tazered by her and *then* arrested.

No, I decided to pass and looked back to the road ahead. And that's when I noticed the pickup with the dented tailgate, backing up along the edge of the road. I almost slammed right into his ass end because I had been looking at the girl, instead of paying attention to the road. I thought for a scary moment that our mirrors were going to clip each other, but thankfully that didn't happen either.

It was two-tone, some God-awful, mint-green and white. The left taillight kept flickering, and a steady, dark stream of smoke sputtered from the tailpipe. The driver's side mirror was a rectangle of motion as it vibrated with the engine's uneven rumbling. There were two guys in the cab: one with a red-and-black checkered flannel shirt and thick, reddish beard; the other one had dark hair in a ponytail and a red, tattered-looking baseball cap.

As I passed the truck, I could see the side was all dented up, and both hubcaps were missing. I had a brief thought about stopping, because I thought the truck might be bad news. In my rearview, I could see the girl facing the truck as it backed up, her arms crossed, her hair still being toyed with by the breeze.

She looked like she was on stage, bathed in a spotlight, as her headlights reflected off the back of the pickup truck.

The driver was getting out of the truck as I came to a slight bend in the road, the scene behind me abruptly cut off from view. I closed my eyes tightly for a few seconds, my hands nervously drumming on the cracked steering wheel.

"Dammit," I muttered and looked for someplace to turn around. It took awhile, but I finally turned into the gravel driveway of some farmhouse placed well off the road.

I backed out of it quickly and reversed the way I came, having to pump the accelerator so the engine would quit misfiring. I could smell the familiar scent of burning oil, the tired engine using more than it should, and watched as the needle creeped up close to fifty. Cursing my inner Boy Scout, I rounded the bend.

The SUV was still there, but I didn't see the beat-up pickup truck. I braked and looked for the girl, but I didn't see her, either. A sense of dread filled my chest as I easily pictured the two guys overpowering her and stuffing her into the pickup and driving off to rape her.

Why didn't I stop the first time?

I gnawed on the index finger of my balled-up fist as I thought about what to do. With no cell phone, the next place to go for help would be the farmhouse up the road. I started feeling sick to my stomach as I pulled over in front of the SUV. I had to see if she was here. Maybe the pickup had left?

I knew that wasn't likely, but I had to check first, before I went for help. Coming around the side of the vehicle, the passenger door was still open, beckoning to the cornfield along the side of the road. I was careful not to touch anything. I'd seen enough crime dramas to know better. And, I wasn't entirely sure I wanted to get involved, anyway. If something looked sideways, I didn't want any part of this thing.

I looked into the front seat and noticed her purse was spilled on the floor of the passenger seat. Its long strap was caught on the seatbelt fastener near the console. A Slurpee cup was wedged into one of the cup holders and an iPod winked at me as it continued playing music to no one. I guess the volume was turned down, because I didn't hear any music.

It was then that I realized my ears were ringing more than I thought they should be. I guessed it was probably because the van's engine was chugging so loudly and had covered it up. The silence surrounding me was speaking in that loud hum that filled my ears after a gig.

I noticed that a bright green tether was hanging around the rearview mirror. The breeze made the plastic card twist a bit. It was an ID badge from the local children's hospital with her picture on it. It made my stomach twist into even tighter knots and I exhaled a breath I didn't even realize I had been holding.

I was about to check the backseat when something caught my eye. It was something white and wedged between the seat and console. The reason it caught my eye was the fact that I recognized the words typed on it. It said *Beautiful Envy*. I realized it was the request list for tonight's gig.

She had been at MJ's tonight.

It had been a pretty small crowd by our usual standards, but they were at least enthusiastic about us. The club's management was happy with the turn out and that's all that matters in this business. Whether there are five people or a hundred, as long as the club owners and management are happy with it, we're happy with it, too.

But, it had apparently been big enough that I didn't notice the brunette with the short skirt. I looked at the name on the ID. It said, Deanne Blanchard. I shook my head, trying to picture her there at the bar, but couldn't. There was an upstairs section there, so it's possible she came in the back entrance, which lead directly upstairs.

I stepped back from the car and looked around again. With each heavy thud of my heart, my resolve was shrinking more and more. I realized that I should probably just get back in the van and head to the farmhouse and call the police. I ran my hand through my long hair, pushing it out of my eyes and let my breath come out in a long hiss through my clenched teeth.

That's when something else caught my eye. It was down the slight incline from the road and near the edge of the corn that still needed harvesting. Something white stood out in the darkness along there. It was an odd shape.

I walked down the incline, not liking to be so close to the corn. As I came up to it, I crouched down and realized it was the same hat that the guy with the ponytail had been wearing, the one in the passenger side of the pickup truck. It was the white underside of the cap. The cap was red and it was dark, but I could've sworn there were a few drops of blood across its bill. And that's when my legs felt like they were beginning to fill with water.

Something rustled back in the corn and it drew my attention. I tried to stand up quickly, but wasn't able to, my legs too weak. I stumbled to one side, almost falling down before I stood up. The rustling stopped as I looked into the corn, cautiously backing up the small hill leading to the roadway.

The rustling started again, and I felt the hairs stand up on the back of my neck. I pushed my hair back from my face again and tried looking into the corn. It was so dark that I couldn't tell who was in there.

Or what.

"Help me!" came a cry from somewhere out in the corn. It was a girl's voice. It made me shiver as goose bumps ran rampant across my lower back and arms.

"Hello?" I asked, before I even realized I was speaking.

I stood on my tiptoes and tried to look out over the corn, but I wasn't able to see anything or anyone moving out there. It was just too dark.

"Help me, my ankle is messed up and I can't walk. Please, before they come back," she said, her words ending in choking sobs.

"Where are you?" I asked loudly, cupping my hands around my mouth to project. My voice was rough from singing, smoking and drinking all night.

"I'm over here," she said, and this time I noticed a light sweeping from left to right. I realized it was a lighter.

"I saw you that time."

"Can you call the police, please?"

"I don't have a cell phone."

"You're kidding."

I rolled my eyes. It wasn't the first time that someone had commented about the fact that I didn't own a cell phone.

"No, I'm not. I'm sorry. There's a farmhouse up the road a little bit. I turned around there and came back to see how you were doing. We can call for help there."

She didn't answer for a few seconds.

"Are you still there?" I asked.

"Yeah. I don't have a cell phone, either. Not one that works, anyway. It died tonight when I went to MJ's with some friends."

"Hey, I played MJ's tonight and I saw you there," I lied. "I'm with Beautiful Envy."

"Wait a minute. How do you know it was me, if you can't see where I am, now?"

I smiled for a moment, before saying, "Sorry, I saw your ID badge in your car. I'm Dave Bishop, by the way."

"You guys sounded really good tonight. I'd seen you play down at Barneys, too. Since you already know my name, I won't bore you with saying it again," she said, laughing a little bit with that.

"That's cool. I appreciate it."

"So, are you going to help me or are we just going to keep talking 'til the sun comes up?"

I nervously rubbed my palms against my shirt rapidly a few times, before saying, "Uh, sure. Do the lighter thing again, so I know a general direction."

The light moved again, between the stalks, about forty yards away.

"See it?"

"Yeah, on my way," I said, smiling as I thought that there was no way that anyone would have ever believed me if I had said after the gig I'd be walking through a cornfield toward a really hot girl. I'm sure that everyone would've thought I was crazy.

I came up to the wall of cornstalks and paused for a few moments. I'd seen that movie where the kids were killing all the adults in the town and worshipping something in the corn. Granted, that was a movie, but it still tickled my unease a bit as I parted the stalks and began making my way through the corn.

The rustling really made me uneasy as the breeze worked through the cornfield. It was a dry rustling, like old seeds moving in a weathered husk. I looked at the sky and wished the moon would fight through the clouds, so I could see better.

"Say something, Deanne, to make sure I'm going in the right direction."

"Something," came her voice, followed by a giggle.

"Very funny," I said, smiling in the darkness.

I turned a little more to my right, trying to get closer to the sound of her voice.

"I can honestly say that I've never had the pleasure of rescuing a girl in a cornfield before."

"Wow, then I should feel doubly indebted to you."

I smiled at that and the playfulness of her voice. I could see the orange light glowing, just about ten yards away. I parted the last few stalks and finally came into the small area that Deanne was sitting in.

She looked so out of place, amidst the dirt and dry cornstalks, corn silk shining in her hair.

"Well, hello there," she said, her smile so warm and welcoming.

"For a minute there, I wasn't sure I'd ever make it," I said, my own smile matching hers.

I looked at her legs, stretching out from her short skirt. She had fishnet stockings and I couldn't help but stare for a moment. Her legs were parted just a bit, and I was able to see the hint of purple panties.

"So, do you want to stare awhile longer or would you like to help me up?" she asked, a knowing smile stretching her lips.

"Sorry. I…oh, never mind. I was looking and you caught me," I said, and laughed a little bit.

"Wow, a guy that admits he got caught looking. Now *that* is something you never see. And besides, it's ok," she said and reached for my hand.

I helped her up and she stood for a moment, testing her ankle. She was a little wobbly, but managed to put weight on it.

"So, what happened?" I asked, as we started moving toward the road.

"Well, I realized I was in trouble when those guys showed up. They both got out of the truck, acting nervous. And the smiles were unsettling. The guy with the big beard spit out into the road. I could practically see the drool at the corners of their mouths. I knew they were bad news. And I knew I was in some kind of trouble. I never did replace the mace that I used a couple of years ago, when some college idiots wouldn't take no for an answer."

"You know, I almost stopped when I went past. I should've stopped," I said, helping her move along.

"Hey, it's not *your* fault. They didn't say anything. They didn't ask if I needed help. Nothing. They just walked toward me. So I took off. I left everything: my keys, my purse, my money. I just knew I needed space between them and me.

"They chased me, and as I took off into the corn, I twisted my ankle pretty bad. These heels are not meant to run in and especially not in a cornfield."

She leaned against me and I kept getting slight whiffs of her perfume or shampoo or both, I wasn't sure which. From my vantage point, I could also get a nice view of her cleavage. The soft bounce of her breasts with each step was hard to look away from.

"So, I just ran as fast as I could, changing directions as much as possible so that they would have a harder time following me. They finally gave up after what seemed like forever. I'm sure it was only a few minutes, but it felt like forever, anyhow. They were probably scared that a police car would come by. They ran back to their truck and took off."

I hadn't been paying attention to what she was saying all that much, eyes still looking at her breasts, mind still picturing her undressing in front of me. A couple of minutes passed and I realized that I didn't really know what direction we were heading in. After a couple more minutes, I realized we must've made a wrong turn.

We pushed aside a clutter of stalks and came upon a pickup truck in the middle of the cornfield.

"That's weird," I commented, before looking closely at the truck.

"What do you mean?" she asked.

I didn't answer, but instead, looked over the truck. It was two-tone, just like the one I had watched backing up on the road earlier that night. I stepped closer to the truck and walked around the back. It had the same dent in the tailgate and the two hubcaps were missing from the driver's side.

"This is their truck," I said, quietly, in the rustling corn.

"No, it can't be. I'm sure it's some farmer's truck or something. Those guys took off."

I looked into the open driver's side window and peered into the cab of the pickup. It was dark, so it was hard to see, but it was very easy to catch the smells that were swirling around the small confines of the cab. It reminded me of my childhood, when my dad would hang his cleaned kills in the garage. That smell of blood and death mingled in the cab, just like it used to in my childhood garage.

Fear twisted my stomach into knots filled with ice, and my legs threatened, again, to spill me to the ground.

"Deanne, we have to get out of here. I can't really tell, because it's dark, but I think those guys were killed. It reeks in the truck," I said, turning toward her.

She wasn't there.

I suddenly had a glimpse of someone following us through the corn and taking her, just like they took the two guys in the pickup truck. Someone darkly dressed, to blend with the night, holding a sinister-looking hooked blade of some sort, thirsting for even more blood, now that it had its first taste tonight.

I realized that I didn't have my lock blade with me. It was back in the van in my leather jacket and I suddenly felt even more vulnerable. Not that I'd ever had the balls to pull the thing out before, but it was comforting to feel its weight in the front left pocket of my jeans when playing dicey clubs.

I looked around the pickup truck but didn't see Deanne anywhere. I had been relying on her to direct me before, so I hadn't been paying that much attention as to the direction we had been going. So, I guessed which way I needed to go. I fought through more and more stalks, the corn silk coating me, and my clothes, in the darkness.

I muttered to myself, the tingle of fear settling at the base of my spine. A little flower bloomed in my stomach, its icy fingers of fear taking root. I thought I heard some voices and almost called out for help, but stopped myself. They sounded muffled and oddly exaggerated.

That's when I stumbled into my van in the middle of the cornfield. The radio was playing, turned up loud; the voices I'd heard were announcers on the air. I didn't try and explain why it was wedged in the middle of the cornfield. All I knew was that the keys were in, because the radio was on. I just wanted to fire her up and peel out of the cornfield. I didn't even care if the band gear was still inside or not.

I opened the passenger side door and slid across the console to the driver's seat. The keys were dangling in the ignition. I turned them quickly and the engine roared into life. All those horses running strong, I put it into gear and pushed down the gas pedal. I was now sitting high enough that I was able to see the road over the top of the cornfield.

Deanne's SUV was still there, the hazard lights perpetually blinking; red splashes of crimson reflected back on the state route sign just behind it. And then I saw *her*. She was standing beside her car and smiling as another car pulled off just ahead of hers.

It was a young guy and he had his cell phone out. The kid was talking to her and was offering to call for help. Deanne lashed out quickly with her hand and knocked his phone away. It skittered across the pavement. Something about her hand seemed really strange, though. It moved so quickly that it was almost impossible to follow its arc, as it now made contact with the kid's face. He stumbled backwards, obviously shocked that the girl had hit him.

I gunned the van's engine and it leaped forward, the corn getting mowed down by the bumper. A drum pattern played out across the grill and hood as the stalks fell again and again. I closed in on the roadway, my lights still off.

The kid fought back. Looking at his stance, it was apparent that he wasn't as scared as I was. He fended off her next two strikes, but his back was now against the bumper of his car and he had nowhere else to go. Her face contorted into a tight mass of wrinkles and rage. She was no longer the beautiful girl that had caught my eye, but instead, something dark and sinister.

Breaking through the line of corn, the van bounced and shot up the embankment leading to the roadway, lurching a little as the loaded down leaf springs creaked in the back. My subconscious had apparently made the decision for me, because I hardly realized what I meant to do, before the van leapt upward along the embankment.

The kid pushed her away from him and jumped to the side of his car. She moved, animal-like, and hunched down, before turning toward the rumbling, drunken movement of the van. She shrieked with an impossibly inhuman voice, the pitch far too guttural to be female. I watched her eyes as she looked at me, just as the van tore across the embankment, the front tires becoming airborne.

The bumper clipped her just under her chin, her head snapping back at an odd angle, sections of her hair coiled around the grill as the van leapt up and then folded down loudly upon her. It flipped up momentarily on the two right tires, before it spun back down and I completely lost control.

It had been built before the advent of seat belts and for the first time since I bought the beast, I really wished I'd had them in the van. It tumbled once to the left and flipped, my head colliding into the door's window, then the steering wheel, and then against the dashboard; my right arm wrenched at an odd angle, getting caught between the gearshift and steering wheel. My kneecap slammed into the console and twisted awkwardly.

Finally, my trip around the van ended, as it came to rest on the driver's side. The smell of burnt rubber and burning oil attacked my nose. It burned my eyes and made me cough a few times. Each cough sent a flash of bright pain to my head. I struggled to grab the passenger seat, but managed to pull myself up, even with my injured arm. I stepped up onto the arm of the chair and poked my head through the passenger side door.

"Hey, buddy, are you okay?" called the kid from the highway.

"I'll live," I managed, blood trickling into my eye from a cut somewhere up in my scalp.

My head was thrumming, a high-pitched whine ringing in my left ear. I realized, as my tongue made the rounds inside my mouth, that I had chipped a tooth.

The kid came down the embankment and helped me climb out of the van. I realized that my leg really wasn't working right, as I tried to make my way up the slight grade to the roadway.

"I guess I should thank you," he offered, his arm around me as he helped me up to the back of his car.

"It's okay. You're welcome. She almost got me, on the other side, in the corn. I watched her as she started messing with you. I thought I should help."

"Yeah, she was pretty pissed," the kid said.

"Looked like it," I commented, as I leaned against the kid's car.

"She always gets that way when her feeding is interrupted," he said, smiling at me. The same light glinted in his eyes as in Deanne's, earlier.

And that's when he stabbed me in the lower abdomen. It was something long and sharp. When he withdrew it, an icy chill settled over me, my legs not wanting to hold me up any longer. That was in contrast to the warm sensation against my hands that were desperately trying to hold my entrails inside. I fell to my knees, and cried out in pain. I fell forward and landed on my left side. My eyes still open, though my vision dimming, I saw someone coming out of the wash of white light from Deanne's SUV.

It was her. I thought for sure I'd crushed her beneath the van. I saw it clip her beneath the chin, and she did have a savage looking injury there, but she wasn't dead. The terrible gash there was an open, gaping mouth that spilled blood down the front of her blouse.

I struggled to try and get to my feet, but nothing seemed to pay attention to what I wanted it to do. It was as if my body was revolting against me. My legs wouldn't move; arms were ruined as well.

I could only listen to her heels clicking on the pavement and watch as she smiled. The gaping wound made her face seem like a hideous sideshow clown – teeth missing from that side of her mouth – her eye drooping toward the wound. I couldn't even get my words to come out, begging for my life.

Thankfully, she took it quickly.

And as things settled back to normalcy and the hazard lights of her SUV still splashed the crimson swatches of color on the surroundings, she waited.

And waited.

THE SUSURRUS OF CERULEAN SNOW
Randy D. Rubin

She holds my hand in hers as the twilight pulls the dead, gray sky down into the blueberry pools of evening. She holds her teddy bear tightly to her right side, shielding it from the susurrus of cerulean snow blanketing the ground. We walk a deliberate cadence, leaving two sets of footprints behind – hers, a petite and delicate skrit... skrit... skrit – mine, a shuffling staccato of half-dead numbness and stumbling. The wind blows the powdery, blue flakes into our tracks as we leave them behind, helping to hide our movement...just in case.

We have traveled down a dead highway for several weeks now, a freeway far from free; filled with interstate carrion and motorcar corpses. The going is slow, at its best, and riddled with stops – to switch vehicles or move immobile lumps of metal and mutilated meat from the middle of the motorway. Camilla has stayed quiet for most of the journey, shock playing the lead role in our passion play. Grief and inexorable pain have supporting roles. When we see the smoke climbing into the sky like a mystical, foggy beanstalk – silver threads against the blossoming blue of twilight – we know we have to stop, maybe find some food, drink, or, at the very least, human decency and companionship. We stop our 'borrowed' car and jump the guardrail. I slide down the embankment and catch Camilla in my arms as she follows suit. Together, hand-in-hand, we traipse across the scrub grass field toward the source of the fire, with Teddy in tow.

***

The apocalypse was a man-made affair, complete with rockets and missiles filled with a plethora of nuclear explosives and an assorted array of chemical weaponry. These gases and aerosols and nerve agents mixed with the radioactive fallout, causing the most heinous anomalies and irreversible damage to the human race. It changed the very atmosphere we breathe. We now have to run from the fallout of totally new weather patterns and systems heretofore unheard of. There are horrific rainstorms consisting of pelting shards of glass, riding the winds and shredding

121

everything in its path. In some higher altitudes and elevations, there are cases where the snowfall is quite caustic; melting completely through some wooden or plastic shelters and causing certain metals it touches to heat up and sizzle. Other times, it is normal, frozen moisture in the air, falling quietly to earth, and in its way, cleansing a tiny bit of what we have destroyed.

There are lightning tornados now, where the windy funnels drop from the clouds in an instant, with bolts of intense lightning inside them, then, immediately after the thunderclap, they vanish back up into the clouds. Then, there are the wailing winds, whose gale-force howlers are known to tear steel beams in half and sing their shrill, sad songs, that strip your hearing from your stirrups; searing your ears and making you instantly and most permanently deaf.

***

Everything is changed now. Is it self-imposed evolution, or mutation? I can no longer debate. I hold Camilla's hand now and walk into the night, and I am at peace. She shivers against the wind, but I don't feel any of the cold chill against my dead skin. I am frostbit in places, of this I'm quite sure, and it gets harder and harder to push my legs forward on knees that refuse to cooperate in this powder blue snow. It catches in the scrub of my beard and moustache, and covers the hat on my head. Camilla's hood is also dusted with it; it blows away each time she looks up at me. Her smile is all the warmth I need to push on. I stop to pull the scarf up over that beaming grin and her little button nose, so she can smile triumphant against the onslaught of the blustery gale.

We can see the flames through the copse of trees, off in the distance, and we've come to the blanketed remnants of a dirt road, containing twin ruts filling up with powder. Camilla looks up at me and I know she's smiling again, even though her face is scarf-covered. I can see a twinkle in her sparkly eyes, a reflection of the flames off in the distance. The road is curved and serpentine. We skrit... skrit... skrit along, each to our own path rut, quietly straining to hear any sounds from around the bend; any indications of whispered conversations from whoever is tending the bonfire.

Shots, through the woods, from the direction of the fire, crack past our ears and 'twing' off some rocks in the distance, behind us. We freeze, motionless and still in our tracks, like white-tailed deer on opening day of hunting season. Camilla squeezes my hand in terror and wants to bolt back the way we have come. I hold her hand tightly, keeping her rooted where she stands. Another shot pings through the night air and I feel that if I stand still any longer, I'll use up the last of our luck. Camilla screams a muffled note – somewhere three octaves above high "C" – into the fabric of her scarf.

"Don't... shoot... it's just me and my little girl."

"Go back the way you come or I'll put a hole in your head. Now git!"

"We just wanted a drink of water, maybe some food for the child."

"One more step and it'll be your last, Creature."

"Just water, Sir."

"YOU don't really need no water. I see the ashy pallor of your hands and face; see how you're shufflin' through the snow there on dead legs. We're pretty sure the rest of you is the same dead-gray, ashen color, underneath all them clothes. We've come across your kind before, Mister, only they didn't want to talk much, just wanted to eat on us human folk like we're cardboard buckets of chicken parts to them. Only way to stop 'em from dinin' on us, we found out a bit too late, was a clean shot to the head. Now, do you want a whistle-hole run through your head, Gray Man? I'll oblige you or see you runnin' in the opposite direction. Now, I'm through talkin'. Git, and I mean GIT!"

"But, my little girl isn't gray, she's just hungry and thirsty, please!"

"Send her over, Creature-Feature. Let go of her hand and send her runnin' this way. Then hightail it out of here, the opposite way, Gray, or I'll aerate your neck weight. If she passes inspection, we'll see to it she's fed and looked after. If my women folk say she even has a patch o' gray anyplace on her, she's gonna get her ears pierced with this thirty-ought-six. That sound about as humanly decent as can be expected, under the new circumstances, Gray Man?"

"Fair enough, thank you."

"I don't want to leave you, Daddy," Camilla whispers up at me.

"You must, for now, Little Dove. It's the only way we'll get through this, honey. Now go, walk over to them and accept their hospitality, and some food and water. Be polite, be a lady and let no one touch you funny. You know what I mean, Camilla, right? Just like we talked about, honey. I'll be close by. If things go bad, just run back to the highway and I'll find you. For now, you have to go, my love, or you'll die out here. Warm up, eat good, get lots of water in you, clean your body parts fresh, and try to sleep for as long as you can. I'll be out here, trying to stay alive."

"Please, Daddy, let's just go now, together. We'll find someplace else with food and water and warmness."

"No, my sweet baby child, now go. I'll be back for you soon. Let them take you in, Camilla, or we're both as good as dead. Now, don't get us killed, girl. We have to survive. I'm a partial Gray now, Cammy, and these folks are terrified to death of them, 'cause full Grays can't help but want to go 'round and eat them. They hunger for flesh and bloody inner parts. They think I'm gonna want to eat them, so they're shooing me off like an old dog with rabies disease. They'd just as soon see me shot and killed and put out of my misery. Go! Run! I'm gonna head at them, and they're gonna start shootin' at me again, but I'm gonna dodge all their bullets and get away. Run to them, and I'll head away into the woods. I'll be close. Maybe hole up in one of the cars back at the road. Go."

"I'm afraid they'll kill you, Daddy."

"They just might. But, honey, this is our best chance of living through this, now. We're running out of time and luck. Go…go now…and know that no matter what happens, Daddy loves you."

"Bye, Daddy…Come back for me. Promise?"

"Promise."

"Cross your heart and hope to die?"

"Stick a needle in my thigh. Now, run, Camilla. Run like a rabbit in the snow, honey."

Warm tears fill her eyes as she runs up the bend toward the voices of the shooters. I can't cry for the loss of her, even though I'm dying to; just one more tear for the little girl I love so very much. No tears, no cold, no feelings of any kind course through me anymore. My limbs died away weeks ago. My heart stopped pumping life's blood through my heart and veins three day back. It has taken every ounce of willpower I can muster, every last drop of humanity, manhood, and fatherhood – whatever I used to be – not to feast on the flesh of that precious little girl. My baby-girl…my sweet daughter, Camilla: who carries this plague, this virulent Gray virus in her chemistry – immune to its effects.

"I already died, Sweetheart, when my heart crossed off."

I'm running – I'm ambling, really – towards them and their spitting, stinging rifles – more like a cardboard cut-out than a person – out into the onslaught of azure snowflakes. The cerulean tears from the heavens stick to my frozen, ashy-gray face. The night sky weeps for me, tonight. I turn toward the bonfire flames and the muzzle flashes, wanting sweet and everlasting release.

Aim for the head, gentlemen. For God's sake, aim for the head.

EDEN SAW PLAY
Stephen McQuiggan

There hadn't been a single customer in the last hour. The sound of Gina's snapping gum, her heavy, cardiac breathing as she squatted behind the cash register, was Eden's only company. Things could not go on like this; in a matter of weeks, the new LUKA supermarket would open and whatever regulars he had left would desert him, like rats from the hull of a plague ship. His little corner shop would die, un-mourned.

Perhaps, he thought dolefully, *I'll even look back on Gina's wheezing fondly.* He doubted it, though. He had only hired her because he knew her mother. God knows why she even bothered turning up; it wasn't the pittance he paid her – that was certain. Maybe it was the chance to read the magazines cover to cover, for, she had the air of a girl whose only friends resided between the glossy pages of the celebrity gossip rags.

If he popped out now for a smoke, someone was bound to come in. It happened every time. As soon as he sparked up a coffin nail, a customer was sure to appear, requiring something he invariably didn't stock, had never stocked, but with a bit of cajoling, Eden could usually persuade them to buy something else. He stood in the doorway and looked out upon the real source of his disaffection this morning: at the small, silent house with the drawn curtains.

He glanced at his watch, then back to the house. "Has Mrs. Muir been in yet?" He had already asked, already knew the answer.

"No," Gina sighed, as if even a monosyllable had the power to exhaust her.

Her weary indifference only served to heighten his anxiety. It was bad enough that LUKA planned to construct a soulless superstore in sight of his shop, when they already had one in town, but now, the very fabric, the last fraying threads of his business, seemed to be unravelling. Mrs. Muir had been coming into his shop at ten O'clock, sharp, every morning, buying dog food for her little Petey, for as long as he could remember. It was after eleven now, and there was still no sign of her.

It was simply unacceptable.

It wasn't the loss of her miniscule trade; god knew, half the time, he gave her the dog food for nothing or at the very least, undercharged her. It was because she was a connection to a past that was fading daily, gobbled up by concrete megaliths like the ubiquitous LUKA.

"Has she any family? Her husband's dead, isn't he?"

Mrs. Muir was ancient, had been old when Methuselah was in shorts; surely there had to be someone further down the family line to look out for her, thought Eden, though he had never heard her mention anyone, save her beloved pooch.

Across the street, he thought he saw a curtain twitch; what if something had happened to the old dear?

"He ran off," said Gina. It always amazed him how much she knew about other people, as if her body stored rumours in its fat cells. "It was her son that died, but they say he wasn't all there to begin with. Retarded or something. I think she got the dog as a replacement."

I'd be better off getting a dog to replace you, mused Eden.

That's an uncharitable thought, he chided himself, *one worthy of a LUKA branch manager.* The thought of the new superstore caused acid to roil in his belly. "People get lonely," he snapped. "Surely *you* can understand that."

Gina glared like he had spat on her and guilt burnt his face; she would be dead by forty, her bloated heart giving out to indifference or else, her future husband would sober up one morning, see what he had married, and bludgeon her to death with a mallet. He had no right to make her any more miserable than she already was.

"I just mean...we all get old, someday."

"Some of us sooner than others," she pouted. Eden bit back a retort; *I deserve that,* he thought.

He began rearranging the cake display for the fifth time that morning, his eye never leaving that sad-looking little house across the road. It looked hollow, somehow, like an empty shell lying on a beach.

"I think I'll pop over and check," he said. "I'm sure I saw the curtains move again. Old dear might be trying to get our attention. Does she still have the phone in?" He couldn't imagine Mrs. Muir with a mobile. Her hands could barely prise open her ratty little purse; the veins ran down them in translucent blue like the scribbling of a determined, autistic child.

"You can't leave me here by myself!" protested Gina. For a girl so mousey and anonymous, she had the voice of a juggernaut airhorn.

"Don't be so dramatic, I've left you in charge before, you're more than capable—"

"Have you seen the time?" She pointed at an imaginary watch on her bevelled wrist, smiling smugly as realisation dawned on his face.

The school kids would be getting out for lunch soon, descending on his shop like the diseased little locusts they were. *Now that's an uncharitable thought,* he told himself. *Still, feral little brats, the lot of them.* He would have been glad of their custom but they only came in to rob him blind. He had caught one last week stealing parsnips of all things. Parsnips! Little idiot probably thought it was an albino carrot; they would lift anything that hadn't been nailed down.

Ah well, they wouldn't be his problem much longer, they'd be Mr. Big Boots LUKA branch manager's — and good luck to them, he hoped they swiped the whole damn store and decimated the (room for 400) free carpark whilst they were about it. He had a flashback as he thought of the little hellions, of how they once jostled Mrs. Muir, knocking the dogfood from her frail hands and mocking him as he stooped to help her. That settled it.

"I'm going to check on her," he told Gina, relishing the death of that self-satisfied grin on her fat, slug lips. "You'll just have to manage. I won't be long, in any case."

She made a flapping gesture as she tried to find the words to protest but he was already on his way to the storeroom to fetch a ladder. He had noticed her top window was slightly open; if anything *had* happened to her, it might be his only means of entry. By the time he returned, Gina was wearing a face he feared might turn the milk. He rested the ladder against the bread shelves and tried his best to placate her.

"She might have broken a hip or something, been lying there all night." That made him shudder. How long could an old woman survive a fall downstairs? What if he got into the house only to find...

He tried picturing a more positive outcome, of a laughing Mrs. Muir, putting the kettle on and smiling maternally at his unfounded worries. "I just had a wee lazy day to myself," she'd say, as he ruefully shook his head and sipped at her weak tea.

Gina stared at him, sphinx like, unmoved.

He put a couple of tins of dogfood in his apron pockets, and some biscuits, too (Mrs. Muir was partial to a digestive when she could afford them), as talismen to ward off all the unhappy scenarios queuing up outside the shiny new superstore of horrors freshly opened for business in his mind.

Lugging the ladder over his shoulder, he made his way across the road to the forbiddingly quiet house opposite. *I bet the new LUKA manager wouldn't cart a ladder to break into a customer's house to see if they were still alive, I bet he wouldn't give one good goddamn; they would just be monotonous beeps on the checkout to the likes of him.* It was the first uncharitable thought he was prepared to stand by that morning.

He propped the ladder by her front door, half-hoping the police would pull up and ask him what the hell he thought he was doing. Maybe he should just call them, let them sort it out, but what if they took their sweet time and...

He was pressing the doorbell repeatedly, shifting his feet impatiently as the irritating, jolly chimes echoed down her hallway.

Across the road, Gina stood in the shop doorway, her large, wrestler's arms folded, her mouth pursed in anticipation of failure. He was struck by the sight of her legs; it wasn't often he saw her standing up, away from the sanctuary of the counter. *She's waddled out to see me fall off the ladder, see me fall and break my—*

Was that music he could hear?

Faint, annoyingly vague, like a word on the tip of his tongue that bursts just before recognition, but music all the same.

He flipped the letterbox and peered in. The hall was dim, but there was no body sprawled at the foot of the stairs and that was something, at least. Yes, there was definitely music playing upstairs, a tune he knew well but couldn't quite place.

"Mrs. Muir?" Eden called. "Are you there, Mrs. Muir?"

Nothing. He let the letterbox snap and went to the window, ignoring the monolithic, judgmental statue of his assistant on the other side of the street. Peeking through the fingernail gap of the curtains, it was too dark to make out anything, other than a few nebulous shapes in the gloom. Was that Petey lying by the fireplace? No, he squinted until his vision blurred, just a bunched up rug. An easy mistake to make, for he had never seen Petey; barely capable of walking herself, let alone a dog, Mrs. Muir never brought the poor mutt out.

He imagined Petey as a fat sausage of a thing, spoiled rotten, lying up like an emperor on the sofa, perpetually panting; not a bad life, all told, when he thought about it.

One of the upstairs windows was open a crack and he placed the ladder beneath it. *If anything has happened to her,* he promised himself, *I'll take the dog and look after it for her until she's better.* It was the least he could do. Then he told himself not to be so morbid, everything would be okay. *I can still walk it for her, I should have volunteered before now.*

He let his guilt sour to anger as he climbed the rungs. Gina should be over here now, holding the ladder instead of gaping like a—

Now he had reached the window, he could hear the music more distinctly, even make out the tune: Morning Has Broken. Wherever the music was coming from, the needle had stuck in the groove and the hymn was doomed to an eternity of repetition; morning had broken, indeed.

Pulling the window up, he hoisted himself into the house, remembering how Mrs. Muir had told him she would play hymns for 'little Petey' to calm him down as he got 'so frisky' at night. The fact it was still playing did not bode well.

Clambering over the sill, he found himself in what could only be the old dear's bedroom; a bed like a big, boiled sweet, a harem of tacky figurines, the air awash with the lung-hammering scent of lavender, a scent that was ambrosia to the elderly.

But underneath the cloying floral barrage there was an undersmell of rancid milk, of urine and, well, there was no charitable way to say it, shit. Old people wrapped themselves in a palette of unpleasant odours like a comfort blanket. Their sense of smell went and their hygiene lapsed.

There was a thud somewhere out on the landing that caused the needle to finally jump from its rut and finish the song.

Eden opened the bedroom door and stepped out into the narrow corridor. On his left was the staircase, on his right, a damp lilac wall. Directly in front of him was a door with a hand painted sign that clutched his heart – PETEY'S ROOM.

From where he was standing, it smelt more like Petey's toilet. Suddenly, he had no desire to open that door. He was totally convinced of what lay on the other side, that what he smelt was not the toxic reek of dog turds but the decaying body of an old lady left to rot after a fall in her rundown little home.

He wanted nothing more than to climb back down the ladder and return to his shop and listen to the heavy, bored breathing of Gina, as the schoolkids filled their bottomless pockets. He had this awful idea that if he opened that door, he would not only find the putrefying carcass of Mrs. Muir, her face frozen in unheard agony, he would also find her darling Petey feasting on her in lieu of his usual *Chunky Chunks*.

He opened it all the same, instincts honed from a lifetime serving the public, too ingrained for him now to ignore.

But the images Eden saw play across the dark theatre of his fears were a child's prelude to the horror that greeted him as the door creaked wide. At first, his mind could make no sense of the tableau offered up before it. The body of Mrs. Muir was slumped on the floor of the unfurnished room, just as his fear had predicted, but that wasn't what clamoured for his attention.

The body he had expected, but not the naked man crouched in the cavity of its broken chest, sucking the desiccated marrow and stringy flesh from its ribs.

The man dropped the bone, crawling out from the corpse with a squelch, pawing slowly toward Eden on all fours, leaving thick clots of blood on the bare wooden boards. The man growled, the chains on his ankles and wrists scraping in time to the click of the stylus on the old gramophone in the corner.

"Petey," growled the man, his face hidden in a nest of hair and guts; only his eyes, wild and lucid, shone out from the tangle. "Petey hungry, Mama."

By the far wall, beneath a faded picture of a youthful Mrs. Muir and a scowling boy, Eden saw holes in the plaster where the chain bolts had been yanked free.

"Petey?" asked Eden, backing into a corner, standing in a mound of shit that was soft on top and crunchy on the bottom. "Good boy, Petey."

He took a can of dog food from his apron and waved it in front of the crawling man. *I've fallen off the ladder*, Eden thought eagerly, *and any moment now, I'm going to wake up with a smirking Gina above me, an 'I told you so' look on her balloon of a face, and he would laugh and—*

Petey pounced and Eden found himself face-down, in the excrement, as sharp claws raked his back. From the angle at which he lay, he could make out several tins stacked up by the door: LUKA CHUNKS, they said on their bright happy labels.

Just before the teeth closed on his throat and a long fingernail punctured his eye, Eden had his last uncharitable thought.

ENTANGLED
Katherine Sanger

First, let me say that I was drunk. If I had been sober, I wouldn't have been surprised that the hotel was actually a giant spider web, meant to lure in unsuspecting prey. There were clues. The rooms were arrayed in a giant web-like pattern. The cars out front ranged from sleek 1960s that had run to rust to brand new sedans with a fine layer of pollen. The most obvious clue, though, was the fact that people were stuck to the hallways with huge threads of sticky, fly-paper-looking strands, like something out of a really bad Hammer horror.

But, like I said, I was drunk. Really drunk. Drunk enough that when Wendy (at least, she said that was her name) invited me back to her room from the hotel bar, which had a massive "No Smoking" sign and was strangely empty, except for the two of us, even though it was only 11 p.m., I agreed and let myself be led back through the maze of doors and hallways and encased human bodies, some of which were still wriggling.

She explained the bodies away with a wave of her hand.

"They're doing renovations."

I nodded, as if most renovations included people being held captive for their bodily fluids. All I knew was that Wendy was hot, and she had invited me back to her room. After six months of celibacy, I think I may have gone along, even if I had been sober.

We eventually got to a door and Wendy paused, and then knocked on it. Even at full drunk, my alert flags raised. Dead people were one thing; getting rolled like some stupid John was another.

"Why you knocking on that door, honey?" I said, doing my best to affect a Texas drawl. (Thinking back on it, it probably came out more like, "why-you-konking-onna-door-hooey," but at the time, it sounded very suave in my head.)

"Shhhh."

I nodded again. I guess, by then, I was under her magical spell or whatever it is that evil seductresses use to feed unsuspecting prey to their arachnid overlords.

She must have heard something I didn't, because after shushing me, she opened the door to the hotel room and gestured for me to go ahead in.

And, being the drunk idiot that I was, I went in.

The door swung shut behind me, and I was face-to-face with the arachnid overlord itself. It didn't take up the room; it *was* the room. Big, black, bristling with hair and eyeballs. Fangs. I remember a lot of fangs, although, thinking back, there were probably less fangs than eyeballs, but the eyeballs weren't as scary, so they kind of faded into the rest of the body. But the fangs just looked evil and mean. It cocked its head and looked at me. I bumped into the door, tried to fumble with it, but there was no handle on the inside. I shifted my head slightly to the side and realized that there was no lock on the door, either.

Fear is an awesome motivator. With a stream of pee running down my leg, I flipped around and dug my fingers into the edge between the door and the frame. The drinks I had consumed had been purged from my system the minute that spider metaphorically licked its lips at me, and I was not going to die, stuck to a hotel room wall, waiting for that giant monster to stick those fangs in me and suck out my blood.

Rustling noises sounded behind me, and I knew that spider was shifting, so I kicked it into high gear – literally. I tried to go all martial arts ninja and kick the thing while spinning around to face it. I missed. Completely missed. Such a catastrophic miss, that I fell on my ass, landing hard and knocking all the breath out of my lungs. I looked up at the spider looming over me, making a weird chittering noise. I knew I was dead. The spider was going to kill me. I was going to die in a hotel room, eaten by a spider, just as my high school yearbook predicted.

But when I looked up, the spider had stopped. It stared down at me, and I swear that there was confusion in its eyes.

"Ummm…hello?"

The spider kept staring. I wondered if it was like a preying mantis, only able to see when there was movement. How long could I hold still?

I sneezed.

The spider was still staring.

"Help."

I didn't say help. The *spider* said help. Why the hell did the spider ask me for help? What constituted helping a spider? Was I supposed to offer up my own neck to it so that it didn't have to struggle with me? Did it want me to attach myself to the wall?

My beer goggles had been fading, and now I could see that the spider, as terrifying as it had been just seconds ago, wasn't in good shape. The fangs had streaks running through them that almost looked like cavities, or maybe, like it drank too much coffee and smoked unfiltered cigarettes. The bristling hair had split ends. The eyes were rheumy, and I thought I spotted a cataract on at least a few of them.

"Are you okay?" I whispered. The tables had turned fast enough that I thought I had given myself vertigo.

The spider stopped looking at me and stared at the door. No way to open it from the inside. The room was a trap, not just for me. If the spider wasn't the bad guy in this scenario, and I wasn't the bad guy...Wendy? Wendy was the bad guy?

How did I not see that coming? Oh, right, the drunk thing. I told you I was drunk, right?

"Kill," the spider said.

Ummm.

"Me," the spider said.

"Oooooh. You want me to kill you?" I was still whispering, trying to keep as quiet as the spider.

There was a knock on the door.

"Trust," the spider said.

Another knock.

For being in such bad shape, the spider moved quickly. One second, I was staring into its eyes, and the next, I was staring at its ass, and it was shooting silky, sticky strands on me, coating me into near motionlessness.

"Trust," the spider said, again.

The door opened and Wendy came in. The woman who had seduced me and convinced me to come to the hotel didn't exist anymore. This woman had much longer, sharper teeth and two extra sets of arms. She looked like a human/spider hybrid. And not in a sexy way. Not that I'm attracted to spiders, mind you. But I'm sure there could be a sexy spider woman.

She hefted me like I was a foot-long corndog at the county fair, my legs the wooden stick, and carried me out into the hallway, where she found some free real estate on the wall and smacked me onto it. I stuck. She shot out her own sticky strips that worked like seat belts, holding me tight across the chest and waist. She smiled, then wandered down the hall, poking at the squirming bodies with one of those additional arms.

I shifted my weight and realized that the spider had spun me into a web that was tight on the outside, but loose on the inside. I could move, a lot more than the squirming people down the wall seemed to be doing, anyway. I thought about "Kill Bill" and that hot chick trapped in a coffin, slowly working her way free and through the dirt. Could I do that? It was a plan, at least. And then, I'd get to show that yearbook committee wrong.

I flexed my hand – fist, poke with fingers. Fist. Poke with fingers. And the web around me got looser and looser. The belt-like straps were still holding me on the wall, but I could move. I kept doing it, shifting from fist to fingers, pushing harder, until I felt the silk strands separate. Then, it was just a quick thrust forward, and I fell to the floor, unable to break my fall, but taking the hit for the sake of survival. I did manage to take most of it on my right shoulder. But it still hurt more than I thought it would, seeing as how I'd only been a few feet above the ground.

My eyes teared up, and I blinked them, needing to keep my vision clear, so I could look for Wendy. I didn't know if she would feel the vibration of my body hitting the floor. I didn't know how much time I had before she came wandering back down the hall. And I had a mission.

I had to kill the spider.

I checked my pockets for any good spider-killing implements. I was sadly lacking. A wallet with some spare change, a few credit cards, and my driver's license. A pack of cigarettes. A lighter. If this was a movie, I'd have been carrying a machete down my leg or a gun in my waistband, but this was real life. My options were to kill the spider slowly by giving it paper cuts (well, plastic cuts) from my credit cards until it bled out, give it a pack of cigarettes and hope it got cancer (if spiders get cancer), or set it on fire. And the fire had the added bonus of potentially wiping out Wendy. And I really wanted to wipe out Wendy.

But, the credit cards were good for something. Their limits might have been maxed, but they still had semi-sharp edges. Sharp enough to cut through the straps and silk casings. I went to the closest squirming bundle and began sawing away with the edge of the Mastercard. It held up well enough to get through, and soon enough, another body had hit the floor.

"What the—," she said.

"No time. Here. Start saving people." I handed her a credit card. She had the pruney look of someone who had fallen asleep in a sauna, and her legs were unsteady, but she took the card and crept to the next person.

I went in the other direction and took down another squirmy sac, handed out another credit card, and kept going down the line until I was out of credit cards.

Then, it was time.

I didn't want to kill the spider anymore. I didn't even like to kill small spiders, the kinds that jumped around. I would shoo them outside or move away from them. And this was a huge spider. The kind that would probably make popping or squishy noises. Sure, I wasn't going to be smacking it with a newspaper, but if it caught on fire, it would definitely be unpleasant for the spider. And it wouldn't die very quickly. And...I could make excuses, but the bodies from the wall were gaining in number, and I had to do something or risk Wendy coming back. She'd had the spider doing a lot of the dirty work for her, but that didn't mean that Wendy couldn't do her own dirty work.

I walked to the door that I knew had the spider behind it. The spider who wanted to die, I reminded myself. I ignored the noises from the people who had been freed. I ignored the fact that some of them might die. I didn't know how fast the fire would catch or spread. I wasn't a practiced arsonist. And, let me remind you, I was also still just a little bit drunk. Which was why I hadn't considered the sprinklers.

When you light a giant spider on fire, it dies pretty quickly. I had been right about that part. I was also right that the noises were extremely unpleasant, but the spider didn't fight me; it clearly wanted me to take it out of whatever miserable existence it was living in. But, the minute the smoke started billowing, the sprinklers turned on. Wet, burned, giant spider is a thousand times worse than wet dog. It's like wet wildebeest mixed with the nastiest burned meat you've come across, left behind on a BBQ pit at the park, after a birthday party gone bad, and the police had to come arrest everyone.

The sprinklers made the ash into slush, but it was too late to save the spider. They were, however, in plenty of time to save the hotel.

The sprinklers turned off, and I made it back into the hallway. And there she was — Wendy. There were still sacs attached to the walls, but none of them were moving. Wendy made up for that; she was down on all eight, scrabbling towards me faster than I could back up. I backed into the sticky wall, pushed myself off, shoulder still hurting from my fall, and stumbled into the soggy carpet. She slowed her approach, and I knew why. She was moving in for the kill. I was dead. Goddamn those yearbook geeks.

I had been trying to stop smoking, but it seemed like it wasn't a bad time to light up. Surely, a single cigarette wouldn't set off the sprinklers again. And, if I was going to die without a blindfold, a cigarette would almost make up for it. I lit up, inhaled deeply, and exhaled a lungful, just as Wendy reached me.

She *freaked* out. The smoke touched her, and she flew back, coughing – or doing the spider approximation of coughing, anyway – and tried to shake her head, but she was already falling to the ground. Her arms and legs splayed out, and instead of looking like a spider, she looked like a cockroach in twitching death throes. I didn't wait to find out if that's really what it was. I did the first smart thing I'd done all night and ran out of the hotel as fast as I could.

It wasn't until I was sober and I was on my computer, cancelling all the credit cards I had left behind, that I wondered if the night had been real. I did some research. Right there, under all that information on spiders, that caused me to feel so sick to my stomach, I suddenly saw a little factoid that, if I had known it from the start, would have saved me all that insanity. Nicotine is a natural pesticide, known to kill aphids, thrips…and spiders.

THEY LIVE IN THE TREES
Daniel Marrone

I know that these words, painted by my pen's ink, will not register as truth in the mind of whomever reads this hastily written note that I leave atop my kitchen table. That is, if those *things* don't destroy it. I know they're outside. I can hear them, those tiny, impish voices, masquerading as the rustling of leaves or the swaying of branches. I am not a naïve man, I do not think anyone will find this paper, let alone believe its preposterous implications. But, if a single pair of eyes, with an open mind behind them, finds sincerity in my words and seeks to save others from falling prey to a similar fate, then I will not have died in vain. Death looms over me as I write this. I will have to be quick, before they get me.

***

It was two days ago from today that my three companions and I were in the misty, densely vegetated Pine Barrens of south New Jersey. We were driving down a lonely stretch of road that seemed to extend onwards infinitely. The needle-like pine trees outside my passenger seat window became a single, rolling blur of green as the car raced forward at a reckless, irresponsible speed. We laughed, we cheered, we sang, and we conversed. Underneath it all, however, hidden beneath the façade of cordiality, there was a seething hatred for each other, a malignant tumor of disdain that was rotting us all from the inside.

Our small group was comprised of my older brother, Richard, my younger sister, Shannon, and her husband, Trevor. Just as the air outside our car was bitingly frozen, the relationship Richard and I had with Trevor was correspondingly icy. He had married Shannon four months ago, when he was thirty-six and she was only eighteen.

We pulled off the road and parked in a small, dirt-covered indentation big enough to hold five cars, right next to a trail that led into the woods. One by one, we piled out of the SUV, opening the trunk to remove our backpacks that accommodated our personal belongings.

Everything seemed normal as we were preparing to enter the woods.

Our spirits were high, despite our secret loathing for one another. However, that all changed the millisecond we set foot on that dirt path. A chill shot through my body, like being thrown headfirst into a glacial body of water. It started from the feet and ran up through my veins, until it filled me completely, my hair standing on end, before disappearing. It lasted for all of three seconds, and I thought it a peculiar, isolated incident that only befell me, but upon looking at the faces of my companions, I knew they had felt it, too.

Nobody said anything. Although the iciness left my bloodstream, I knew there was something in me, a microscopic demon clawing his way through my blood vessels. I thought it crazy at the time (although it makes perfect sense now), but I felt that the *forest* was inside me, filling my lungs, pumping my heart, digging through my brain and unearthing my fears, my hatreds, my weaknesses. I felt shrunken to the size of a pin, intimidated by the wooden, bark-covered behemoths surrounding me. The woods were in my head, and the heads of my company.

Richard and I walked next to each other, while Shannon and Trevor ambled hand-in-hand in front of us. At one point during our hike, Trevor spoke, completely unprovoked, as if prompted to speak by an imaginary friend, "This is my first time camping."

The random comment hung in the air for a few moments of silence, except for the intermittent cawing of unknown birds and cooing of owls. It was the kind of statement meant to express a meek civility, to show Richard and I that he wanted to spend the duration of the camping trip, and perhaps beyond that, in peace. Richard broke the silence after a few moments by responding with a weak, "Yeah." The only sound after that was the crunching of leaves under our feet.

I didn't make any attempt to socialize, even with Shannon or Richard. I felt completely drained, but not in a physical way. My legs weren't tired, my stomach wasn't weak, and not a single trace of sweat was evident on my forehead. I just felt *empty*, like a hollow shell. My mind wandered everywhere and nowhere. I would stare at my surroundings for an indeterminable amount of time, as reality slowly dripped away like wax down a candle's spine, without even realizing it, and then all of a sudden the world would put itself back together and I would return to the Pine Barrens, walking with Shannon, Richard, and Trevor. These episodes occurred frequently, and when they ended, I wouldn't know whether a second, a minute, an hour, or a year had gone by.

I was brought out of one of these peculiar reveries by Trevor's indignant voice shouting, "What is your problem, man?" and I realized we had stopped moving. I looked up at Shannon, whose pale face, agape mouth, and piercing eyes, all aimed in my direction, made it clear to me that she was appalled at something I had done. I turned to look at Trevor, but when I saw the fire in his eyes and his red face, I averted my gaze and stared at Shannon. "What? What did I do?" I asked, innocently.

"Don't play stupid with me, you f—," Shannon defused Trevor's violent outburst with a tight squeeze of his wrist.

I turned to Richard for some answers. "What did I say?" I whispered to him.

He just shook his head and said to the whole group, "Come on, guys, let's just walk a little farther. We'll look for a clearing or a grove and then we can set up camp and have some food."

"I don't want to hear another goddamn word out of him!" Trevor roared, pointing a meaty finger at me.

"All right, you made your point," Richard began, as calm as he could muster, with signs of agitation seeping through the cracks in his demeanor. "Now, turn back around and keep walking."

Trevor and Richard stared at each other for a moment. Trevor's eyes left Richard and met mine, before he fixed his gaze back on Richard and nodded his head somberly, as if words were shared telepathically between him and my brother – words they didn't want *me* to hear.

Before we started walking again, I could have sworn I heard a tiny, mischievous laugh to my left side. I turned my head, but only saw a few leaves blown about by a light breeze. I shrugged my shoulders, assuming that what I had heard was nothing more than dried up, dead leaves rubbing against one another. I could not have been more off from the sickening, macabre truth.

We reached camp and began setting up our individual tents without uttering a single word to anybody. As I scanned everyone's face, I saw that nobody was smiling. In fact, everyone looked gloomy and desolate, as if they had just attended a funeral. I couldn't wrap my head around what had changed in us. We used to be somewhat friendly and could ignore our detestation for one another, but all of our civilities were slowly fading away into nothingness, vanishing before our eyes. It was those goddamn woods. I wish I had never set foot in them. I wish they had never set foot in *me*.

A burning pile of kindling and wood was erected in the center of our campsite, around which we gathered, sitting on logs, to eat our dinner. In a voice equally as soothing as the crackling fire, Shannon said, "The way the fire illuminates the dark is so beautiful."

Putting his arm around her, as she rested her blonde-haired head on his shoulder, Trevor said, "You're right, baby. This *is* beautiful."

"How about we take out some wine?" Richard inquired rhetorically, digging through his bag without waiting for an answer.

Procuring two bottles of wine, he used the glow of the campfire to read the labels. "Here, Trevor, you'll *love* this one," Richard began, leaning forward, handing the wine to Trevor, "she's aged about sixteen years."

I laughed at Richard's words, interpreting them as a discreet, subtle slander against Trevor for marrying an eighteen-year-old. Whether or not he meant the double entendre, I do not know, but after he said it his eyes grew wide and he stuttered out a pathetic apology. Trevor threw the bottle at the ground furiously, foaming at the mouth. The bottle shattered into dozens of dagger-like shards.

"Why the fuck do you treat me like this? If you have something to say to me, then just say it!" he bellowed.

Richard tried to repair his slip of the tongue like a ship's captain frantically bailing water out of his sinking vessel.

"No! I wasn't making a joke, I swear to you! I didn't mean anything!"

I was laughing hysterically while this confrontation took place, not because it was inherently funny (which it wasn't), but because I didn't have a choice. I felt like a marionette, completely at the mercy of the monstrous branches above me that pulled the strings. I wanted to stop laughing, I *tried* to stop, but I couldn't.

"Tell him to shut his mouth!" Trevor demanded.

"Don't tell my brother to shut up! You're the one who is blowing things completely out of proportion!" Richard shouted in my defense. "Now, sit down and calm yourself."

Tears were falling from my red cheeks like raindrops from a leaf. In a deep, slightly demonic voice, several octaves lower than my own, someone said, "What are you gonna do about it, child-fucker?"

I looked in all directions around me, to see where the voice had come from. Using everyone's reaction as a guide, I discovered that the voice came from my *own* throat. But I swear to you, whomever is reading this note, that I spoke no such words!

Richard and Shannon had to restrain Trevor from lunging at me with balled fists. She was making an effort to calm him down.

I backed several steps away from the rabid man, our eye contact not faltering the tiniest bit. "What is the matter with you?" My sister asked me, more disappointed than upset.

"I'll tell you what's the matter with him," Trevor promised fiercely, breaking away from Shannon and Richard's grip.

"Trevor, this is not the–," Shannon's attempt at a peaceful, nonviolent resolution was interrupted by her berserk husband.

"No, this *is* the time! It needs to be said! Your brother isn't mad because I married you at a young age, he's mad that I am married at all!"

"Trevor, don't you dare!" Shannon pleaded.

"He envies me! He wishes he had a wife that didn't fucking kill herself!" Trevor spat the last three words.

It wasn't I who reacted after that – it was Richard – who punched Trevor so hard that they both fell to the ground. I rushed to Richard's side and picked him up, gripping him by the shoulders so as not to let him kill Trevor. Shannon did the same with her husband.

"I ought to kill you for saying that to my brother!" Richard howled, rubbing his bruised knuckles.

Trevor didn't respond immediately. He was too busy wiping the blood from his nose and mouth to say anything. He stormed off with Shannon and yelled back, "I don't need this shit! We're going to the car."

I let go of Richard, who seemed calm enough to not completely lose control of himself. I called after them, "Wait. It's not safe to be out at night."

Shannon and Trevor stopped walking and turned to face me. We were all panting as if we had just run a marathon.

"Let's all go to our tents and stay out of each other's way. We won't stay the rest of the weekend and we'll leave for the car in the morning," Richard said.

My sister and Trevor both nodded slowly in agreement, and we each entered our individual, dome-shaped tents. As I zipped my door closed, I thought I saw a small figure, about the size of a rabbit, run behind the tree nearest my tent. Not thinking anything of it, I closed my door and descended into the boundless realm of dreams.

***

I was awakened from my sleep by a feminine voice shrieking, "Trevor? Trevor? Trevor?!"

I stepped from the comfort and familiarity of my tent out into the mysterious, unpredictable moonlight, and saw Shannon, her hair a complete mess, with bags under her eyes and a horrified demeanor. She was desperately scanning the black gloom surrounding us. When I asked about the cause of her apprehension, she responded with tears in her eyes, "Trevor's not in his tent. I went by to see how he was feeling but he wasn't there."

Richard emerged from his tent as well, having overheard Shannon's assessment of the situation. "I wouldn't worry about it, Shannon. Maybe he had to go to the bathroom."

"But he's been gone almost forty-five minutes!" Shannon was growing more panicked with every second that ticked by.

Holding my sister's wrists gingerly, I began speaking words of comfort and reassurance. Her fear changed to bewilderment, and I noticed she was staring at my hands. Tilting my head downward to see what she was looking at, I uncovered the source of her confusion. My hands, as well as the rest of my clothes, were covered with dirt. There were tiny pebbles underneath my brown fingernails.

"What the hell happened to you?" Richard asked, his voice concerned.

It was then that the dream I was awoken from came back to my memory. I couldn't remember every detail, but fleeting bits and pieces came to my mind like notes from a jazz musician; they seem scattered and unrelated, but encompassing them was a central idea that tied it all together.

I remembered wandering off into the woods, seeing Trevor a short distance ahead of me, searching in front of him, oblivious to my presence, advancing slowly – as if some unknown entity was provoking him. The next image that came to mind was of an oddly deformed, hollow tree, with a kidney-shaped hole in the trunk. Out of the hole in the misshapen tree, came a torrent of small creatures, which I couldn't remember the looks of. They were obscured in shadow. The last thing I remembered of my dream was standing in front of the tree, my head sticking into the hole, calling out Trevor's name. The inside of the tree was completely dark, and I heard an echo, as if I was shouting into a well. I recalled wondering, *How deep does this go?* Somewhere in the bowels of whatever lay at the bottom of the tree, a deep, sonorous voice, sounding like an operatic baritone, said, "We're waiting for you."

I did not verbally relate this dream to my siblings. I was not granted enough time. Shannon began jumping to conclusions in the midst of her frightful panic.

"What did you do?" she asked, backing away from me slowly.

"He probably just went out for a walk last night and fell down," Richard rationalized to Shannon. This only made her more suspicious.

"Why are you answering for him?"

I approached Shannon with my arms outstretched in a show of peace.

"Shannon, just take a breath. We can go out and look for him at daybreak. We won't be of much help, bumping into trees in the dark."

Shannon was pale and trembling, trying even harder to avoid being near her brothers. "What did you do to him?" she wept.

"We didn't do anything to him!" Richard said, losing his patience and consequently raising his voice.

"Stop it! Stop it! Stop it!" she screeched, starting to frantically flee the campsite as her hysteria reached its climax.

"Get back here! Shannon!" I cried out, not realizing that yelling was not helping her plight.

She was already far gone into the woods. Richard exclaimed in exasperation, "Fuck!"

Sprinting in the direction of Shannon's reverberating cries for help, with our flashlights in hand, Richard and I descended deep into the woods, traveling far off course from the designated trail. The beams of light shining from our flashlights darted back and forth as we ran. We continued our pursuit, until Shannon's pleas morphed into a bloodcurdling scream, and then stopped all at once. The chorus of crickets chirping drowned out our wheezing breaths. Richard called her name several times before I told him to be quiet.

"We don't know what the hell is out here with us," I rationalized.

Richard nodded in silent agreement, trying his hardest to remain calm but failing miserably. We slowly advanced; wincing each time we stepped on a twig, out of fear that our predator, or predators, would hear us.

It was at this point that I started to feel a *warm vibration* in my head. I looked down and stared at my legs, which became one solid, blurry mass. My vision didn't fade to black and I didn't dramatically crumble to the ground, as I might have expected. In the amount of time it takes to snap your fingers, my vision was crystal clear and my headache vanished, but I wasn't sure where I was when the symptoms began. There was an entire period of lost time, which I could not account for, starting from when the headache was born and when it subsided. If I had the choice, I would extend that period of "lost time" just a few minutes more, so I wouldn't bear witness to what happened to Richard; an event forever seared in my brain.

***

It chills me to the bone. Even now, it makes me want to destroy this paper and puncture my eyes with this pen to erase the grotesque images. But the memory of my brother being butchered – desecrated before my repulsed eyes – whirls and whips around inside of me like the winds of a sandstorm.

When I re-entered consciousness, I was pointing my flashlight at Richard, who appeared to be convulsing on the ground, lying on his back. As my eyes adjusted to the brightness of my light, I realized he wasn't convulsing; he was desperately struggling to shake off his body the dozens of hideous creatures – each about the size of a chipmunk, but shaped like minuscule, hunchbacked humans – that were swarming him.

Their skin was bubbled and red all over, as if they had contracted smallpox and the symptoms never wore off. Their minuscule spines protruded from their backs; the only white part of their scarlet exterior. There were six of them near Richard's head. Two were pulling and clawing at his hair with their tiny, dagger-like fingers, while the other four climbed on his shoulders, tearing and biting off chunks of skin. The rest of them, which had to have been close to *one hundred*, were climbing all over his stomach, chest, arms, and legs.

They were so densely packed together in their large numbers that they looked like a sea of pustules rolling over Richard in waves. Their combined body mass kept him pinned to the ground as they tore and chewed their way through his skin, muscle, blood vessels, and eventually, his bones. He opened his mouth to scream, but two of the creatures climbed into his mouth and down his throat. His head jerked violently, as the creatures plowed their way down his esophagus; blood cascading down his chin, adding to the enormous pool of red liquid that was accumulating underneath him. I could hear a very faint scream that was muffled by the gut-wrenching beings.

They had already chewed his limbs into several, mangled pieces, when the two monsters that climbed into his mouth burst out of his stomach, spraying internal organs and blood for yards. They tugged at his ribs, and each creature climbed off of him, grasping their own individual bone.

They carried his mutilated remains like a family of fire ants, each one holding a rib, a chunk of meat, or a small body part over their tiny, hairless, reptilian heads, and marched in a single-file line to the base of a tree. As I shined my light on the tree they were filing towards, I discovered it was the very same tree I had seen in my dream earlier that night; the deformed tree with the kidney-shaped hole.

I watched in absolute shock as the beings jumped through the hole in the tree, and disappeared. The tree had to have a tunnel in the bottom of it; it would be impossible for a hundred of those *things* to fit in a single tree. When the last of the creatures entered the tree, and all that was left of my brother was a pool of his bodily fluids in the dirt, I let the flashlight fall from my numb fingers. My head was pulsating, beating in sync with my out-of-control heart. I started dry heaving, but all that escaped my mouth were nauseating sounds of gagging. From my eyes, fell my body's entire supply of tears. I leaned against a tree and crumbled to the ground. Finally, I was able to vomit.

Then, I felt that ominously familiar warmth in my head. In a futile attempt to escape my inevitable fate, I crawled as far away from the tree as I could get, before the blurriness in my vision returned.

***

This time, when my vision returned to normalcy, I was laying on the ground at the mouth of a cave. I could tell I had wandered a far distance over a long period of time, because the pitch-darkness of night had become the revelatory light of day. Struggling to my knees, which were too weak to hold my body weight, I leaned against the nearest tree to catch my breath. When there was enough oxygen in my lungs to speak, I spoke into the cave's opening.

"Hello?" The only response was my own echo. I made the decision to enter.

The cave was darker than the night had been several hours previously, and without my flashlight, I aimlessly walked, with my hands serving my eyes' duties. The sound of water dripping from the dirt ceiling was the only noise besides that of my feet stepping in puddles of it. It was a constant downhill descent.

Off in the distance, I could see the light of a fire. Advancing towards it, a large, circular compartment came into view. For a brief instant – a fraction of a second – I felt the slightest bit of hope, for safety, for another human being. Hope for *anything*.

My hopes were shattered, shortly. The walls and ceiling of this compartment, which was about the size of an ornate ballroom, were completely plastered with decomposing bodies in various states of decay. The light of the room came from candles within the eyeholes of skulls dangling from the ceiling around the perimeter of the room. Bones and rotting intestines, kidneys, livers, lungs, hearts, and brains, littered the floor like discarded wrappers left after a snack. There were several open doorways along the circumference of the room, each leading to a complex system of tunnels.

Of all the bodies atrociously ornamenting the walls, one in particular, caught my eye. *It was Shannon.* It was only her head on the wall, fit like a puzzle piece between the assorted body parts. I approached it, slowly, unsure of what to do. I noticed a slight movement in her eye, like a muscle twitch. Before my confusion could bring me to the ridiculous conclusion that she might be alive, her eye exploded, leading a river of small eggs and larvae to pour out, like pus from a popped zit. The scream that escaped my lips must have alerted the creatures in the cave, because I could hear their feet splashing in the wet dirt as they hastened in my direction. I have never run faster in my life.

***

That is my story. That is everything that happened, verbatim. I have not exaggerated a single claim, nor did I leave a detail unwritten. I understand nobody will believe my story. They will search my house and find my clothes, painted in Richard's blood, and immediately accuse me of killing him.

Nowhere is safe for me to hide. They live in the trees, you know. Those goddamn oaks in my backyard are antagonizing me, deriving sadistic pleasure from pushing me over the edge, into the unfathomable chasm of insanity.

I'm okay with dying, it's only a matter of time before those horrible things come and rip me apart, just like they did to Richard. I can hear them. Or is that just a breeze blowing into some leaves? Are they on their way in? I don't intend to find out.

Hopefully, when the police find this note next to my hanging body, they won't put it in an "evidence" bag in some cluttered filing cabinet. I have to warn people. I have to warn *you*, whoever may end up reading this.

If there is no body, you will know for sure that those creatures are very real, and are probably waiting outside *your* house, right this very second. If there is no body and no note, you will go about your life, oblivious to the horrors that lurk in the dark shadows of even the most beautiful forest. I wish I could live in such ignorance, but it is far too late for me.

To my mother and father, I love you. To Ashley, my beautiful wife, I'll see you soon. Goodbye.

A LETTER TO MICHAEL
Edward R. Rosick

I watched the sun die over the Western horizon, the air in the cramped eighth story room of the Jasmine Hotel humid and stale. Looking out a cracked window, Detroit appeared old and tired, a caricature of American industrial might turned impotent.

But, matters such as those didn't mean much to me, anymore. They didn't mean anything to the long-limbed, red-haired, twenty-year-old army private, still dressed in fatigues and sprawled dead on the floor, lying in a pile of his own intestines.

We had met earlier in the day at a riverfront jazz concert, one day after I had gotten back into town. He was getting ready to muster out for a tour in Afghanistan after completing his final twelve months in Iraq. He saw me as a kindred soul, a man who could understand—unlike his friends and family—why he was going back to that caldron of hell. It wasn't because he was a rabid patriot, or filled with some sense of greater destiny; it was because that's where his brothers and sisters, his true family, were. After half-a-dozen beers, he considered me his best friend. It was easy to talk him into coming back to my room for more alcohol and war stories.

I closed the window overlooking streets filled with garbage and rats and sat down on the mattress next to my scimitar, its razor-sharp curved blade stained with the private's blood. The bloodlust and black rage that pushed me over the precipice was still inside me, driven by the never-ending parade of young men and women feeding the Middle East machine of war.

But, perhaps this night would be different. If anyone could end it, it would be him. I called Michael at his law office and prayed to gods that ceased giving a shit about me long ago that he was still there.

Michael picked up on the second ring. "Hello?" he said. It was funny, hearing his voice. It sounded soft and civilized.

I waited a few seconds then cleared my throat. "Michael. It's me."

There was a pause, then a loud sigh. "Look, I don't know who this is, but—"

"Twenty-seven point two klicks north of Rafah. December 17th, 1990. You took two slugs in your gut. I took one in the right bicep, just above my skull and crossbones tat—the slug went clean through and I was back out on patrol in a week."

Another pause. Finally: "Where are you?"

I gave him the address and told him to come alone. He said he would and I believed him. Even after all these years, I knew Michael as well as one man could know another. We had shared too many battles for it to be any other way.

I pulled out three single pieces of carefully folded paper from my shirt pocket. I don't remember if I was ever going to send the letter to Michael or not. Sometimes, I think I had written it just to put into words the madness that entered my world, to try and give that horrific time meaning and context.

I kept it—I read it over and over—to remind myself of what I was and what I hoped I could be again. Its words were smudged and faded, but they still held tight their dark chakra of that night, twenty-four years ago and 6000 miles away.

***

Tuesday morning, January 3, 1991
Somewhere north of Rafah

"ENEMY AT THREE O'CLOCK!!"

That's how it started, Mike, with some private first class (your replacement, can you believe it?) fresh from the states, screaming his lungs out at four in the morning.

But you know all about the craziness here as much as I do. At least, up until that night. Because that night, man...that night took the insanity that was our normal up to a whole new level of fucked.

I've tried to write my folks and explain to them about what happened. But unless you've been here and had this 24/7 living hell burrow under your skin until you want to join the Shaikh who dance like madmen in the streets of Riyadh, it's just not possible to understand.

That's why I'm writing you, Mike, even though I don't hold any hope that the censors will let this letter get through. But I need to tell someone that I'm not crazy.

And if I am, I need someone to understand why it happened.

Anyway, this PFC—name was Jacobson—started screaming like a round of magnesium tracers had hit him. I poked my head out of my tent into the starlit night, expecting to see a squad or platoon of Iraqis. There was sand, some scattered tamarisk shrubs, and eight tents of our demolition squad nestled in a small ravine.

There were no enemy soldiers.

"Jacobson—calm down and get over here!" I yelled in my best commander voice.

Private Jacobson—he looked so damn young, I bet he didn't even have hair on his balls—who was about 10 meters away on the near edge of our perimeter, looked at me with wide eyes that were full of fear, then dropped in a dead faint.

By that time, Andrews, Cooper, Matthews, Zitek, Kaufman, Davies, Davidson, and Johnson—all of the old team that had gone out with me for another Recon mission looking for the mythical Iraqi weapons of mass destruction (you'd think with our billion-dollar satellites we wouldn't need to send men into harms way before the 'real' war starts and we turn Iraq into one big sand dune, but hey, what the hell do I know?) —came out of their tents, ready for a fight. They had AK's in their hands (yeah, I know, the brass wants us to use M-16's, but we both know what an unreliable piece of firepower the 16 is here, hell, if yours hadn't jammed up, you'd probably still be here and I'd be minus one potential medal of honor) and were led by Andrews, who gave a war cry and ran full out into the night while his AK sang a 150-decibel song.

I know you're thinking—"where's the L-T's usual standard military protocol?" My only answer is that I was getting tired, Mike. Fucking exhausted. Weary of going out for weeks at a time to blow up shit Saddam—if he really had it—had hidden and buried so deep in the fucking desert that he probably couldn't even find it. Of watching fellow warriors get shot and blown up into chunks of lifeless flesh. Of seeing you, my best friend, get almost killed. It was wearing on me, Mike. I didn't tell you, but I was going to ask for a transfer once my tour was over. Get me a nice little desk job in Germany or Korea, find some blonde Fraulein or little Mama-san to screw day and night, and spend the rest of my time collecting government paychecks until I was old and fat and retired.

Funny how some things don't work out.

So I didn't do a damn thing as the rest of the boys followed Andrews' lead and started running and shooting and having a grand old time. Just pulled back into the tent, put on my flack jacket, and waited for them to run out of ammunition so I could go see just what was going on without getting shot to hell.

But then it got quiet. So quiet, I swear I could hear the thick layer of cordite from my boy's guns fall onto the dry, parched earth. So fucking quiet that I could hear my heart pounding like Alex Van Halen on his drums, five seconds before I realized how scared I was.

Besides the unreal muteness, I could smell something over the gunpowder, over the omnipresent heat of the land, over all the death and hate and bullshit that infected the entire Middle East. It smelled like something rotted, infected, old—no, not old—ancient. It scared me down to my cynical soul and all I wanted to do was lay there in my own sour sweat and pray to Jesus to come take me back to Detroit.

But these were my men—my family—and I just couldn't lie there. I took two deep breaths to clear my head, grabbed an M-60, loaded it, threw a couple belts of shells over my shoulder, and moved slowly out of the tent.

The camp was nearly deserted. One second, my boys had been filling the air with thunder and lead, and the next second they were gone. It was totally empty except for Jacobson, who was still lying on the ground next to our encirclement of razor wire.

There were no bodies. Absolutely nothing! I tried to think—gas, some exotic Iraqi bio-weapon—but nothing clicked. Almost all of the men had disappeared into the blackness of the night.

I think I would have lost it right there if it wasn't for Jacobson, who finally came to and started wailing like a six-month-old baby for his momma's tit. I walked over toward him and finally saw what had turned his brain into curdled mush.

You have to believe me, I was straight that night, as straight as anyone can be and still function in such an insane place. This thing wasn't a hallucination, no bad DT's, no after-effect from some bunk uppers. It was real, Mike. And more terrible than any sane man can imagine.

It was 10 klicks outside the camp at three O'clock. It stood up...and up...and up, at least 15 meters tall. Its skin was a sickly, decaying yellow, like sand that had been pissed on by fifty men. Patches of festering sores oozed congealed puke-green seepage off its scarred torso. And its face was straight out of some cheap-ass horror flick: sickly red eyes, smashed in nose, and a mouth filled with more sharp teeth than in that huge shark we caught off the coast of Ra al Khafji. This fucking monster looked at Jacobson, looked at me, then walked toward us like a drunken giant on legs as big as tree trunks.

My finger squeezed down on the trigger of the M-60 with no thought involved. I hit the freak square on. I know I did. I saw a line of gaping holes appear in its chest and thick, black stinking fluid pour from those holes. I must have hit it at least a hundred times.

My arms ached from the recoil, my ears sang from the bullet reports, and that bastard kept walking without missing a step. He got to the razor wire, reached down, and picked up Jacobson, who was still squealing like a pissed-off baby.

What could I do? I had just put over a hundred rounds of death into the ugly fucker and he didn't flinch. Like some giant garbage disposal, his shark mouth opened wide and he stuffed the private into his mouth. A few pops, a few chews, and one Alan Jacobson, PFC, gone. Two more steps and the freak was standing over me. He reached down with hands as big as a Jeep and I dropped to my knees, grabbed the crucifix at my chest (you remember, don't you, as they were taking you away in the Cobra, you pulled the chain you had the cross hanging from around your bloody neck and made me swear to wear it), and waited to become another midnight snack.

I must have been kneeling all night. The next thing I remember was the sound of choppers in the morning that carried me away to Jubbah. A week later, I asked about getting a report on that night and was ordered to keep my eyes closed and my mouth shut even tighter.

Yeah, right. Like I'm any good at following orders from assholes.

I learned from a Sufi holy man that the area we were in that night was holy ground for them. Holy might not be the right word though; more like an epicenter of their culture, a place where the first Mesopotamian was formed out of the warm sand and where the last will be buried at the end of time. The Sufi told me that Ghuls, a type of Djinn, were placed there to keep watch and ensure the land wasn't desecrated.

I don't know, Mike. A year ago I would have laughed the whole fucking story away, but now, who am I to say what is and isn't anymore? I only know I've been in this damn psycho-ward in Saudi Arabia for two months now and if I don't tell someone, I really will go insane.

I hope by the time you get this letter you are able to read it, and I hope by the time I get home (seven more weeks if I can believe my doctors) we can get together.

Maybe then you can help me figure out what happened. Help me understand why I'm the only bastard out of the mission still alive.

***

The knock on the door was solid and loud. "Come in," I said.

Michael pushed the door open, the hissing fluorescent light in the room silhouetting his tall frame. His formerly athletic body was covered in the baggage of extra weight from twenty-two years of living well, and his kinky, thick Afro of youth was now graying and sparse. He carried a large-caliber semi-automatic pistol in one meaty hand and I smiled to myself. He hadn't lost all of his edge.

I think he recognized the smell of the carnage before he saw the body of the soldier. Michael walked in two more steps and slammed the door shut with his foot.

"I never believed all the stories I heard." He motioned with the barrel of the gun at the dead young man on the floor. "At least, not until now."

"What happened to you?" His voice cracked with emotion. "You used to be the guy who would do anything for his men…" his voice trailed off and he pointed the gun at me, "and now you're killing our brothers!"

He paused again, probably waiting for some type of explanation.

I said nothing.

"I tried for so long to get in touch with you," he continued, "even after you disappeared when you got stateside. Then a year later, the boys from the brass started showing up and told me that you massacred all the men in our unit. They asked me a million questions and showed me pictures of things they said you did. I never believed them. Then in '92 things went quiet until '03, when they showed up at my door and said you were again on your killing spree. But in all of these years, I never believed them. You were the best C.O. we ever had, the best friend I ever had. There's no fucking way you could be a stone-cold killer."

He glared at me, and I could see in his light green eyes the betrayal I knew he felt. With his free hand, he pulled a cell phone out of his pocket. I heard three beeps as he punched in some numbers. I assumed 9-1-1. He put the phone to his ear and said the name, address, and room number of the hotel.

I took hold of the scimitar and stepped toward him as I felt the deep, ravenous swelling grow inside the smoldering pit of my soul. Michael clicked off the safety and pulled back the hammer of the gun in one smooth motion.

"Pull the trigger," I said, trying with all my might to hold down the beast. "Mike, pull the damned trigger before it comes out!"

"What the fuck are you talking about?" He stepped back until he was against the closed door. "Stay where you are, man, or I swear I'll—"

"He let me go so he could send some part of himself over here with me," I said, my voice becoming garbled as I felt my mouth stretch and widen and my will to die shrivel away. "He wanted to come to America. To where all the men who desecrated his home lived. He's killed them all, Mike. Every man from our unit, or any unit, that walked over that area. All except you and me."

Michael dropped the phone and gripped the gun with both hands as I smiled. A very wide, extremely hungry, razor-sharp smile. Michael fired the gun three times. Before he could get the fourth shot off, I severed him completely through the waist. The black, viscous fluid that poured out of the three bullet holes in my chest quickly congealed and dropped off my perfectly healed skin like bloated leaches.

Michael's upper torso rolled over next to the body of the young soldier. I carefully stepped around the wide pool of blood that spread across the cheap linoleum floor and moved over to my dying friend. He looked up at me with confused eyes as his frantic heart quickly beat away the last remaining seconds of his life.

I unhooked the chain holding the crucifix from around my neck and carefully placed it around Michael's. As his eyes glazed over in the universal sign of death that I knew all too well, I felt the dark, vengeful side of the beast become silent in the hidden crevices of my soul.

The hallway of the hotel was empty and quiet. A large, gray rat moved close as its keen nose picked up the scent of a possible meal in the room. I kicked at it and it scurried away. In the distance I could hear the sound of sirens.

"Maybe now he'll consider all the dues paid," I said out loud to whatever gods were listening. "Maybe now, he'll let me rest."

The rat reappeared and leered up at me. Tiny, dark eyes shined with a malevolent hatred as it clicked together its mouthful of razor-sharp teeth. I was just about to strike it with the scimitar when the first police officer burst out of the stairwell and leveled his gun.

"Drop your weapon!" he screamed. Even before I had taken the first step toward him, I realized with maddening certainty that the demon had tasted too much American blood for him to ever rest again.

BAD BONE
John Howe

The man called Hucklebone walked down the sidewalk with a worn burlap sack slung over his stooped shoulder, with its open end wrapped around his large, grimy hand. He carried a small, pointed shovel in his other hand and mumbled to himself as he turned the corner at the edge of town. People in the street gave him a wide berth as he passed; he acknowledged no one. A few teenagers laughed and jeered but kept their distance. Hucklebone walked on.

Officer Wesley Hornsby leaned on the fender of his squad car with suspicious eyes concealed by mirror lenses and spoke as Hucklebone shuffled by.

"What you got there, Huck?" There was just a hint of menace in his voice.

Hucklebone stopped and nodded at the bag. "In here, you mean?"

"Yeah, what's in it?"

"Got a couple of cats need burying."

"Let me see." Hornsby pushed his bulk off the car and strode forward.

Hucklebone upended the sack and dumped two mutilated carcasses onto the sidewalk. "Just a couple of cats."

Hornsby jumped back in disgust. "What the hell, Huck," he said, his hand resting on his sheathed nightstick. "What'd you do that for?"

"How else you gonna see 'em?"

"Just put the damn things back in the bag, Christ almighty."

Hucklebone picked up each cat and dropped them in the sack. He wiped his hand on his soiled trousers and attempted to scuff the blood off the sidewalk with his shoe. "Gonna bury 'em in the field over there." With the shovel, he pointed at the vacant property with a sign that said, *Future Home of Brookside Memorial Park.*

"What happened to the cats?"

"They're dead."

"Right," the officer looked skyward. "How'd they die?"

"I found one on my porch." Hucklebone took a labored breath. "The other one was in the driveway."

"So, you happened to find two dead cats and now you're coming all this way to bury 'em, instead of on your own property?" Hornsby shook his head and turned up his palms. Hucklebone stood there and said nothing. "What else you got going on, out your place, Huck?"

"Nothing," he said. "I need some things at the store, anyway."

"Just go bury the damn things and get on home."

***

Megan Larson watched the bedraggled man emerge from the convenience store with a bottle of something wrapped in a paper bag. She'd seen the episode with the cats and she, too, wondered what else was going on. She thought about the missing twelve-year-old girl; the one from the wrong side of the tracks, who disappeared about two months ago. There had been an extensive search by local police and volunteers, but no sign of her materialized. Eventually, it was assumed she was just another runaway, but Megan wasn't so sure. She'd been with *The Gazette* for six years and had yet to break a story bigger than an occasional drunk driving arrest. Yes, she could smell something about this guy; something foreboding, something bigger than dead cats.

***

When it was dark and the streets were quiet, Megan crept through the tall grass that glistened with dew in the pale moonlight. The ramshackle house was barely a shack, small and unpainted, with a tumbledown front porch and a rusted metal shed in the back. The house was dark except for a feeble light from one window. She carefully peered through the dirt-streaked glass and saw the old man sitting at a table wearing jeans and a dirty undershirt. The *Wild Turkey* bottle was half empty, a smudged shot glass near it. Hucklebone rose, scratched under his arm and left the room. Megan relaxed a little and waited for his return, hoping to see something she could investigate further.

"What the hell are you doing here?" Hucklebone looped an arm around her neck and a clenched fist jammed into her back.

Megan fought to get loose, but the man was stronger than he looked. "I just came to talk, that's all."

"You came to snoop around is what you did." He breathed heavily, then sighed and loosened his grip, slowly. "I'm sorry...I didn't mean to hurt you, if I did."

She turned toward him; he smelled of whiskey and sweat but his eyes were not threatening, as she feared they would be. "I'm not hurt." Megan trembled and rubbed her neck. "Scared to death, but not hurt."

"Well, come on in then, if you want to talk." He walked up the rotting porch steps and she hesitated then followed. "This thing's getting out of hand, anyway."

**

At the table, he offered her the bottle. She shook her head. "What's getting out of hand, Mr. Hucklebone?"

He poured a shot and downed it. "Just…I don't know…everything." His hands shook as he poured another shot.

"Tell me, please," she said. Hucklebone eyed her distrustfully.

"Hey, aren't you the one with the paper?" Before she could answer, there was a loud crash from the front of the house. Hucklebone sprung out of his chair. "This way, quick!"

Megan screamed in protest as he pulled her into a doorway and onto steps leading downward, slamming the door shut behind them. He turned a deadbolt latch and placed a thick board into brackets that blocked the door from swinging open.

"What's happening?" she said.

"Stay quiet." Hucklebone listened intently at the door. "I think he went back outside."

"Who?" She trembled in the dark, her voice a whisper.

"My son, Carlton."

"I didn't know you had a son."

"Hardly no one does," he said, still listening at the door. "He keeps pretty much to himself."

"The cats," she said. "Was that him?"

"Yeah, I'm pretty sure."

"And that missing girl…" Megan's trembling began to subside. "Do you think he had something to do with that?"

"I don't know what all he's done. I spend most nights here in the cellar." He took a long breath and lifted the board from the brackets. "I never see him in the daytime and not too often at night, either."

"Do you think he'd hurt you?"

"I don't know." Hucklebone turned the deadbolt and cracked the door open. "Yeah, I think he might."

The door jerked from his hand and a dark figure, dressed in black, pulled the old man through the doorway. There were shouts and they tumbled and fought in the kitchen. The whole thing happened so quickly; Megan couldn't tell who was beating whom, in the mayhem. There was more struggling, then screams, and Megan distinctly heard Hucklebone shout, "Carlton, no!" And then silence. Megan pulled the door shut, turned the latch and fumbled with the board.

"Mr. Hucklebone?!" she cried out through the door.

There was no sound; she prayed that Carlton was gone. Suddenly, the door rattled violently under a volley of great blows, as if someone were crashing into it over and over. The wall shook, plaster dust rained down, and wood crackled. Megan backed away from the door. It seemed solid enough, but she didn't trust it to hold for long. She felt for a light switch, found none and groped her way down the stairs. Her phone, damn it all, was in her purse on the kitchen table.

At the bottom, she brushed cobwebs aside and moved slowly with outstretched arms. The sounds from the doorway stopped. Her hand found a dangling string and she pulled it. A ceramic fixture with a bare bulb hanging from the overhead floor joists, cast meager light into the small cellar.

The hard-packed dirt floor sloped upward to what, she assumed, was the rear of the house. There was a slanted cellar doorway with a simple hand-turn latch secured with a thick steel chain, most likely put there by Mr. Hucklebone. She climbed the short, makeshift wooden ladder and started to unwrap the chain, aware that Carlton might anticipate this, but she couldn't stay there. He would have means to break in the door with a crowbar or even power tools. She turned the latch with breath held, her entire body shaking with fear. The door jerked from her hand and flew upward, and she fell back, screaming.

***

The dark figure jumped through the doorway, onto the cellar floor, with legs crouched and hands spread. Megan swung the chain as hard as she could and felt solid contact. Carlton recoiled and groaned, sounding more like a man than the hideous monster she'd expected. She saw his bloodied face with long wild hair in the dim light; he looked up at her with narrowed eyes and a thick, black beard, as he tried to rise. His face drooped on the left side and had an oozing, ugly cut on the cheek, either from the fight with his father or from Megan's chain. He rose to his knees and spat out some teeth.

"Stay down, you bastard!" Megan said, with the chain readied for another swing. He lunged at her and she whipped the chain around. It caught him in the face again.

Megan dropped the chain and ran up the stairs, toward the kitchen. She struggled with the board and managed to free it, just as she heard Carlton climbing the stairs, snarling now, like a cornered wolf. As she turned the latch, he grabbed her ankle and pulled her down the stairs.

They both tumbled to the dirt floor and Megan realized the thick plank was still in her hand. He pulled her up by the hair and wheeled her around. She swung the board and hit him in the side of the head; there was a loud thud, like a watermelon falling to the floor. Carlton's eyes opened wide and he collapsed. She didn't wait to see if he was alive or dead. She dashed up the stairs and saw Mr. Hucklebone's body in his dirty undershirt, sprawled face down on the floor, with a pool of blood beneath his head.

She ran out the front door, to her car parked alongside the road, jumped in and hit the lock button. Megan cursed and cried and pounded the steering wheel when she realized she'd, once again, left her purse on the table – including her keys and cell phone. The decision to stay in the car or go for help weighed on her. Then, a miracle occurred. Headlights appeared in the road and she jumped from the car and ran toward them, waving her arms frantically. To her utter relief, it was a police car; it stopped and Wesley Hornsby opened the door, heaving himself out of the seat.

"Is that you, Megan?" he said as he reached in and flipped on the flashing lights.

"Oh God, oh God," she sobbed and started toward him. Then she stopped. Her throat went dry and her eyes widened; she tried to speak, to warn him. The man in black had appeared from nowhere, behind Hornsby; the wood board she had hit him with raised, a horrible smile on his face. She screamed and Carlton, his black beard dripping, swung the plank. It hit the officer with a grotesque-sounding roundhouse blow that twisted his large head and sent him face-first onto the pavement. Thick blood oozed from the side of his head and brain matter glowed red and blue under the flashing police lights. He didn't move.

Megan was frozen in place, paralyzed with fatigue and horror; too gripped with fear to run. Carlton stood with the board on his shoulder, as if he'd just hit a home run in a game with demons, and he howled a surreal shriek, filled with hate and lust and a thirst for more. His open mouth revealed toothless gaps and split lips; blood ran down his neck. He turned to her and dropped the board, holding out his hands, fingers apart and trembling. A repulsive, snarling cry radiated from his demented mouth. His face was contorted with pain and rage, his wild hair dripping with sweat – or blood, or both – and quivered in all directions. Megan stared in terror, resigning herself to a horrible death and holding up her arms in an effort they both knew was futile.

***

There was an incredible roar and Carlton twisted sharply and lurched to the side. Then, another roar, and he lurched again and fell. He rolled onto his back and looked at the sky with wide eyes. She saw gaping holes in the side of his chest and his abdomen – the black material of his shirt torn and ragged and wet.

***

Hucklebone lowered the double barrel shotgun and let it fall at his feet. A siren sounded in the distance and then another. Megan slumped against the police car and slid down to the pavement, unable to move. Both barrels of the shotgun oozed smoke as it lay in the road. Hornsby and Carlton lay in the road, one atop the other, unmoving.

Hucklebone limped slowly to Megan and collapsed into a sitting position next to her, facing away from his fallen son. His head was bleeding from a deep wound above one eye. There was considerable swelling already and his breathing was nothing but a weak rasp. The sirens were getting closer. Flashing lights from the first car appeared over a crest and the cruiser came to a screeching stop.

"I guess you got yourself a story after all," Hucklebone said, with what sounded like his last breath, but he sat there in the road with Megan and he almost smiled. A young, blond police officer, uniform freshly starched, got out of the car with gun drawn and unsteady orders for everybody to freeze. The second police car arrived.

Megan looked at Hucklebone, her breaths swift and audible. "I'm sorry about your son," she said.

"Well, he wasn't much good." Hucklebone was fading, his breathing labored and he held his hand over his wounded head.

***

The police officers had questions, many questions. They treated the old man badly because of his tarnished reputation. As a precaution, they said he was to be handcuffed. Megan rose to her feet and said, "This man needs medical treatment at once!" She jabbed a finger at the blond officer. "He saved my life and killed his own son to do it." The officer ran to his car and radioed in for an ambulance.

***

Hucklebone sat with his head against the dead cop's squad car door with eyes closed. Megan prayed he was asleep. She squatted and gently shook him and told him help was on the way. She pleaded for him to wake up, to hang on, but the old man was no longer breathing. Megan touched his cheek, her tears flowing and her heart swelling.

"Thank you," she said.

SHEOL
Paul Stansfield

The end came quickly for Keith Murray, and relatively painlessly. In fact, it was precisely the sort of death that most people, given their choice, would pick: dying while asleep. It was a brain embolism in Keith's case. He was even dreaming when it happened. Like other outside stimuli, such as alarm clocks going off, or conversation, the slight pain and confusion of dying was actually briefly incorporated into Keith's dream. One minute he was having anal sex with Brooke Shields, the next he was sniffing cocaine with the members of Mötley Crüe. The coke, when inhaled, caused some irritation, and then weird images went through his mind. (Keith had never actually done cocaine, so he was unsure of how it felt or what it did, exactly. So his mind threw in an approximate cause for his real life trauma.) But then, his brain shut down and he died, all without waking up.

The next thing Keith was aware of was standing in a strange place. The sky was purplish-black, with no sun, although a dim sort of light nevertheless still could be seen. All around him were many, many people, more than he'd seen at one time ever, including at a rock concert in a huge stadium. Thousands and thousands, perhaps millions. All naked, too. Here and there, Keith noticed huge piles of worms. Two kinds; white, tiny maggots and larger, brown-reddish earthworms. The ground, or more properly, the floor, was a dingy, light gray, and it felt like concrete. That was all.

He turned around, several times, to see if he could find anything more. He couldn't. The same people, worms, and sky in all directions. Keith looked closely at himself. Aside from his also being naked, he looked basically the same. Same body hair, same height and weight, same moles, same scars. Well, he did look extremely pale, even by his light Irish ancestry standards. But maybe that was because of the light.

He looked around some more, and grinned. What a strange dream! This observation always cheered him. Whenever he realized, in a dream, that he was dreaming, he usually chose to change it, make it more fun. Keith tried to do this now. Thought of float-flying, but nothing happened. Pictured himself in a zoot suit, standing in a garish, Monte Carlo casino; again, nothing. Imagined hitting the World Series winning home run for the San Diego Padres, without success. Oh well, might as well make the most of it.

Keith wandered over to his nearest neighbors (a short trip) and started talking. First, he addressed a man in his sixties, who was sitting and staring off into space. "Hi, where are we?"

The man didn't even look up.

Keith tried again, with a fortyish woman with a potbelly. Again, no response.

He asked perhaps thirty people this question before a teenaged girl finally answered. "Sheol," she said in a quiet monotone.

"Where's Sheol located?" he asked his helpful informant.

"I don't know."

"Well, what's your name? I'm Keith. Keith Murray."

"I don't know."

"You don't know your name?"

"No."

Keith shook his head bemusedly at this, and after it was apparent she had nothing more to say, walked away. He stared some more at his comrades. He noticed that although all the various human races were represented, they all looked pale somehow. White, black, Asian, Indian – all pale colors of whatever shade they were. Strange. As he looked, he abruptly saw a woman blink into existence. She resembled all the others. After a moment, she sat down on the hard floor next to some other people. There was complete silence, Keith noted. Probably millions of people together, none talking. He shook his head again.

A few minutes later, a boy popped into being. He was Asian, probably nine or ten years old. This time, Keith ran up to the newcomer. "Who are you?" he asked.

The boy looked back at him, in Keith's eyes. A first here. "I'm Randy Wilson. Who're you?"

Keith answered, and continued his interrogation. "Where are you from?"

"Fort Wayne, Indiana."

It went on like this for several minutes. Keith learned Randy's address, phone number, what grade he was in, how many siblings Randy had, what TV shows he liked, what his father did for a living. Finally, he paused, having run out of immediate questions. Randy took this opportunity to ask one of his own.

"Where's my family? We were driving to Gary to see my Nana. Then I was here. Where are they?"

Now it was Keith's turn to say he didn't know. Just as he did, a very old, tall woman interrupted. "If they died like you, they're here somewhere. If not, they're still alive. You can look, but you probably won't find them, even if they're here."

Randy took this news calmly. Before Keith could scold her for her insensitivity, she stared at him and said, "You're quite curious, aren't you? So was I. I got here hours before you did. I managed to learn some."

At last! He forgot all about Randy. "Okay, where are we? One person called it 'Sheol', but where is it?"

"That person was right. This place is called Sheol. As to where, I don't know. But I do know this is the afterlife. You died and were sent here, like everybody. And there's no escape from here."

Keith smiled at this. He still thought it was a dream, but he didn't feel like arguing that point. "So, is this Heaven or Hell?"

"Neither. They don't exist. The dead come here. Although, as you can see, and as you'll experience, it's closer to Hell than Heaven."

"All right, then, how come more people don't talk, and just sit there?"

"Because this is The Land of Forgetfulness. Once you're here for a while, you forget who you were, and other personal details. Then, after that, you forget how to talk. It happens to everyone."

"What's the deal with those worms?"

She sighed. "I don't know why they're here, but they are. In great numbers. We all use them to sleep on, and to cover us at night."

Keith shivered and laughed. "Yeah, right! Some bedding! I'd sooner lay on the ground."

"No, you won't. The ground's hard. And it gets cold. The worms and maggots provide some warmth. You'll see."

"So, there's day and night here, huh? And we need to sleep?"

"Yes. Apparently night lasts about nine hours. The total 'day' lasts about as long as on Earth. And you do get tired."

"What about food and water? Do we also eat the worms?"

"No. We don't need food or drink. You'll see. You won't remember what it feels like to be hungry or thirsty."

"Who's in charge here at Sheol?"

"No one. I guess whomever or whatever runs the universe puts us here, but no one rules here. There's nothing to rule, really."

"No one dies and leaves here?"

"Nope. We can't die again. We're here forever." As she finished this sentence, Keith noticed a change in the large crowds. All those who were sitting, stood up, and everyone trudged over to the nearest mound of worms. As he watched, each person scattered an inch-thick pile of maggots on the ground, lay down, and scooped piles of earthworms on top, until they were covered. Then, these people closed their eyes and went to sleep. Keith stared, both fascinated and revolted, as, one-by-one, the millions of visible people all did this. He noticed too, as the old woman had said, it was getting distinctly darker and colder. Even his source finally went over, gathered up a worm bed, and fell asleep.

Keith was fairly tired now, too, but couldn't stomach the thought of putting worms on himself. He peered around in the semi-darkness for other objects. Nothing. He lay down on the hard, cold ground and tried to sleep.

Quickly, it became unbearable. Resignedly, he stumbled over to a still large pile of worms and threw some maggots down. After a minute of revulsion, he lay down. They weren't as bad as he thought. Like the people, they seemed subdued. Only slightly squirmy. He gave in entirely and tossed earthworms on himself, keeping them away from his face. After what seemed an eternity, he also fell asleep, thinking just before he did, *I'm gonna be working out this dream in therapy for years.*

***

Day broke, albeit, in a subtle way. Keith awakened to find the temperature had risen back to the original 60-65 degrees, and the lighting had gone from utter black to dim, but visible. This also caused Keith to think, perhaps, he wasn't dreaming, maybe they were right, and that he'd died and gone to the afterlife. He thought of this grim prospect for a good fifteen minutes or so. Finally, he sighed and joined his fellows in gathering up his wormy bedding and shoving it into rough piles. With great disgust, he picked out several maggots and worms that had crawled into his ears and his ass. A maggot had even gone into the tip of his urethra. He managed to get it out and threw it on the pile, shivering with revulsion as he did. Keith tried to put the incident out of his mind by finding the old woman he'd talked to the previous day. It wasn't difficult. She was standing twenty feet from him.

He quickly approached her. "Remember me?"

She smiled, slightly. "Yes. We were talking about this place yesterday."

He returned her grin. "Exactly. And I have many more questions. Most of them philosophical and religious."

"I don't know as much about that. But I know someone who did. Maybe he still does. Come with me." She led him away from their area. They walked perhaps a hundred yards away, his hostess looking carefully at each face. Eventually, she pointed to a Latino looking man in his fifties. "Father Swan might be able to help you."

At this, the man looked up. His eyes, unlike his neighbors, weren't blank. He motioned Keith to sit down. "How can I help you, son?"

Keith sat down and got right to the point. "Why is God punishing all of us by putting us here?"

"Is it punishment?" Swan's green eyes glittered.

"I'd say so. I don't see any angels playing flutes, or people basking in loving bliss. I see zombie-like, mute people doing nothing, forced to put worms on themselves to warm up at night."

"When you forget everything you won't be so unhappy. You'll just be. And I wouldn't call it punishment. Every person comes here. Good and bad people. I saw a vicious, unrepentant serial killer here – whose name escapes me – along with several people I know to be nearly saints. Or take myself. I was a pretty decent fellow on Earth, yet I'm here."

"So was I! What is this? I was taught that good people go to Heaven, and bad to Hell. Why didn't we?"

"I share your confusion, in part. I do remember reading of this place in the Old Testament, in the early parts. They just changed the discussion of the afterlife, gradually, until they got the Heaven and Hell bit. Apparently, they were right the first time."

"So, was being a good Christian a waste of time? Should I have just been a hedonist, had fun?"

"My gut feeling is, no, you did the right thing. But, at the same time, it wouldn't make a difference in where you went after death. Whether you were Christian or not doesn't matter, either. I've met members of all the major religions. Buddhists, Muslims, Jews, Hindus, etc. Some good and some bad. All here, just the same."

"This doesn't bother you?!" screamed Keith. This apathy was driving him nuts.

Swan's tone stayed mild and calm. "It did, at first. But I've come to accept it. Besides, I'll forget everything soon enough."

"Well, fuck that! I'm not going to accept it! I don't want to forget!"

"It won't matter. You will."

That was it, for Keith. He stalked off angrily, leaving Swan and the old woman without another word. He walked for about ten minutes, until he was in the midst of a different set of people. He had some serious thinking to do.

***

Dawn broke, and Keith fairly leapt up out of his pile of vermin. It was his fifth day here, and he had a busy day planned. It was nice to have a plan that involved action for a change. He'd spent the last three days praying feverishly. On the second day, to God. Then, when nothing changed, even his internal feelings, he'd prayed the next day to an amorphous, non-Christian Creator being. The fourth day, which again was identical to the others, prompted Keith to pray to Evil, and to Satan in general, out of desperation. Again, no change.

So today he was an atheist. No more praying to anyone. He was his own deity, free to do what he wished. And he had certain questions he wanted answered. The foremost being, what happens when you try to kill someone here?

And so, imbued with his zeal, he looked at the faces of his immediate comrades, studying them. After a few minutes, he found a guy who resembled someone he'd hated back home in Jersey. That guy had been a bully who'd picked on Keith. This one was close enough. He walked up to his intended victim, who sat there unmoving, looking arguably like Rodin's "The Thinker." The man's hair was a sickly yellow color.

Keith reared back and hit the man with a haymaker, using all his strength. The man flew backward, landing flat on his back, his nose trickling blood. Even this was slow, though. Keith waited to see what the guy would do.

The man resumed his sitting position and made no sound. Didn't even take notice of the slight wound. Didn't even look up at Keith, who was standing right in front of him.

That was the most infuriating thing of all. Keith knocked him over again, jumped on the man's torso, and started pummeling his face. Punch after punch, letting all the anger and frustration of the past few days pour out of him. The man's face broke and bled some more under the attack, but, as always, not as dramatically as on Earth. The man made no effort to defend himself, however, and still made no sound. Finally, Keith gave in completely to his rage. He grabbed the man's throat with both hands and slammed his head against the hard ground eight times, until the skull was broken thoroughly, and his victim's brains and blood lay strewn in a big mess over his body. Keith paused for a second, unsure of what he'd done. Ashamed, he looked up and around. No change. All the people were in the exact same positions as before. As Keith stared, one woman raised her head slowly, casually took in the kill scene, and then lowered it again without changing expression. This renewed Keith's fury. He gave the corpse's head a few more slams for good measure. Then he stared into the man's eyes (or what he could see of them through the cuts and bruises), and watched the entire body in general. No movement. No sign of life.

Keith crowed triumphantly, "I killed someone! He's dead! I killed an already dead person!" He let loose some curses, too, daring any gods or goddesses to punish him for his crime. Again, nothing happened. He thought some more, and smiled. He'd always wondered what human flesh tasted like. Here was his chance.

He tore a chunk of flesh from his victim's ruined face and popped it in his mouth. Forced himself to chew. It was awful. Not bad tasting, exactly, just a complete lack of taste. Spitefully, he kept going, and forced himself to swallow. His esophagus didn't help much, either. It took him several minutes to actually get the flesh down. Disappointed, he turned back to the corpse. Grabbed a handful of slimy, wet brains. Keith put these in his mouth, too, and gagged. No taste! Worse than plain rice cakes. Resignedly, he spat out the brains and walked away. Spent the rest of the day alternately feeling guilty and victorious, and ultimately, just hollow.

***

The following day, he again woke up, somewhat happily, as he had another idea. Sex! He'd try to have sex. Why not? He wasn't concerned about being punished anymore; might as well.

Thus invigorated, he removed the worms and maggots from himself (and as always, from within himself, although he'd gotten used to this) and walked around, searching for a prospective mate. Keith tried to ignore the nagging doubt he had with this idea: He had no lust, here. He was naked, and everyone else was, including many young, attractive women, but he'd yet to be turned on. He remembered what it was like to want someone sexually, but he didn't feel it. Really, the only reason he was enthusiastic at all was the idea of doing something different.

But these thoughts, he managed to suppress. Then he had a revelation. As he watched, dumbstruck, a woman popped into existence. A very familiar woman. An ex-lover, in fact. An astounding coincidence, considering he'd only bedded seven women in his life. But, sure enough, it looked exactly like his college girlfriend, Sheila. And the new people had better memories! He wasted no time in approaching her.

"Sheila, is that you?" He already knew the answer. Could see the characteristic, largish mole, right below her belly button.

"Yes," she said.

"It's me, Keith Murray," he said, and waited to see if she said anything else. She didn't. He was afraid of this; roughly half of the newcomers seemed as dull and sedated as the veterans, right away. Of the others, most of them forgot everything within hours.

But, maybe in this case, it didn't matter. "You want to have sex?" he asked.

She shrugged and just stared at him. Thus encouraged (or more properly, not discouraged) he set about making love to her.

It was a disaster. Completely disappointing. Kissing her, caressing her, was like kissing or touching a warm, fleshy robot. He felt nothing, and it was obvious she didn't, either. He kept at it though, again, angrily trying to get some pleasure, any pleasure, or at least, something new. She didn't seem to care, one way or the other. Keith tried to warm her up, using both fingers and tongue, to no avail. She seemed disinterested and dry. Quite a contrast to the excitement this had caused her back in college. He did have a moment of joy when, with her willing if jaded help, he achieved an erection. Even that was wrong, somehow, though. He was happy only because he did get it up, not in the act itself. But he had to see it through. Keith entered her, pumping away madly.

And madly. And madly. It must have been forty or fifty minutes. Still, no indications that he would come, or that she would, or anything. Ironic really. There had been times in his life when women had said he'd come too fast; now he wasn't at all, but no one was benefiting from it. This was so pointless, and joyless. Had he ever really enjoyed this? It was hard to believe. And Sheila looked like she was reading tax forms. Completely dead. Well, they both were, but animated. At least, he was, otherwise. Finally, he stopped. Withdrew. He started to apologize, but stopped as he looked back at Sheila. She simply sat up and stared off into space. Didn't appear to notice him. Probably, she didn't. It was a familiar sight to Keith. Just especially depressing this time.

Without another word, he stood up and walked off. Before he'd gone fifty feet, he stopped in shock and horror. The murder victim of the previous day sat in front of him, wounds healed, "living" again. Even this unfortunate action had failed.

***

Keith was up and about at first light, walking around briskly. It was one of the few fun things left. Not all that stimulating, but much better than sitting or standing around, as his comrades did, constantly. It was also one of the few new or different activities he'd tried that worked properly. He had tried. He always gave himself credit for that. In the three days since the ill-fated sexual encounter with Sheila, he'd tried to buck the trends and learn things about Sheol, at every turn. One night, Keith had attempted to stay awake. He'd managed to hold out for two or three hours before the cold had driven him back into the familiar cocoon of invertebrates. The lack of light, even dim lighting, hadn't helped, either. Walking around had been pretty futile, as he'd kept running into worm-covered people. As he'd stood there then, shivering violently, he hadn't felt all that rebellious, or innovative – just foolish. So, that experiment had failed, too.

The next day, he'd studied the worms more. He was very curious about them and why they were here. They clearly didn't eat either, yet still survived, if in the same subdued manner as the humans. Out of boredom and cathartic cruelty, he'd dispatched several wondering if they, too, would appear unharmed the next day, a la his blond murder victim. Of course, how would he tell? All worms pretty much looked the same. Keith had eaten a few as well. Which had caused him some measure of mirth, remembering the old kid's song, "Nobody loves me. Everybody hates me. I'm going to eat worms and die." Alas, the worms were as tasteless as the human flesh. In addition, their slight squirming did nothing for their charms. He'd choked down a few and then quit.

For his next attempt at distraction, he'd tried self-mutilation. He'd systematically sat down and destroyed his left pinky toe. Had banged it against the floor until it was shattered, then continued damaging it until he could actually tear it off. It hadn't been very difficult. His sensitivity to pain was significantly less than on Earth. The pain was more annoying than agonizing. And this act was also as useless. The next morning, he had been miraculously restored. Keith figured that even if he found a way to "kill" himself, it would also be temporary. No escape.

The only good thing about this place was he had plenty of time to think, especially about himself. He remembered hearing stories that portrayed ghosts as being overpoweringly envious of the living. He could strongly identify with that. If he was given the opportunity to be on Earth, haunting someplace, he knew he would be. It'd be tough to refrain from abusing the living, incredibly tough, knowing what he did now. Keith's regret was acute. All the opportunities he'd missed haunted him. Every night he'd stayed in because he was slightly tired, all the hours wasted watching moronic TV shows, all the bullies he'd avoided, all the women he'd been afraid to ask out. Or shit, there was much worse. All the general moralizing he'd done, every hedonistic pleasure he'd left undone, because it was "wrong" or "sinful." For what? It had made no difference. It was funny – blackly funny – but he couldn't laugh at it; it was too fresh and real. Although, it could have been worse. He could have been a priest, or a complacently poor person. Wasting his life for a later eternal reward that, surprise! – hadn't been granted.

Yeah, life had been more precious than he'd dreamed. There'd been crappy times, true, but more good times to balance it out. Even pathetic, miserable lives sounded better than this. And altruism was bunk, he'd decided. Let anyone see what waited for them after death and then see if they ever sacrificed their health or life for someone else. Not likely. Not even for their own kid. Sure, you loved them, they were cute, but so what? You'd all be in Sheol eventually, mute, mindless drones for eternity.

Thoughts like these disturbed him. Keith was still capable of feeling guilt, feeling that he was being too pessimistic, too selfish. Then, existing even an hour or two in Sheol crushed these optimistic, selfless thoughts. Shit, this place would turn Norman Vincent Peale to despair! Was he dead? Keith didn't know. Oh well, it was only a matter of time. 'Course, old Norm most likely wouldn't be depressed for long. He'd be without memory, just like all the others, soon enough.

That was the root of Keith's problem: memory. Obviously, his was unusually good for this place. No one he'd met (and the number of people he'd met here was well into five digits, so far) had retained memories as well as he had for so long. Randy Wilson, the old lady, and even Father Swan had all lost even the ability to speak, days ago. As far as he could tell, his mind was pretty intact; his memory seemed about as sharp as when alive. Of course, it hadn't been particularly great then, but now, comparatively, it was astounding. Was this a blessing or a curse? Sometimes he thought joining the herd might be a relief, other times not. One of his few satisfactions left was feeling special, feeling superior to the loathsome zombies. But knowledge undeniably caused him so much pain at the same time.

Not that, ultimately, his opinion mattered. He could yearn for stupid numbness, but he wouldn't necessarily get it. Or, he might dread it, and forget everything all the same. No choice. No power, no control whatsoever. Why he alone had this memory was also puzzling. The answer to this was similarly unknown to him, frustratingly so.

This thought was on the periphery of his mind now as he strode about. It was his new calling of the moment. Keith was curious about the borders of Sheol, if any. He planned to walk and walk, and see if there were rivers, or walls, or a fiery moat to keep people in. Or, if this was a planet: see how long it took to circumnavigate it. It was something to do.

It was a casual stroll. He stopped often to observe people. Another hobby of his was seeing if he could recognize famous dead people. This was problematic too, though. Anyone who died before the advent of photography might stay anonymous, since they looked different from paintings. Also, the people themselves usually didn't recall their identities, of course. Still, it passed the time. Keith told himself he'd seen Einstein, Lindbergh, Teddy Roosevelt, and a recently deceased supermodel whose name he (and she) didn't remember. Whether they really were these people was beside the point.

As he bedded down that night, probably twenty miles from his previous home, Keith hatched another possible scheme. Maybe he could convince some vegetables to lay atop one another in a large stack, like in "Yertle the Turtle"? Maybe he could enjoy a better view, or amuse himself by high diving off them into a large pile of worms? Might be (gasp!) diverting, even fun. Worth a shot. He drifted off in a slightly more pleasant mood.

Around him, Sheol continued.

AT DAY'S END
Leonard Apa

Walter Dayton, still called Day, by what was left of his (sort of) friends, thought he had adapted to his life on the street quite well over the spring and summer months. Even into the first weeks of December, Day thought he had a handle on things. As the weather cooled throughout the fall and into winter, it started to change from crisp to biting. Day *acquired* convertible, fingerless gloves/mittens, work boots, a heavy jacket, and a pair of new (to him) jeans, from various sources, including a thrift shop and a couple of department stores. Those items, along with the heavy, olive, drab duffel bag, strapped to his back and everything it contained, were all his worldly possessions.

Over the spring and summer, he had scouted for places where he thought he might be able to keep warm when the weather cooled; this act made him proud, made him feel proactive, like things would still turn for the better. While he still thought that they would, while he still held onto hope, he had his moments of doubt, especially when he saw the first flakes of snow and felt the howling wind cut right through his heavy clothes and gloves, like he was wearing nothing at all.

Day rubbed at his chest, hoping to warm it and hoping the hands would warm from the friction. Didn't he see that in a movie or something? He shook the thought from his mind; he had bigger things to worry about. The snow had been so unexpected that he wasn't anywhere near any of the warm spots, as he thought of them, so he had to come up with something around the immediate area. He took the dying, pre-paid cell phone from his pocket and checked the time. Close to ten, most places would be closed for the night, so going into a store to warm up was out of the question. He checked the minutes, they were nearly as depleted as his phone's battery, and he had no money to put more on, so Day preferred not to call anyone and possibly waste the minutes. Besides, who would he call, anyway?

He stood, still rubbing at his chest, with no real relief coming from the action. He squinted his eyes, searched the area as the snow's fall thickened. Across the street, set in the darkness of a building was a dimly lit area. Day stared at the lit up building and felt stupid. It was so simple and so perfect. Stepping to the edge of the sidewalk, he checked both ways, although, since the snow's sudden and rapid falling, the streets had become deserted of cars. It never hurt to be cautious though, just one of the few lessons he had learned from his alcoholic parents, the other lessons could be considered the cause of his roaming the snow riddled streets with no place to go at ten in the evening. He hoped the bank didn't have any all-night security, but it wasn't like he was in a big city or anything, all the banks he had been in didn't even have security guards during the day.

Inside the dimly lit ATM room, an old receipt fluttered across the floor, and Day could hear the soft purr of a motor. Heat. The ATM room was heated, and that skittering receipt was his promise of a warm night indoors. Reaching into his back pocket, Day pulled out his wallet, now empty, aside from his expired driver's license and a debit card to a dead bank account. Both items were technically useless, along with the wallet, but he couldn't bring himself to let them go, and now he was thankful he hadn't. Day looked at the magnetic lock and removed the debit card from its spot in the wallet. He looked down at it with a sad smile, and held it tenderly like a talisman from his past, from better days.

Swiping the card through the slot at the door, Day placed a hand on the door's handle. Nothing happened. No metallic clink of the lock disengaging, no red light turning green. Nothing. Day swiped it again. The light remained red. He swiped a third time, and again, nothing happened. Did the card deactivate when the account did? It couldn't be; any card with a magnetic strip should work. Hell, even gift cards with the strip should work. With a frantic hand, Day swiped the card again. The light turned green and his stomach dropped in excitement. He pulled the door, but it remained locked. The light held its steady green, as if mocking him, but there was no metallic clink, no lock disengaged. Just the green light staring at him.

Day felt something inside him break. He wanted to just fall to his knees and weep. His ears ached and felt numb at the same time. His fingers felt like he had run them through glass, cutting them to ribbons, and still, the green light taunted him with the promise of heat.

"Please. Please, just open." Day was aware of how pathetic and crazy he sounded, talking to a door, or a higher power that never seemed to favor him.

But his luck must have been changing, because the solid green light blinked and he heard the lock disengage. Day pulled the door open fast, before the door could change its mind and he was stuck outside all night. The warmth that enveloped him was like heaven. The smell of stale cigarettes, not so much, but beggars can't be choosers and all that.

"Thank you," Day said, again not sure if he was thanking the door or that mysterious higher power, but he didn't care which, now that he was in the heat.

The small ATM room would be just big enough for Day to spread out in. On one wall was a small counter for writing out deposit slips and overnight deposit envelopes; Day saw that if he moved his head just right, he could use the counter to block out just enough of the light from above, so it wouldn't keep him up when he tried to sleep. On the other wall, a garbage can overflowing with ATM receipts sat bracketed, about a foot off the ground; a perfect spot for his feet when he lay down to sleep.

Day fished around in his duffel bag, his fingers brushing against thick, cool glass, his own warmth in a bottle he was saving for later, his extra socks, a pair of sneakers, and finally, pulled out a battered paperback of David Morrell's "First Blood." One of his favorite novels, he had read it more than a dozen times, and until he managed to get something new to read, it would do for another go. At the part where Rambo had been arrested and has his POW flashback, the cell phone in his pocket bleated out its generic ring.

Confused by the sudden noise, as someone who had gotten used to an electronically silent world, without the constant ringing of cell phones or chimes of e-mails, Day looked around for the source of the sound.

Realizing where the ring was coming from, he reached into his pocket and pulled the phone out as if it were an alien object. He hadn't received a call in months and mostly kept the phone off. The display screen read 'Brian'. Even as he debated answering, his finger clicked the button and accepted the call.

"Hello?" Day tried on a chipper, but tired voice. Brian was an old friend that stuck with him, even after rehab (not quite the fix they all had thought it would be) and the ensuing divorce.

"Day, what's up buddy?" Brian's voice was genuinely chipper. It always had been.

"Hey, Brian, not much." Day stared at the white letters on the blue screen of the ATM. The screen flickered and the letters seemed to change form, but Day couldn't tell for sure at the angle he sat.

"How are you doing?" Brian's voice distracted him from the screen.

"Actually, tonight I'm doing really good." Day looked around the ATM room, the ice in his body slowly melting away and being replaced by wonderful warmth. "How about you?"

"Can't complain. It's been so long since we spoke, what are you up to these days?"

"Working construction," Day lied, staring at the work boots on his feet for inspiration.

"Nice, nice. Hey, pal, you want to grab a drink? A soda or coffee, of course. Me and the boys from the office are at—"

"I wish I could, but it's no good. I've got to get up early tomorrow and work."

"On a Saturday?"

"Time and a half. A man's got to eat." His stomach rumbled, conceding the point. "Maybe another time?"

A moment of silence; Brian had something he wanted to say, and though Day was worried about his battery and minutes, he wanted to hear what his old friend had on his mind. Maybe he would argue that coming out to hang for a bit wouldn't kill him. Or, maybe he would say that with the snow fall there was no way he could go into work the next day. But after the considerable pause...

"All right, Day." Brian said. "Take care, buddy."

"You, too, Bri. Night." Without looking at the phone, Day replaced it in his pocket. His gaze drifted back to the blue screen on the ATM; he stood to read what it said.

Insert Card

The screen twitched and the letters flickered again, but the message never changed. Day shrugged and sat back down, propping himself against the wall. He picked up his beat up paperback again and began to read.

As the words he read turned into sentences, and the sentences into paragraphs, and the paragraphs into pages, Day shivered from a chill that ran down his back. He felt like he was being watched. He looked through the glass windows of the booth. Nothing but the empty parking lot, rapidly filling with snow, looked back. Day couldn't shake the feeling. He dropped his book and stood up. His breath fogged the glass with his face almost pressed against it. He looked out into the darkness. The snowfall came down in full fury, blanketing the open air as much as the blacktop of the lot. The effect of the whirling twists of snow was dizzying, but pretty, and Day watched for a few minutes. Turning away from the window, he surveyed the little room he was in. It was clear no one watched him from inside the room. Looking from floor to ceiling, he noticed the mirror in the corner. Most likely it hid a video camera, but more immediately, it was probably the culprit he felt watched by. Day stuck his tongue out at it, smiled, and sat back down.

The toasty temperature rose and Day stripped his coat and gloves off, feeling cozy as a King. For the third time, he picked up his book and began to read. Beads of sweat broke out on his forehead, as the temperature continued to rise. Day now removed his sweater, and a second sweatshirt underneath, so he was left in only a stained t-shirt with holes in both armpits. He ran a bare forearm across his forehead and decided to remove the heavy work boots as well. His big toe stuck out of the thick, woolen sock of his left foot, and despite the heat, despite the hunger in his belly, and despite his situation, Day laughed because it reminded him so much of something he would have seen while watching Charlie Chaplin as the Tramp.

The sweat on his brow grew heavier, as did the air around him. The heat, now sweltering, was suffocating him. Day's heart began to race and a headache began to form at his temples.

"What the hell is going on in here?" he asked, and felt his eyes drawn to the flicker of the ATM screen again. Day stood up with the intention of cracking the door to let some of the cool air in, but he was drawn to the screen. The white letters *had* changed, and the message was no longer *Insert Card*, but now *Insert Tongue*. And Day, for whatever reason, didn't think it would be a bad idea to obey. The card slot blinked an angry red, Day was sure it had been green earlier, but that was in the back of his mind. Staring at the message, he felt his tongue start probing the inside of his mouth, just behind his teeth. His mouth opened slowly and his tongue began to peek out like a shy groundhog, as he moved closer to the machine. His tongue poked further out, nearly fully extended now, and the angry red lights beckoned him closer.

A crash at the window startled him and he spun to see a wad of snow sliding down the glass. Day shook away whatever fog had taken control of his mind and stared out into the whiteout of snow. There was no one out there. Wiping away the sweat on his soaked forehead, Day turned to the ATM again.

Insert Card was the message. The heat was getting to him – that was all, nothing but the heat. He swiped at his forehead and shook the remaining fog away.

"Insert tongue." Day felt like laughing, and he did.

Sitting down against the wall again, determined not to get distracted by phantom messages from inanimate objects, Day opened his book. As he had learned over the years, and should have realized right away, when you want to do something, something else tends to get in the way. The thrumming motor of the heater, that Day had learned to ignore since first stepping into the ATM room, started to cough and sputter. The motor grew louder and then lower, in wheezy puffs, reminding Day of a heavy smoker on their deathbed. He found the vent and stared at it. The coughing grew louder again and then louder, still. Somewhere, deep within the wall, there was a bang and rumble and then silence, followed by a cloud of dark, gray smoke and dust from the vent.

Still watching the vent, Day hoped the heat would kick back on. It had gotten hot in the tiny room, set somewhere between the Sahara desert and Hell, but it was better than the Fortress of Solitude outside. Enough silence passed and Day began to worry. If the heat didn't kick in, it would still be better indoors than out in the snow, but...

The thought never finished, as the soft purr of the motor kicked on. He let out a sigh of relief and relaxed, with his back to the wall. The heat didn't only start again in that steady, if not overwhelming way, but began to pour out in a solid wave that grew hotter and hotter. The sweat poured down his face, soaked his t-shirt, and made his underwear stick in a very uncomfortable fashion. He stood and made a point not to look at the ATM screen on his way to the door. Day pushed the handle but the door didn't budge. He looked down to the foot of the door; there wasn't enough snow to block it from opening, so he should have been able to push through without a problem. But the door would not move. Pushing harder, Day felt a gnawing in his stomach. He tried again and again, throwing all his weight into the door, but it remained closed.

His thoughts jumped back to when he swiped the card. The green light had lit, but the door wouldn't move. Was there a solid green light on the other side, right now, laughing at him? *You wanted to get in so bad, now sweat.* Day turned to the vent. The motor's rhythmic drone revved up and softened again.

"This place is fucked." Day pulled the shirt from his chest, but it fell back with a wet smack.

Looking over the enclosed space, something else felt off, but Day couldn't figure out what. Urging his eyes to look anywhere but at the blue screen of the ATM machine, they did just that, like a tourist trying to mind his own business on his first trip to New York City. The screen flickered and the letters went wavy. The message began to change in mid-wave, but fell back into place.

Insert Card

It wasn't the machine that was different, though. No. That remained just as screwed up as ever. Something else. It nagged at him, but Day could not place it. He tried to shake the feeling. Tried to relax. He was just hungry and tired and sweating. Day unbuttoned his jeans and pulled them off, now in only his under shirt, boxers and socks. He just needed sleep, a couple hours, at least.

Reaching into his duffel bag, his hand touched the bottle again. How he wanted to take it out and take a long pull on it. He wanted to feel that fiery liquor course through his body. He licked at his lips, closed his eyes, and took in a deep breath. Day removed, instead of the bottle, a tightly wrapped blanket and spread it across the floor. He would read some to relax and then get to sleep. Day sat with his back against the wall, the counter just above his head and his feet nearly touch—

No, they didn't nearly touch, his feet fell flat against the other wall, and either he grew taller or the counter lowered, so that his head nearly bumped it. The garbage can on the opposite wall, that provided plenty of space for his toes before, now brushed the tips. Day stood up, too fast. He heard the thud of wood before he felt the shooting pain course over the back of his head.

"Son of a—"

He winced, rubbing the ache away. The small room, his shelter, his solace for the night, was closing in on him. He stood in the center of the small(er) room and reached out, his fingertips not even grazing the walls. His eyes plastered to the flickering ATM screen. The screen flashed like hundreds of the same frame in a movie, but between flashes, there was something else. There was something *hidden*. He strained to catch a glimpse of it. Just a peek at the force that held him hostage, the force that wanted to do him harm.

There it was, on the left side of the screen. Just a series of dots, but Day knew: he knew it was an eye. The right side, more dots: another eye. Mocking eyes, hungry eyes, wolf eyes, watching him. The tips of his fingers now brushed, just barely, the enclosing walls, as something formed at the bottom of the screen. Another set of dots, only this time, it formed a manic joker's grin. The heater sputtered and coughed, sounding alarmingly like laughter. The taunting laughs of a bully. His fingers now pressed hard against the walls.

With his fingers flat up against the imprisoning walls, Day dropped his head and instinctively began to stoop his shoulders. He glanced up and saw the ceiling drop closer as well. The claustrophobic ATM booth forced his back forward and his face closer to the screen, stilling laughing with its maniacal grin. Now his hands were flat against the wall and his back continued to bend, his face peering, closer still, to the screen. Day knew, and he didn't understand how he knew, but he knew that if his face touched that screen, he would be swallowed, not just his tongue, but swallowed whole by the flashing of the sinister blue.

The deep-throated chuckle of the vent continued as the gleeful grin waited expectantly for its meal. Day, nearly bent in half now, was mere centimeters from the glass of the screen. The moments of darkness between each flash of blue grew in length. The series of dots that made up the face in the screen twisted into a look of such hunger that Day thought his heart would stop. He could feel his nose, just the tip, barely touching the screen where the mouth gaped in ravenous pleasure, and on (through) the screen, Day felt something wet.

The walls continued to box him up, continued to force him onto the screen. Day squeezed his eyes shut, ready for the worst. Pressure built in his arms as they were forced to bend to the will of the closing walls – his knees, as they were compelled to buckle under the weight of the ceiling, and his back, as it arched and pushed him forth. Fingers wrapped around his wrists and ankles. With his eyes squeezed shut, he had no way to be sure, but he knew that if he looked, he would see nothing holding him. He sure felt it, though.

He squeezed his eyes tighter, with his cheek now pressed to the glass, a feeling of wetness and nothingness. The humid, dank breath of machinery, like burning motor oil and old grease, assaulted his nasal cavity. Something sharp pressed against his ear, biting softly, nibbling. Something else wet and thick ran across his cheek.

Just a taste. The thought invaded his mind in a voice he did not know and the sensation of being licked came again. *For now, just a—*

A noise broke through the alien thought. A ringing. His phone (and as it turned out, his salvation), as all at once, the vent's laughter stopped, the wet tongue receded, the grip on his wrists and ankles were released, and the pressure from the walls pulled back. Day didn't want to open his eyes, but by the fifth ring, he slowly did.

The room was back to normal. The soft chug of the motor was still in the background but no longer sounded like laughter. The blue screen of the ATM no longer flashed or shimmered, or flickered. No face beaming at him expectantly. It was just the steady white letters.

Insert Card

Day absently reached into the pocket of his discarded jeans and pulled the phone out. Without looking at the screen, he answered.

"Hello?" His voice was light, almost giddy. He ran a hand over the cheek that had almost been eaten off by an ATM machine – a fucking ATM machine – and it came away wet. Without so much as a thought, Day wiped the hand on his soaked t-shirt, his eyes never leaving the machine. His breathing felt labored and if he had to guess what going into shock felt like, he'd bet that he was halfway there.

"Walt?" *Elise.* She was the only one who called him Walt. He never thought he'd feel so happy to hear her voice. It had been a bitter divorce, a spiteful one, and she tried to hurt him throughout it, but he knew he deserved it all. Still, as much as he deserved what he got, her treatment of him had stung, and he couldn't help feeling *some* resentment toward her. Now though, in the moment, she was his savior.

He reached into his duffel bag and this time, when he found the bottle, he pulled it out. He had wanted to save the small amount of amber liquid, for what he didn't know, but he pulled the top off and took a deep whiff, then a second. Then, he screwed the top back on. He let the heavy glass drop from his hand.

"Walt? Are you there?"

"Yeah, Lee, I'm here." Day eyed the room with suspicion, sure that at any time, the room would begin to crush him again and the ATM machine would no longer be satisfied with *"just a taste,"* but would devour his crumpled up body and pulverized bones. He knew he might already be dead if it wasn't for the unlikely call from his ex-wife. The woman who had forbidden him from seeing his son until he was sober, the woman who had told him not to call, or write, or even send an e-mail, and now she had saved him.

"Thank you," he said, trying to keep his voice steady, as he began gathering his things. He would risk the cold. He would find someplace else to sleep – anywhere there wasn't a demonic fucking ATM machine intent on playing with its food before deciding to chow down.

"What? Walt, the phone cut out, what did you say?" Lee said in the annoyed tone she always reserved for him.

"I said, thank you."

"Thank you? What are—"

The line went dead and Day eyed the machine set into the wall. His heart pounded so hard that it hurt. He looked at the screen of the phone but it was dark. He tried the power button but it would not turn on. It set him at ease, but barely. He knew the phone would die, and sooner rather than later, but he still had the suspicious feeling that it wasn't the battery that ended the call or drained the remaining juice.

Dropping the phone on the small counter (that remained at the correct height) to write out deposit slips, Day pulled on his jeans. The heater still ran but an odd sense of cold was forming in the pit of his stomach. He rolled up his blanket, nowhere near the neat bundle it had been before he had removed it from his duffel bag. He tossed his paperback and the blanket back into the duffel and finished dressing.

Sliding his gloves on his hands, Day pulled the mittens over the tips of his fingers. He dropped his useless phone back into his pocket and strapped the bag to his back. Standing in front of the door, Day took in a deep breath, knowing that if the room wasn't done with him, the door would never open. He sucked in another deep breath and held it. As frightened as he was of the room, somehow, he was more frightened to try the door and find it locked.

He placed a tentative hand on the door's handle and slowly let the breath he was holding out through his nostrils. Day firmed his grasp on the handle, took one last, deep breath and yanked. The door came toward him, just a crack, and let in a small burst of cool air, and then pulled back shut. Day's resolve was breaking. He watched through the glass of the door, out into the howling, swooping wind and snow and tried again.

The door came open, but slowly, and then burst open so hard that Day was pushed back deeper into the shallow room. Cold gusts of wind cooled the remainder of the drying sweat on his brow and sent chills through him. His body bumped against the wall next to the ATM machine and Day jumped away. The door out, the door to his freedom, stood open, and Day felt a determination he had never felt before. Not when it came to kicking his drinking habit, not when it came to saving his job, his marriage, nothing. But this was his life, now. More so than ever, this was all or nothing. He took the first step forward and nothing tried to stop him. Feeling encouraged, Day took another step. A crying laugh of victory escaped his lips.

Day placed another foot forward, and another. The door started to close and he moved faster. He slid his fingers between the metal edge of the door and the metal doorframe. When nothing happened, he laughed again. Maybe the damned thing wore itself out? Day looked back into the room and shook his head, only half believing that all he had gone through truly happened at all. Then, he eyed the glass bottle, still where he had dropped it. Sitting in the middle of the floor.

Turning back to the door, Day knew he should just go. His gaze drifted back to the bottle. He eyed it with longing. Only a few swallows remained, barely a few. He should let it go. Just get the hell out of Dodge, to paraphrase the saying. Still, that amber liquid called to him. He knew he'd want those few sips, want that taste, especially after all he'd gone through. With his hand holding the door open, Day stretched, trying to reach the bottle. He could not grasp it, didn't come close.

He pushed the door open as wide as it could go, held it as he braced himself for the grab. Day rushed into the small room again; the bottle so close, yet feeling so far away. Like doing the forty-yard dash in gym class, he reached down for the bottle, his body already twisting back toward the door as his hand clamped onto the cold glass. The gap of the door closed in, but Day knew he could make it. It would be impossible not to. With his hand nearly on the door's push bar, Day's foot was pulled out from under him. Falling down hard, a throbbing pain rushing through his back, Day looked around for the hands that had gripped him earlier. Looked and waited for their caressing touch, but it never came.

Sitting up, he saw his foot wrapped around the strap of his duffel bag, and didn't remember taking it off. Day looked at the door. It had closed. He stood in front of the door, his hand hovering over the push bar. He knew he had to try, but was already sure of the result. Day pushed and the door did not budge. He stared out at the snow, twisted the top off the bottle and took the final swigs, strangely relieved that he hadn't thrown his life away for nothing.

Just a taste. The words invaded his mind. The deep-throated chuckle of the heater assaulted his ears. When the phantom hands intertwined their fingers through his, he tried to break free but was tugged toward the machine. Glass shattered as the bottle fell from his hand and his face was pressed hard against the sticky, moist glass of the ATM machine.

Day screamed loud as the wet something probed at his face again. Screamed as the sharp something began to nibble again.

Above his screams the coughing laughter of the vent was louder than ever.

ABOUT THE AUTHORS

Sylvia Greenwich is a high school English teacher by day and harbinger of doom by night, spinning spooky stories for fun and very little profit. She likes to tell her students that a good writer knows the rules of writing, and a great writer breaks them with impunity. While she's not sure she's gotten either part of that advice right herself, she keeps making the attempt because, as she's also fond of reminding her students, there's no shame in failing as long as you give your best in the effort. Supporting a household of imperious cats and supported by an infinitely patient husband, Sylvia aspires to add a few humble tales to the world's great library.

If you are interested in following Sylvia Greenwich's career as a fledgling author, please look her up online at: www.sylviagreenwich.com. On her website you will find free original fiction as well as links to her other published work.

Gregory L. Norris grew up on a healthy diet of creature double features and classic SF TV shows. He once worked as a screenwriter on two episodes of Paramount's modern classic, *Star Trek: Voyager*, and is a former writer at SCI FI, the official magazine of the Sci Fi Channel (before all those ridiculous Ys invaded). Norris's short stories appear regularly in fiction anthologies, and he has published several collections and novels, two of the latter appearing on Home Shopping Network's "Escape with Romance" line, the first time HSN has made novels available to their customers. The idea for "Wealth and Hellness" came to him after a visit to a nursing home to see his beloved grandmother, Rachel, who was supremely well cared for -- the cautionary tale's creation owes to the question of what if she *wasn't*.

Follow Norris's literary adventures on Facebook or at his tiny slice of virtual real estate, www.gregorylnorris.blogspot.com.

John H. Stevens lives with his lovely wife, Geraldine, and daughter, Katie, in the suburbs of Chicago, after growing up near Wrigley Field. During the day, he's a mild-mannered Systems Programmer. At night, he tries to come up with ideas for horror stories, despite his dogs' demand to play with them. His scariest secret is that he's a Cub's fan.

He's truly honored to appear in the inaugural issue of Creepy Campfire Quarterly. If you'd like to see more of his work, please visit his website at http://www.johnhstevens.com.

Nicholas Paschall is a collegiate graduate from the University of Texas at San Antonio with a degree in History, which helps him research ideas for his stories. He's been published in over twelve anthologies and magazines, including *Shrieks and Shivers* and *Demonic Visions*. Nicholas regularly maintains an author website: http://nickronomican.blogspot.com, where he posts stories for his fans to enjoy for free. Drop by the old graveyard to pay him a visit and he'll spin a tale from the finest spider silk for you, chilling you to the bone and leaving you with a sense of dread sitting heavy in your stomach and a feeling that you're still being watched. You can find his work online from numerous sources, with his latest online works at Creepypasta. Just head on over there and take a look at what he has to offer if you want some spine-tingling tales.

Mijat Budimir Vujačić is an economist by trade, storyteller at heart. He is a published author of three horror novels written in Serbian: *Krvavi Akvarel*, *NekRomansa*, and *Vampir*. His stories appeared in *SQ*, *Altair*, *Encounters*, *Acidic Fiction*, *Creepy Campfire Quarterly*, *Under the Bed*, and *Infernal Ink* magazines, as well as in professional anthologies *Toxic Tales*, *Silent Scream*, and *The Nightmare Collective*. He believes a strong work ethic is the root of all success, and that it's best to err on the side of action. A fan of all things horror, he's also an avid gamer, hobby blogger, hookah enthusiast, and a staunch dog person. He lives in Belgrade, Serbia. You can message him at: mbvujacic@gmail.com or you can follow him on twitter at: https://twitter.com/MBVujacic.

Unbeknownst to **Robert Stahl**, his body is an empty shell, telepathically controlled by a brain in a jar, which was buried long ago under the floorboard of his home in Dallas. Consequently, his days are filled with the urge to write: stories, letters, articles, whatever. At night he listens to music and when he drifts off to sleep, the brain laughs, a humorless, pitiful sound, as it jiggles alone in the dusty darkness. His work has been published at *Acidic Fiction*, *Urban Fantasist*, *Creepy Campfire Quarterly*, *Odd Tree Press*, and *Whispers From the Abyss*.

Emilio DeGrazia, a longtime resident of Winona, MN, grew up in Dearborn, Michigan. He has had two collections of fiction, two novels, two collections of creative non-fiction, and one volume of poems published. He and his wife Monica also have co-edited the works *Twenty-Six Minnesota Writers* (1995) and *Thirty-Three Minnesota Poets* (2000). *The Nodin Poetry Anthology*, also co-edited, was released in April 2015.

DeGrazia's collected short stories, *Seventeen Grams of Soul* (1995), was winner of a Minnesota Book Award, and a collage of creative prose, *Walking on Air in a Field of Greens*, was one of three finalists for a Midwest Book Award. *Seasonings*, a collection of poetry, is his most recent book, with a second collection of creative non-fiction, *Eye Shadow*, due out in November of 2015. He has just finished a second term as Poet Laureate of Winona, and tells his children he wants to be a poet when he grows up. His web site is: www.emiliodegrazia.com.

John Teel is a union Ironworker from Philadelphia. His fiction has appeared in *Dark Moon Digest*, *Pulp Modern*, *The Literary Hatchet* and Playwithdeath.com's anthology, *The Nightmare Collective*. When he isn't working he spends his time with his wife Rae, their son Charlie and their dog Gizmo, who they never feed after midnight.

Please feel free to look up author John Teel's work on Goodreads at: https://www.goodreads.com/author/show/14155683.John_Teel.

Craig Steven is a member of the Horror Writers Association. He doesn't think he's deserving of this honor, but accepts it regardless. He's been published by *Sanitarium Magazine*, *Jitter Press*, *Under The Bed*, and *Creepy Campfire Quarterly*. He used to be the editor for *Beyond*

Imagination and *Beyond Science Fiction* magazines before they were, unfortunately, discontinued. His first ever full-length novel is being published by the esteemed R.J. Cavender. When he's not writing, he's watching rap battles or reading. His life really isn't that much more interesting than yours. If you want to keep up with him for whatever reason, go to: www.writercraig.com and watch him try his hand at being a writer, an endeavor that promises to leave him disappointed.

A writer of both fantasy and horror, **Marlena Frank**'s work is in a smattering of short story anthologies. Her stories lean toward weird horror, creature horror, and YA fantasy. Her latest story, "Tiny Necks", will be published in Bloodshot Books' *Not Your Average Monster Volume 2*, due out in February of 2016.

She typically thinks up strange tales while sipping sweet tea at her Georgia home, listening to podcasts on her hour-long commute, or while reading a good book with her two cats. Her current favorite fandoms include Batman, Lord of the Rings, and Black Butler.

You can follow Marlena's ramblings on her personal author blog: http://lenafrank.wordpress.com. You can also stay notified of Marlena Frank's new releases by signing up for her newsletter here: http://lenafrank.wordpress.com/mailinglist/.

David J. Gibbs was born and raised in the greater Cincinnati area. The oldest of three, he protected his younger brother and sister from neighborhood bullies and the monsters under their beds. Spending a great deal of time building tree forts while exploring the expansive Muskegon Woods around his home, he let his imagination run wild with stories and legends of the area. He always sought out the inexplicable and enjoyed roaming the darkness of campfire tales and monster stories.

An Eagle Scout, he has always enjoyed the outdoors, camping and hiking all across the country. A gifted athlete, he particularly excelled at soccer and track and field. He has become a nationally certified soccer coach and continues to instill his love of the game through his coaching. He is an accomplished musician as well, playing Cincinnati area gigs regularly with his band Spare Change.

Though he has always enjoyed writing stories, it wasn't until the third grade, when Miss Cummings requested a meeting with his parents over a story he had written, that he began to focus on darker elements and creepy things. That particular story was about an axe murderer lurking in the woods surrounding the school. He chopped up students and stored the parts in a small shack. It truly disturbed his teacher.

Afterward, David began spending hours using his mother's manual typewriter on the kitchen table writing all kinds of stories. His first novel was finished in the back seat of his parent's car in a spiral notebook while on vacation sitting in the parking lot of Saint Augustine, FL. He has since graduated from the manual typewriter to a laptop, but his subject matter remains dark. Never losing touch with the wonder and magic of childhood, he continues to push the limits of imagination with his stories. A web designer by day and rock 'n roll superhero by night, he is always seeking the threads in his daily life that will lead to stories that will excite, delight, scare and, most of all, surprise his readers.

Over the last year, his stories have appeared in numerous publications, including: *Sanitarium Magazine, The Sirens Call, Massacre Magazine, Nebula Rift, New Realm, Aphelion* and *Under The Bed.* He has also published two collections of short speculative fiction entitled *A Taste of the Grave* and *Once, Twice, Thrice* as well as a novel entitled *The Walking Man.* His work has also appeared in the anthology *Tales From The Grave.* Later this year, and into early next year, his writing will also be appearing in the following anthologies: *Dark Monsters* and *Hidden in Plain Sight.*

Authors he enjoys reading include: Caleb Carr, Peter Straub, Stephen King, Jeffrey Deaver, James Patterson, Dean Koontz, H.P. Lovecraft and Michael Connelly.

Links to his available works, blog and updates can all be found at: http://www.davidjgibbs.com.

Randy D. Rubin lives in quiet lunacy in a very old haunted house in Virginia. He is a very proud member of The Horror Writers of America and HWA-VA. He matriculated from Old Dominion University studying Creative Writing/English. He has two novellas published by Secret Cravings Press, "*The Legend of my Nana, Miss Viola*" and "*The Witch of*

Dreadmere Forest". His short story, "Tommy Kitty Cellar Son" is part of the anthology, *Suffer the Little Children*, published at Cruentus Libri Press and "This is a Troll Free Call" is in *Ugly Babies Vol. 1*, by JWK Publishing. His story, "The Water Got Mad" is part of Perpetual Motion Machine Publishing's *One Night Stand* series. He is the featured poet showcased in *The Horror Zine*'s September 2014 issue. He recently won the NECON E-Book Flash Fiction Contest last year and received an honorable mention for his haiku poetry this year. His flash fiction took second place in the January Short Fiction Contest at The Cult of Me.Blogspot.com this year. His dark passions and prose have been turned into podcasts at *The Wicked Library*, Episodes 417 in 2014 & 516 last season, and 613 this year. His drabbles have appeared at *Hellnotes Horror in a Hundred*. And he's just getting started…

His first dark poetry collection, *The Demon in My Head Doth Speak* was just released through Eldritch Press in February. His short story, "T-BONE" has just been published in the *Happy Little Horrors Anthology Vol 2 – ALIENATED* at Amazon, as of Halloween 2015.

Stephen McQuiggan was the original author of the bible; he vowed never to write again after the publishers removed the dinosaurs and the spectacular alien abduction ending from the final edit. His first novel, *A Pig's View Of Heaven*, is available now from Amazon and through Grinning Skull Press: www.grinningskullpress.com.

Katherine Sanger was a Jersey Girl before getting smart and moving to Texas. She's been published in various e-zines and print, including *Baen's Universe, Black Chaos, Wandering Weeds, Spacesports & Spidersilk, Black Petals, Star*Line, Anotherealm, Lost in the Dark, Bewildering Stories, Aphelion*, and *RevolutionSF*, and edited *From the Asylum*, an e-zine of fiction and poetry, and *Serial Flasher*, a flash fiction e-zine. She's a member of HWA and SFWA. She taught English for over 10 years at various online and local community and technical colleges.

You can check out links to Katherine Sanger's many, many blogs at: http://www.fromtheasylum.com or you can also find her on Facebook here: https://www.facebook.com/katherine.sanger.5 or follow her on Twitter @KatherineSanger.

Public records indicate that **Daniel Marrone** was aboard the S.S. Pangolin when it was torpedoed by a radical group known only as "The Triangle." While his body has yet to be discovered, thousands of his manuscripts were found in an airtight safe amidst the submerged wreckage. As the Marrone family's lawyer, I have been asked to write on Daniel's behalf. Through interviews with the surviving family members, who currently reside in an underground bunker in the heart of New Jersey, an agreement has been made to release the entirety of Daniel Marrone's writings sporadically and in seemingly random publications. Prior to boarding the S.S. Pangolin as a "biochemical consultant," Mr. Marrone served, honorably, as a receptionist at his hometown hospital, while devouring horror movies and literature in his spare time. I have successfully published another of Mr. Marrone's manuscripts, entitled, "Grandpa's House," in Issue #6 of *Massacre Magazine*. I sincerely hope you all enjoy his unaltered works, and keep all three of your eyes open for future releases. Trust nobody.

Edward R. Rosick is a writer living in the urban wilds of Michigan. He has had multiple short stories published in magazines, webzines, and anthologies, and has attended both the Clarion and Taos Toolbox Writers Workshops.

By day, **John Howe** designs steel buildings and manages construction projects for a design build firm in west Michigan. At night, he succumbs to his passion for writing short fiction and has had stories published by *Horrified Press*, *EMP Publishing* and *Toasted Cheese Literary Journal*. John enjoys experimenting with many genres but his writing strengths often lead him toward the darker side.

During his day job as an archaeologist, **Paul Stansfield** does everything from finding 2,000-year-old prehistoric projectile points, removing 150-year-old feces from historic outhouses, and exhuming human burials--some so well preserved that the brains and other organs are still intact. Otherwise, he likes to write, especially horror fiction. He's had over 20 short stories published, in magazines such as *Morbid Curiosity*, *Cthulhu Sex Magazine*, *Under the Bed*, *In D'tale*, and *The Literary*

Hatchet, among others. He also has stories in three horror anthologies — *"Undead Living"* (Sunbury Press), *"Coming Back"* (Thirteen O'Clock Press), and *"Creature Stew"* (Papa Bear Press). Paul Stansfield's personal blog address is: http://paulstansfield.blogspot.com and he can be reached at: paulccstansfield@gmail.com. His hobbies include drinking craft beer, tennis, and caring for the humongous tapeworm that lives in his intestines.

Leonard Apa was recently published in the June/July 2015 issue of *Writer's Digest*. His short story, *And Introducing the Scarlet Scrapper* was featured in *CAPED: An Anthology of Superhero Tales*. He has been accepted and has participated in the Borderlands Press Writer's Bootcamp and is a member of the NJ Authors Group. He is currently working on adapting *And Introducing the Scarlet Scrapper* into a full-length novel. Visit him on Facebook at: www.facebook.com/1leonardapaauthor.

www.ingramcontent.com/pod-product-compliance
Lightning Source LLC
Chambersburg PA
CBHW050937120626
46552CB00001B/246